BEYOND MONONGAH

AN APPALACHIAN STORY

JUDITH HOOVER

ARCHWAY
PUBLISHING

Archway Publishing books may be ordered through booksellers or by contacting:

Archway Publishing
1663 Liberty Drive
Bloomington, IN 47403
www.archwaypublishing.com
1 (888) 242-5904

ISBN: 978-1-4808-3619-8 (sc)
ISBN: 978-1-4808-3620-4 (e)

Library of Congress Control Number: 2016914011

Print information available on the last page.

Archway Publishing rev. date: 08/31/2016

LeRoy Collins Leon County
Public Library System
200 West Park Avenue
Tallahassee, Florida 32301

For Tom. If he hadn't kept saying, "Go write that
book," it never would have been finished.

PREFACE

The stories of those living during the early years of the twentieth century are lost to most of us today. This loss of relevance is especially true for those who spent their lives underground, digging the coal that made industrialization possible. Their poverty, their illnesses, and their servitude all seem impossible today, but their hardships were the way of life for miners and their families dwelling in the beautiful Appalachian region of America. The majesty of these mountains hid the dark and often deadly world below. The epic story of the Monongah disaster, to this day the worst mine accident in American history, brings these families and their struggles and triumphs back to life.

ACKNOWLEDGMENTS

I wish to acknowledge the writers of two books, Jason Skog for *The Monongah Mining Disaster*, part of the *We the People* series for young readers, and Davitt McAteer for *Monongah, The Tragic Story of the 1907 Monongah Mine Disaster*. Each of these books provided factual details around which I could create fictional scenes for my fictional characters. The Center for Disease Control's National Institute for Occupational Safety and Health gave me details on coal mine disasters dating from 1839 to 2001. The West Virginia Division of Culture and History and the West Virginia State Archives Library provided contemporary articles from local and national newspapers. West Virginia University's Wise Library gave me access to not only the words and phrasings, but also the voices of West Virginians, through their oral history archives. To all of these, I owe a great debt of gratitude.

CHAPTER 1

Both of her babies were down for their naps and Clemente was at home with a bad cold that day, but the terrible tremor sent all four of them out the door headed toward the mines. Bessie grabbed little Orie, hitched up her skirt, and ran, repeating, "Oh my God, oh my God, oh my God," all the way. Clemente sprinted ahead carrying Ivy, appealing all the while to *Madre di Dio*. Startled from their sleep, both children began to wail, a sound soon heard throughout the small town of Monongah, where every family had a miner missing behind the inferno of flames roaring from both mine entrances. Wives, mothers, sons, and daughters appeared from all directions, held back only by the heat and smoke coming from these portals.

The scene was one of disorder and confusion. A train of loaded coal cars on its way up and out of the number-six mine had broken loose and rolled back down, steadily gaining momentum, and crashed at the bottom of the grade inside the mine. Explosion followed explosion as the accumulated coal dust and the naturally occurring methane sparked and burst all along the way through tunnel after tunnel. The brattice walls and curtains constructed to direct the air flow became useless piles of rubble, protecting none of those further inside from the poisonous gases that killed stealthily, unseen and unavoidable. The fan weighing twenty thousand pounds that had forced life-giving air through mine eight was torn away and landed across the West Fork River. The fan at number six was damaged, but not destroyed. The timbers and machinery that had exploded outward from the mines were followed by streaming black smoke seemingly under enormous pressure.

The mine's powerhouse and other structures on the surface were destroyed by the initial blasts, and more explosions deeper underground followed in rapid succession. Where the portals to mines six and eight had been lay unimaginable devastation, and still, minutes later, fragments of cloth and paper drifted down from the sky and onto the frantic onlookers. Smoke and fire continued to billow from both mine entrances and from newly formed cracks in the earth above the mines. With the hillside over the mines sloping downward, some tunnels lay close to the surface and some existing small openings, locally called "toadholes," had now widened. A man emerged from one of these holes, along with billowing smoke. As those nearby ran to help, he turned and pulled three others out, one badly injured but alive. Scattered conversations could be heard through the restless crowd.

"These four got out—there must be more!"

"My Sammy was working in the same place; he'll come out any minute."

In the afternoon, moaning was heard from another toadhole, and a searcher lowered down on a rope found a miner sitting dazedly on the body of his brother, as if to protect him from rock falls. Though in his delirium, he fought with his rescuers, these two were brought out; one lived, and the other died. Still, it seemed unthinkable just to stand around doing nothing. Two men nearby tried to find a way to help.

"Here, let's see if we can lower someone else down to find the others."

"No, don't you see that hole's got all full of smoke?"

"Let's try hollering down the hole. Hello? Hello—anyone there?"

Only one more survivor would be found, but he died before they could get him out of the mine.

News of the disaster reached Fairmont, where the company was headquartered; calls went out for volunteers, and miners began boarding the streetcar to Monongah all along the way. The crowded streetcar was unnaturally quiet for the short ride, as if the riders knew what they would find. Most of these men had been miners long enough to have experienced cave-ins and explosions, and the news coming over the telegraph wire this time foretold true catastrophe.

Among these miners were Hershel and Jeremiah, returning from their doctor's appointment. Hershel whispered to his father, "Which of the boys went to work with Orie this morning?"

"I think it was Domenic, since Clem was up all night coughing. We may all be damn lucky for the coughing."

As the streetcar slowed to its stop in Monongah, Hershel could see that the tracks beyond were mangled, so he knew that any volunteer rescuers coming that way could ride only so far. He couldn't see the mine entrances because of the milling crowds of women and children pushing forward, crying and screaming. There seemed to be no order; no search parties were being organized, and there were no ranks of injured waiting stoically for treatment. At nineteen, with long years spent underground, he knew the men would have to be rescued now—or not at all.

Running forward along the ruined track, he finally came to a gap in the groups of terrified people and could see the mine entrances, or what was left of them. Of number eight, where he would have entered that morning, nothing was left but a crater in the side of the hill with first purple, then brown, and then black smoke pouring out. The entrance to number-six mine, connected to a trestle over the river, was completely clogged with the wrecked train of coal cars, with blown-out timbers and piles of rock and coal. Now he understood why no one was going in, but as he made his way toward the devastation, he worked over in his mind all the ways he thought that miners could survive such a situation. If they were back far enough, beyond the twists and turns of the tunnels, they could be safe from the initial explosions. If they had enough of the air-directing canvas brattice curtains between themselves and the explosions, they could breathe until rescuers arrived. These mines were supposed to be modern, with plenty of air circulating through the tunnels. Only when he saw the huge missing fan lodged into the bank on the other side of the river did he begin to lose hope.

A call went out through the crowds for volunteers willing to try entering the mine by climbing over the debris at the number-six portal since the number-eight crater still spewed smoke and flames.

"Okay, fellas, who's ready to go in?" shouted a second-shift foreman. "Line up right here in groups of ten, and make sure there's one local man among you."

Many stepped forward, Hershel among them. Though they had no safety equipment, those who worked there had mental images of the underground passages. *I know where Orie will be working today*, he thought, *and I know the fastest way to get there, if they'll just let me in.* Orie and Hershel, friends since boyhood, had worked together, married sisters Bessie and Lucy, served as best man at each other's weddings, and lived together since Lucy's death. Hershel thought Orie would be safe since they had both worked at the far end of mine eight. The explosions surely wouldn't have touched him.

Though he had not made it through the crowds close enough to join the first group, Hershel could see them enter, fanning away the smoke and disappearing into the darkness, but they emerged within ten minutes because of the poisonous gases they encountered. With no ventilation, the tunnel was filled with coal dust, methane, and the black damp that forms after explosions such as these. The methane, pure natural gas, gathered at ceiling level while the black damp, mostly nitrogen, would sink to the floor, so breathing was restricted to a small corridor all along the way. Once the fans were replaced, curtains could be reinstalled to direct the fresh air to the most likely spots to find survivors. But for now, those involved in the rescue could work inside only for short spans of time before they, too, would succumb to the gas.

Hershel clambered forward as this first group emerged, coughing, their eyes streaming, their faces already blackened as if they'd just finished a whole shift. These men had crawled over ruined coal cars and twisted track, had waded hip-deep through mounds of spilled coal, and had come, finally and only, to death itself. They came out of number-six portal stunned and exhausted from trying so hard just to breathe. Hershel couldn't see anyone he knew among this crowd, so there was no one to ask about Orie. There were shouts of, "What did you find?" and "Did you bring anyone out?" But their failure could only be conveyed by downturned eyes and a shake of the head. Someone murmured, "Dead horses and dead bodies," but no one mentioned any sign of life.

As some retreated in the face of this horror, Hershel made his way forward, determined to be included in the next group of rescuers. Surely, ways could be found to get past the immediate damage to reach those farther back waiting for help. Someone said, "Let's go," and the men turned as one to begin this hopeless task that had to be done. They had no masks, no air supply, nothing but a canary in a cage and a lamp that would go out in the presence of the colorless, odorless gas. Before they could enter, though, the company called off any further rescue efforts until a fan could be rigged up to provide ventilation, at least in mine six.

With precious time slipping away, Hershel worked his way through the crowd of desperate families as he looked for Bessie. At last, he saw her on the hillside above the mines, no coat, no scarf, no hat, on this cold December morning, shading her eyes, looking and looking as if looking itself could bring her Orie out of the mine. She seemed to be in a stupor, not seeing anything at all, but staring all the same. Where were the children? he wondered. Where was Clemente; where was his father?

"Bessie, you'll catch your death," he said, immediately cursing himself for a fool with that choice of words. She seemed not to notice him at first, but she glanced up and suddenly collapsed to the frozen ground, still not speaking a word.

"Here, take my coat," he pleaded, trying to help her sit up. Still, she just stared.

"Bessie, where are the children?" At that, she began to cry and pull at her hair; then she began to scream.

"Bessie, please, let me help you," he begged.

"He's dead, isn't he? We'll never see him again, will we?" she said.

"He would have been working far back in the mine, so we'll find him when we get to go back in."

She seemed to come back to herself with these words, so he asked once more about Ivy and little Orie.

"They're with Mrs. Ola—I asked Clemente to take them away from this awful place, but I couldn't go. I kept thinking that they would start walking out of the mine any minute and this would all be over."

"You mustn't stay out in the cold like this. Let's go home for just a minute to get your coat. You'll need to keep your strength for Orie and the children. We'll make you some tea, and maybe you can lie down a little while. I'll go back to the mine, and I swear, Bessie, we'll find Orie before this day is out."

The next rescue attempt would not be made until late that evening, when the fan at number six had been repaired. Once the portal had been cleared, all they found were the bodies of miners and horses, which they left undisturbed in their haste to find the living. At seven hundred feet inside, the gases drove them out again.

"Orie Morris?" cried Bessie, receiving only a shake of the head in reply.

"Sam Duffy?" "Thomas Noland?" "Harry Solas?" "Michael Evans?" "Umberto Gallo?" "Antonio DiMarco?" "Josef Gaada?" "Felix Kovaks?"

Names called out, all receiving the same answer. It soon became obvious that none of those early bodies could be identified because of the severity of the devastation. Those in the path of the explosions suffered the most appalling of injuries: crushing, beheading, dismemberment, pulverization, such that their bodies could never be fully recovered. Those lying beneath tons of slate would wait, unknown but deeply mourned, until the entire length of the mine had been searched.

As more volunteer rescuers entered, they encountered nearly unbearable conditions—intense heat, steadily accumulating gases, mounds of debris, and new fires that swallowed the oxygen being pumped in and caused the tunnels to be evacuated once again. What would happen to those trapped behind these fires? Even if they were dead, would the fires consume their bodies, so that there would be nothing at all to identify, nothing at all to bury? The company denied that any new fires had broken out, but within hours, the smoke pouring from each portal revealed the truth as no company statement could. Within a few days, an even more profound truth would be known: there would be no other survivors.

Those who had lived through the explosions and fires soon died from the gas, some covering their heads as best they could as if to ward off the inevitable. The waiting families clustered on the hillside, even as the December snow began to fall, knew nothing of the agony of their fathers or brothers underground perhaps trying to scribble a note on paper or carve a message onto the tunnel wall, hoping and praying for rescue, but realizing that such a miracle could never happen. Among those would be Hershel's friend, Orie.

Hershel and Jeremiah had been among those entering the mines several times by now. They knew these mines well, although everything inside had changed profoundly.

"Dad, I don't think you should go in again so soon," warned Hershel.

"Now, you know as well as I do that I won't give up till we find Orie and Dom."

As they walked ever deeper into mine eight, their breathing became labored and talking became impossible, so they just moved on. Finally, they came to the workings where Hershel had spent the last day alongside Orie, shoveling the coal they had brought down with a charge of black powder. There, sitting with his back to the coalface, was Orie, seemingly at peace, stopped in the act of pouring coffee into his cup, the coffee puddled at his feet, his lunch bucket revealing the sandwich Bessie had packed that morning.

"My God. Here he is," whispered Jeremiah.

As the rescue efforts turned into the recovery of bodies, the sense of urgency among the volunteers only grew. Still, conditions inside the mines were so deadly that they emerged weak, and some were still being carried out unconscious from exposure to the gas. Doctors who had come expecting to treat miners who had survived now were needed for the volunteers. Several thousand curiosity seekers had flooded into the little town, mingling with survivors and hindering the work that so desperately needed to be done. Police and mine guards were called in from neighboring towns to control the now-circuslike crowds.

A photographer hawking his postcards made the mistake of wandering into the path of a Polish family trying in vain to get close enough to the volunteers to learn about their son. Their lack of English combined with his lack of concern made for a bitter confrontation, with neither side willing to give ground.

"You kids get out of the way!" he shouted. "I've got business to attend to here."

When he pushed one of the children aside and into the mud, the father knocked him down, which caused an uproar with the crowd swirling onto the scene. Those thinking the roar meant that survivors had been found were soon disappointed. Frustration only grew as hours passed with no good news, only countless deaths to report. Once the fires had been extinguished and both mine fans reestablished, recovery efforts began yielding so many bodies that wagons filled with straw were brought to both portals to transport the burned and mangled to the morgue set up in an unfinished bank building. There, long lines of those in dread, yet determined to find their loved ones snaked along the muddy streets. Those who could be identified as Polish were carried to the basement of the Polish church. Caskets were hastily built and lined up along the streets of Monongah, and embalmers came long distances to prepare these hundreds of bodies for burial. The conditions of the corpses were such that often, a body would be claimed by more than one family.

"I know that's my Joseph—see the coat he was wearing?"

"No, it's Anton—I know it is."

"Oh, please, let it be Joseph. I must tell the children they've found their father! Please, oh, please, let it be Joseph."

"Now, now, ladies, let's see if I can help. What might Joseph have been carrying in his pockets?" said an official-looking man standing by.

"He had his missal—he always carried it with him. Is it there?"

The man searched all the pockets he could reach, but came up with only a pocketknife.

"Thank God; it's Anton. The boys gave him that knife last Christmas."

At that, Joseph's wife collapsed onto the floor and had to be carried out for fresh air. The smell of death so permeated the building that those waiting were hurried out, with no further remains identified that day. The overwhelming task of filling the caskets as quickly as possible required volunteers, a job refused by the onlookers, but taken on by survivors as the only remaining gift they could give. From long custom, the dead had been brought home, the bodies washed and laid out by family members, so aside from the condition of those killed in these mines, caring for the dead was nothing new.

The hundreds of coffins soon filled hundreds of graves hastily dug in new hillside cemeteries near the Italian and Polish churches. The Monongah miners had consisted largely of immigrants, new to the United States, although a minority was from old West Virginia families. As news of the disaster spread, even more sightseers, perhaps fifteen thousand in all, arrived from Pennsylvania, Ohio, and New York to stand alongside the victims' families who still waited for any scrap of information coming from the mines. Bodies from farther back showed few signs of distress, which proved to be both a blessing and a curse to the survivors. Everyone knew about the gas, but why couldn't they have been reached in time? The search officially ended on December 12, six days after the explosion, even though more bodies would be recovered during the cleanup phase of reopening the mines.

Orie's body was among the last to be carried out. A large man with a generous and cheerful heart, Orie had seen Hershel through Lucy's death and had prodded Hershel to try to see life as promising rather than defeating. His greatest love was for his small family that had grown to envelop Hershel, Jeremiah, and the two boys from Italy. Although Bessie ran the household, Orie had taken his role as father to mean that when little Orie refused to eat his supper, he would coax the child to have "just one bite," then "just one more," until the plate was clean. Although Bessie was a loving mother, it was Orie who had begun teaching Ivy to tie her shoes and write her letters and numbers and praised her efforts to the skies. Hershel wondered who would do that now. His greatest fear was that little Orie would have the sort of childhood he'd endured.

CHAPTER 2

1896

Hershel was just a boy—a baby, really—fit only for work in the mines, now that he had given up school. Eight years old and already terrified, already angry. His father, Jeremiah, said that fear could never be shown because the men would laugh at them both. His mother, Lucinda, said that learning to read was his only hope, but he had furiously chosen, instead, to throw an inkwell at the teacher and escape out the schoolhouse window, never to return. After that, his mother said nothing at all, but packed the lunch he would carry into the mine on his miles-long journey nearly to the coalface.

On the Sunday afternoon before his first workday, Hershel whispered his fears to his twin sister, Jane.

"Carmine said there's rats big as cats in the mine," he said.

"Oh, surely, they'll be afraid of you," she replied. "He's just trying to scare you."

"Maybe so, but then he talked about the water that drips all the time and rises up like a river in the mine when it rains."

"Have you asked Daddy about that?"

"No, 'cause he won't talk about it. I've heard him and Mama talk about the roof falling in, though."

"Yes, I remember somebody being covered up and Daddy digging him out."

"The scariest thing is looking at the coal fire burning in the grate and wondering what would happen if the mine caught on fire."

"Oh, Hershel, please, just go back to school," begged Jane.

"You know Miss Lawson wouldn't have me back anyway after what I did."

At that point, Jane began to cry, and Hershel did too, even though boys weren't supposed to cry—ever.

Walking to the mine with Jeremiah the next day, Hershel knew he wasn't big enough to use a pick or a shovel, so he wondered what lay ahead for him. He could have asked his father about his worst fear—that they sealed up burning mines with people left inside—but he didn't really want to hear the answer.

Instead, he asked, "Will I work with you, or will I work with the other boys?"

"I don't know," was all his father said. The unanswered, perhaps unanswerable questions of his life began to take shape with those three words.

Hershel spent that day working as a trapper boy, sitting alone in the dark, waiting for the coal to rumble down the chute, waiting for the signal to open a door that would redirect the flow of air from one corridor to another. Bigger boys with more important jobs at least had open flame lamps on their hats, but he did not. His job that day consisted of raising the trapdoor so the coal could fall into the mine cars lined up on the track below. The only other sound was the dripping of water; the only light appeared through cracks in the trapdoor when a new train of cars creaked and groaned its way up to the door, powered by teams of mules. Billows of coal dust surrounded him when the cars were being loaded, and that dust settled on him and in him as he waited for the next load. He dreaded the dripping water and the rumbling coal, and the legendary rats. He hated the silence; he hated being alone; short of talking to himself, he heard no words spoken, so he took the silence into himself and learned to live with it.

As he walked along the tunnel on Hershel's first day at the mine, Jeremiah likely wondered how the boy had made out. He hadn't seemed afraid when they rounded the first bend and the sunlight disappeared. Still, he hoped Hershel hadn't run crying, trying to find his way out.

"Hersh," he called from the other side of the trapdoor. "Son, are you there? Come on, now; it's time to go home."

"Yes, Daddy—I mean, Father, I'm here." *Daddy* and *Mama* might be all right at home, but never should he utter the word *Daddy* at the mine.

"Well, how was it?"

"Oh, not so bad. Better than school, anyway."

"Were you scared?

"First time I heard the coal coming down, I wondered if it would smash me flat, but it didn't, so I was okay."

"Well, your mama will be proud of you as long as you get your work done and don't play pranks with the other boys."

"I'll try."

Hershel's work was a little nearer the mine entrance than his father's. Jeremiah worked at the coalface, three miles inside, drilling the holes for the black powder that broke apart the coal seam and sometimes brought down the roof. Hershel's brothers, Charlie and Jim, worked different shifts from Hershel and Jeremiah—it seemed safer that way. Bill, the oldest brother, loved numbers and had finished high school, so he found a job in the mine office.

"Did you load the holes today, Dad? When the ground shook, I sure wished I could've seen the shot go off."

"Hershel, you don't want any part of that job. Sometimes people get covered up, and sometimes they die. You remember Jake's dad, don't you? Lost a leg and can't never work again. You ever hear 'fire in the hole,' you run like hell, and I mean it. Come on, now, we've got a ways to go before supper."

Indeed, they had a long walk before coming to the mine entrance. There, they washed the black dust from their hands and faces and began the walk home—not too far, since they lived in a company house. Once outside, Hershel blinked his eyes in the twilight, and, like any boy might, he began to swing his lunch bucket by the handle.

"Stop that!" roared his father. "What do you think you're doing? This ain't a picnic ground, and that's no play toy."

Jeremiah had a quick temper that his children knew better than to test, so Hershel walked carefully by his side till they were in sight of home. At that point, he began to run. Though his days of running to the arms of his mother were soon to end, he felt only an urgency to see her and to know that she loved him, even if he couldn't read.

Mother and Jane had supper on the table for Jeremiah and Hershel. The smaller children, Virgil, Leonard, and Debbie, would eat later with Mother and Jane. Those who worked at the mine got first choice.

"You better save some for me," Jane teased. Hershel wasn't a big eater, but he loved dessert, and this day, Mother had made a blackberry pie.

"Maybe I'll just eat it all so you won't get fat and ugly," he answered back. She swatted him with the dishtowel and went back to her chores. He hoped his mother would save a tiny piece of the pie for a surprise in his lunch bucket; it took him some time to realize it would always be her own piece she gave.

Hershel lay awake but exhausted. He'd asked his mother to leave one lamp burning in the kitchen, but thoughts of going back into the dark kept the comfort of sleep far off. When he did finally slip away, it was into a nightmare so real he awoke with a cry, tears stinging his eyes and soaking into the bedclothes. His mother, still up packing the lunch pails for morning, spoke his name and held him tight, saying over and over, "It's just a dream, just a dream." To him, though, it was not a dream. It was his new life, and as far as he could see, it always would be.

Only to Jane and Mama could Hershel confide his fears. His mother had never been beyond the entrance to a mine, but she could understand the terror of being confined. As a child, she'd been held down and tickled by her older brothers till she fainted. While some kids liked to be tickled, she lost her breath and felt like she would die if she couldn't get loose. *Please, God,* she thought, *don't let Hershel have that feeling, too.*

Next morning, before daylight, Hershel heard his parents talking. Lucinda said, "Jeremiah, do you think Hershel could work as a breaker instead of a trapper, at least till he's a little older?"

"Well, trappers make a little more than breakers, and we can use the money, but why would you want that for him?"

"Did you hear him cry out in the night?"

"No, what happened?" his father asked.

"He had a dream that the roof came down and he couldn't find his way out. He felt like he was smothering."

"He said the work was okay when I asked him."

"That's just what he'd say, but the truth of it came out in the nightmare. If he could be a breaker, he would at least be outside in the daylight. They might not make as much, but those boys work hard picking the slate out of the coal. They're just not closed in," Lucinda explained.

"Well, it's best to make all we can to save up for hard times, but I'll ask. You never know what they'll say."

Two years earlier, hard times had come in the form of a strike. Anyone who participated was put out of the house and off the land. Anyone who didn't was labeled a scab, hated, spat on, beat up, or worse. Jeremiah, with seven children to feed by then, chose to work and paid an awful price—loss of hearing in one ear from a blow to the head— but considered himself lucky to be alive after all. Now three of his boys would have that choice to make, if they stayed in the mine. His brother Bill's work in the office put him on the other side of an invisible line that seemed a mystery to Hershel.

Hershel had heard his mother and father talking long past bedtime the night before the strike had begun.

"We'll lose everything if we strike, but I don't know how we'll live here if we don't," his mother said. "They'll pull up anything left in the garden. They'll torment our children at school. It won't be so bad for Hershel, but Jane loves school."

"I know," his father said.

"It's always about pay, but what else is there to strike about this time?"

"It's the gas, Cindy. This mine's so full of black damp, it's a wonder we all ain't got blowed to hell a long time ago. Sometimes, it feels like somebody's behind you, or like a shroud is coming down about your shoulders, but when you turn around, you can't see nothing there. It can explode and kill you on the spot, or it can make you sit down and just die from breathing the stuff. The foreman won't listen, but the men are spooked and want to get someone's attention, so they've called a strike."

After six months of living in tents, rainwater running like rivers through their few belongings, seeing their babies sicken and die of consumption or starvation, the men called off the strike and some went back to their old jobs. Others were blacklisted and forced to leave the state. His brothers, Charlie and Jim, to Hershel's surprise, stayed on at the mine but talked in whispers about finding something else to do. Now, two years later, Hershel had followed the path of most coal-camp boys and gone into the mine, too. Once the teacher, sympathetic to the strikers, had called his father names and singled Hershel out, actually giving the other kids permission to humiliate him, he knew school was not for him.

As they started walking home from school one day, Jane said, "Why can't you just pretend they're not there? They don't have the nerve to say it to your face. They just do it behind your back."

A crowd of boys stood in their way, and she had to watch as a bigger boy backed Hershel up against the fence next to the schoolyard and pounded him to the ground, where he lay crying tears that burned his eyes and clouded his vision of Jane, so helpless to defend him. When the fight was over, she helped him get up, and, with as much dignity as they could muster, Jane and Hershel walked slowly and painfully home.

They had always been together, had always played and schemed and dreamed together, had always protected each other from their father's fits of anger, had always searched, together, for wildflowers for Mother. They found daisies in June, sky-blue chicory and cream-white Queen Ann's lace in July, goldenrod in the yellow-flower season of August, and the orange pods of bittersweet and red leaves from the maple trees in autumn. They were always out in early spring looking for violets to fill Mother's tiny cut-glass vase, a legacy from her Irish great-grandmother. The vase always sat sparkling on sunny days on the kitchen windowsill.

Years later, Hershel would treasure Mother's flower sketches and Jane's diaries, even though her words were just marks on the page to him.

Hershel and Jane had spent their childhood days, first as twin babies in the same crib, and then as perfect playmates with their own ways of talking and of seeing their world. On hot summer evenings, they listened to Mother's stories of lightning-bug princes rescuing regal butterflies from evil dragonflies. They lay on their backs in the yard, studying the stars, waiting for Orion the hunter to rise up over the horizon as the first sign of winter to come. They heard the peepers in the spring and the bullfrog chorus in the summer, the whippoorwills and the owls at night, the distant thunder marching over the hills sending out advance scouts of lightning to mark the way.

Summertime was the best, because everyone took turns working in the garden. With enough rain, they would harvest plenty of tomatoes, beans, and corn. Hershel loved running barefoot in the soft, cool dirt, ducking down to throw clods at Jane between the rows of cabbages and potatoes that would be stored in the cellar under straw and dirt to keep for winter. Winter came early, however, in these hills of West Virginia, and the bounty of summer didn't seem to last very long. Mother could have made a feast every one of those warm days, but she saved and saved, canning and drying, for the hard times sure to come again.

In the fall, the whole family worked at making apple butter. There were several fruit trees in the coal camp, and all of the families could share in the bounty. The night before the cooking began, everyone gathered in the kitchen and spilled out onto the porch to peel and core the apples. Next day, Jeremiah and the bigger boys spent the morning keeping the fire going under the big kettle, stirring the apples with a long-handled wooden paddle, while Mother and the smaller children washed and scalded the canning jars. After a hard day's work, gleaming jars of reddish-brown apple butter sat on the counter, and the family breathed in the sweet smell and looked forward to the sweet taste that wouldn't come till winter was well underway.

Their mother read them stories by the light of the kerosene lamps at night, and when the lending library at the company store ran out of children's books, she made up stories of her own. Hers were better anyway. She had attended school until the eighth grade but married early, never learning to type, as she had intended. Still, she wanted her children to have adventures, at least in their heads, so she encouraged their imaginations.

The children, in turn, especially those two, loved the woodlands and escaped the tiny shotgun house at every chance. Lifting up flat rocks along a narrow stream bank, they found crawdads and salamanders that became the heroes of new stories. Hershel loved the fact that Jane was not timid about these creatures but played with them just as he did. Running home to show them to Mother, Jane chased after Hershel, laughing and threatening him with the crawdad's pinching claws.

Now, of course, she couldn't follow him into the mine—women in a mine were considered bad luck. Still working as a trapper, the request for a job as a breaker being turned down, Hershel spent his days alone in the dark. Jane tried sneaking in one winter morning dressed in Hershel's clothes and wearing a cap over her pinned-up hair. Never anticipating the maze of tunnels and the absolute darkness of the mine, Jane was the child seen crying and running to escape the stifling feeling of being buried alive.

"Is that one of our new boys?" said an old miner trudging his way to work.

"I don't know him, if he is," said another. "Too bad he ain't got what it takes to earn his keep."

Arriving home breathless and grimy, her dirty face streaked with tears, Jane was met at the door by her mother.

"Jane, what on earth?"

"Mama, I had to see what it was like, and I wandered around and around, but I couldn't find Hershel. Oh, Mama, how can he stand it?"

Her mother took her in her arms, wiped her face, and just said, "Hush, now, he'll be all right. He won't go back to school, so there's nothing else for it. Men have worked these mines for years and years, so it's nothing new, Jane."

"Mama, he's not a man—he's a boy."

"Well, if he's not a man yet, he soon will be. This kind of life grows people up fast. Now, come peel these potatoes."

Jane peeled the potatoes and broke the green beans as her mother had taught her, and she vowed that one day, she would be the sort of teacher who would help boys like her brother, who would never make them feel small, who would do everything she could to keep them in school. She missed him terribly, as he did her, but it seemed their paths were now separate.

1899

Hershel and Jane noticed that their mother seemed to grow weaker as she grew larger with the weight of the next baby—her ninth child.

"Why do we keep getting more babies?" he said. "Mother doesn't seem well enough to go through with this one."

"Once it's there, you either go through with it or you die," Jane explained, though she didn't know much more about having babies than he did.

When finally, the baby was born, it was completely blue and lived only a few hours. Their mother, as it turned out, lived only a little while longer. The baby, a boy, left his mother with too little strength, or perhaps too little will, to survive. She lay, propped up on pillows, and called her children to her bedside one by one to say good-bye.

"Jane," she said, "you must take the household chores—the cooking, the cleaning, the canning. You've been such a good girl and learned so much. I know you can do it. Aunt Lorena can show you things you don't remember. Just be sure to pack the lunch buckets at night and make them a good breakfast in the morning."

"I will, Mama," she sobbed. "I love you, Mama. Please don't go."

To Hershel, she said, "When you're not at the mine, you must see to the younger children—love them as I have loved them, go to them when they cry in the night, give them solace when they miss me, since they won't understand. Jane will need your help." Lucinda knew that

Hershel and Jane would love the children, whereas her husband would give them only discipline and his vengeful version of God.

"I will, Mother. I promise."

Hershel was small for his age—never enough to eat. There wasn't much besides dried beans in the long winters, except for the years when they could save potatoes or cabbage. The Ladies Aid Society collected pennies to try to bring in oranges to prevent rickets, but there were never enough of those to go around. Home-canned tomatoes could help, but they always ran out before the pussy-willow tufts made their appearance in the spring. Mother had done her best, but now she was gone and Jane was trying to follow in her footsteps, as Hershel tried to follow in his father's. Too bad he seemed to have inherited his father's temperament, his impulsiveness, the bright flame of his anger, though Hershel remembered his mother's efforts to keep him from that path.

The life of a trapper, filled as it was with fear, left no room for mistakes. Other boys played pranks on each other, and Hershel's concentration on his work made him vulnerable. Caught between the possibility of his father's wrath if he failed at his job and the fun and friendship of the boys, he more and more often became the butt of jokes and the victim of hazing rituals. The one he dreaded most was called "greasin' the trapper." A gang of boys would grab a younger boy, pull down his pants, and smear grease from coal-car axles all over the most private parts of his body. The result was burning and stinging for the rest of the workday, until the child got home to wash it off as best he could. His mother's lye soap did its own share of burning and stinging the now-raw skin. Sometimes, the same torture would happen again the next day, and the next, until they moved on to another victim. Hershel had received this treatment as an eight-year-old and knew it would happen to him again sooner or later if he couldn't figure out how to fight back.

Two new boys appeared one morning in May, already friends and bigger than most. Their families had moved to Monongah for work in the mines, and the boys chose to work rather than finish out the last few days of the school year. Bobby was the real joker of the two, his laughter ringing out in the mine, and he quickly made friends, including Hershel. Orion, who liked to be called Orie, a bear of a fellow, took his work as seriously as Hershel, but he also liked to have fun.

"Hey, Hersh, want to play baseball on Saturday?" he asked.

"Don't know how," Hershel replied.

"Aw, we'll teach you. We need to round us up a team—you and me and Bobby will make a start. We had a good team in Fairmont, and we need one here. So will you play?"

"If you'll show me how, I'll try."

Hershel felt that he finally had a friend in Orie, but he wasn't too sure about Bobby, who would play a trick on anybody, friend or not. Learning to play baseball was a lot more fun than he'd ever imagined, and the best part was that he was good at it. Hitting the ball came naturally, and he loved running the bases. His years of duck-walking through the low-ceiling mine made crouching as catcher easy as pie, he thought. They played every weekend all summer, and Hershel dreaded the long winter to come.

CHAPTER 3

1900

At the age of twelve, Hershel could notice a change in himself that was both good and bad. He'd grown so much that his pants didn't fit right anymore, but being taller meant that maybe he could work a different job in the mine. He'd been a trapper long enough, he thought. He'd like to work with the mules, but he knew that required more strength than a little boy would have. He felt not only taller, but stronger what with all that baseball playing, so he asked Jeremiah what he thought about it.

"Well, you know, son, a mule can kill you if it wants to. If you don't treat 'em right, they'll kick you in the head or mash you up against the wall, and there's some mules that nobody can handle. Are you sure that's what you want to do?"

"I can't imagine not treating them right. What does that mean?"

"I've seen men beat and kick the poor sons-a-bitches when they refused to move or they wouldn't go fast enough. That mule might just bide his time and then pay the guy back with a couple a good kicks of his own."

"I'm too old now to just stand around opening and closing doors. I'd like to try my hand at mule wranglin' if you think they'd hire me."

"Nothin' lost from tryin', so just go ask about it."

Hershel got his chance, but word got around and on his last day as a trapper, three of the other boys decided to give him one last little present, a good greasin' that he'd remember for a long, long time. Gathering as much grease as they could take off the coal cars, they whispered and giggled about the plan. When Orie heard about it, he came up with a plan of his own. "Come on, Bobby, let's go find Hershel before they can catch him," he said.

"Why? Don't you want to get in on the joke?"

"I can tell you've never had this happen to you. It's no joke, and Hershel's done nothing to deserve it. The joke's gonna be on them."

With the workday nearly over, most of the trappers were on their way out of the mine as Orie began to gather a group together. He didn't know, though, that Hershel had already gone home, so they wasted some time looking for him. Starting back in to find the culprits, they were met by two old miners leaving for the day.

"Wonder what they're up to," said one.

"No good, I'm sure," said the other. "We best leave well enough alone."

Rounding a corner, the three boys met up with Orie and his group.

"Where you think you're going? It's time to go the other way," said one fearfully.

"Where were you going? We heard you had a surprise planned for Hershel on his last day. Did you find him?" asked Orie.

"No, we musta missed him."

"What's that you've got in your hands?"

"Oh, just a couple a greasy rags. That's all."

"And what were you gonna do with greasy rags?"

A nervous laugh slipped from the boy. "You know what we do. It's just a joke. Hershel would have had a good laugh with us by tomorrow."

"Well, if it's such a good joke, let's see how you'd like it if we played it on you."

"No, you can't mean—"

"Yes, that's just what I mean," Orie replied.

"No, it's not fair. There's more of you than there is of us."

At that, the crowd of boys behind Orie moved forward.

"This ain't right!" cried the boy.

"It's just as right as it would have been as you planned it. And just as wrong, too. We need a better ball team next summer, and you can't be good teammates and good friends and do this kind of stuff to each other."

"So are you gonna let us go?"

"We'll let you go this time, but if we hear of any more of these little jokes, there'll be hell to pay."

On Monday, Hershel was introduced to his mule. The boss said, "Now, Hershel, this here's Ol' Jess, and he's been around a long time. Treat him right and he'll work hard for you. Do something he don't like and he'll stand there like a statue for the rest of the day."

"Yes sir, I'll try my best to get along with Jess, and I hope he'll try to get along with me. Do you think he'd like an apple?"

"I think that would be a good way to start out."

Hershel and Jess worked together well that first day, Hershel giving the commands he'd been taught and Jess trudging along pulling two loaded coal cars at a time up and out of the mine. At the tipple where the coal would be transferred into railroad cars, Hershel unhooked Jess and they turned back to begin the process over again. At day's end, he led Jess to the mule stable inside the mine, gave him food and water, and spoke softly into his ear. "Thank you, Jess. I'll see you tomorrow." Hershel would repeat this day again and again, thinking of himself and Jess as partners in the real job of coal mining, him no longer a trapper alone in the dark.

It was a blustery February day, and now that she had hung the clothes to dry, flapping and snapping on the line in the yard, Jane turned to the dusting and sweeping needed to get the smell of coal dust out of the house. The children were playing under the kitchen table, the boys, Virgil and Leonard, making a fort of the chair legs, the girl, Debbie, walking her paper dolls beneath the rungs. Hershel had cut the dolls from a sheet of brown butcher paper and drawn on faces and clothing with Mother's charcoal pencil. In his haste to finish Debbie's dolls before time for work, Hershel had forgotten to fill the coal-oil lamp on the mantle, so Jane began the process, spilling a few drops down the front of her apron. That would soon dry, she thought. As she replaced the top part of the lamp back onto the base, she was distracted by the clattering of dishes in the cabinet, a daily occurrence when the black powder went off in the mine. Placing the lamp back on the mantle, she failed to notice that the two parts weren't fully attached.

Sweeping and dancing with the broom, Jane hummed a melody she had heard her mother sing. Debbie came out from under the table to join in the dance, adding her own version of "Ring Around the Rosie." Laughing and collapsing on the floor, they were joined by the boys for a wrestling match that neither Mother nor Father would have approved of, had they been there to see it.

Jane and the children ate a lunch of boiled potatoes and cabbage, and then she put them down on pallets on the floor for their naps. She wanted to get the dusting finished and the supper started before Father and Hershel arrived home, their shift over for the day. Once again, she hummed her mother's song as she began reaching up to dust the mantelpiece, catching the hem of her apron on fire. In her haste to put it out, her dust cloth struck the lamp and the coal oil spilled again, this time down the front of her dress. Her first thought was to get help, but running screaming into the yard was the worst thing to do; the cold winter wind fanned the flames. The engineer on a coal train that ran behind the company houses tried in vain to stop when he saw her fall in the yard, but by the time the train slid shrieking to a halt and the trainmen ran back along the track, it was far too late to save her.

Jeremiah and Hershel arrived home at the end of the shift to find the children and the neighbor ladies weeping and wailing on the porch, seemingly at a loss to deal with such a tragedy. No one had seen fit to send word to the mine. No one had blown the disaster whistle, because this disaster had happened in their home and not in the mine.

Taken from him less than a year after their mother's death, Jane would remain in Hershel's heart throughout his life, always just beyond the edge of his consciousness, but always a disturbing, yet comforting presence. He agonized over the question of why Jane, a lively and gentle girl, had to die with such violence and pain, and what he could have done to prevent it or, worse still, what he had done to cause it. Someone had refilled the kitchen lamp that day, but he never could bring himself to ask his father about it. His father only ever said, "It was God's will, so we'll say no more about it."

1903

The weather had been bitter, as it generally was in that part of West Virginia, but once inside the mine, the temperature was always the same—the only thing that changed was the level of the water. When it rose above his knees, Hershel was glad he'd brought an extra pair of pants; the wet ones froze soon after he emerged from the mine, and they became too stiff to walk home in.

This day, January 31, however, was most peculiar—his fifteenth birthday, and a warm, sunny, windy day. Though it was not a workday, he awoke early, and before opening his eyes, he realized that his face was not cold. When he emerged from his cocoon of quilts, the room was not freezing, as it had been for weeks—just chilly. Through the tiny dormer window, the sunlight streamed gold on the floor, and he jumped to that spot and hunkered down to bathe his whole body in the light.

The sky was whitish-blue and cloudless. Hunger and the movement of the sun soon drove him from the spot, and once he had washed his face, dressed, and eaten his breakfast, he took his tea out onto the small porch below his window. This enclosure faced south and also provided shelter from the blustery wind that whipped the fallen leaves in circles. Only when the breeze came directly toward him did he feel a chill; overall, he thought this a perfect winter day as he sat with his back against the sun-warmed wall of the house. Yesterday, he had seen the frighteningly magical sight the older miners called "flowers of the darkness." Jeremiah put no stock in such imaginings, but Hershel had been told that the coal itself was created many years ago from leaves and ferns and that the remnants of those ferns glowed white against the black of the coal when touched by the light of a miner's headlamp. Seeing this ghostly image himself for the first time had been both shocking and reassuring that even in the absolute blackness of the mine, beautiful flowers could be found in the dead of winter. He would look for them forever, he thought, and be lucky to see one ever again.

A red wasp lumbered by, groggy from being awakened ahead of season, and the black-and-white cat "lying guard" on the edge of the porch batted it down, only to lose track of it in the leaves. Hershel's hand moving along the edge of the railing seemed to the cat a steadier target, and she pounced three times, until he finally petted her head and shooed her away. She took up a position on the top step and waited.

He thought of winter days generally as silent, but this was a noisy day. The wind rattled the oak leaves that stubbornly remained attached and caused the fallen ones to seem to walk, point over point, along the dirt track that served as a road past the fronts of the company houses. The wind hummed in the long-needled pines across the road, sometimes blowing the song toward him and sometimes away. Some sounds, like trains hauling coal, started as low notes a long way off down across the valley, and they grew louder and higher in pitch as they arrived. Armloads of leaves were flung onto the porch and fine, gritty dust settled into the long-since-cold last swallow of tea in his cup.

The cat, not yet fully grown, demanded his attention by walking resolutely onto his outstretched legs. It moved onward and upward until it stood peering up into his eyes, as though he had the only answer to its unspoken but burning question. It had white paws and a white tip on its nose, and the rest of it was black. It reminded him of a coal miner who had just blown his nose and washed his hands. The cat had tried unsuccessfully to drink his tea; he gave it the last sip and then went inside to wash out the grit and put the kettle back on.

His father had taken the younger children to church, but Hershel had refused to attend since the deaths of both Mother and Jane, so close together. His three older brothers had moved off to a boarding house and would one day marry and start families of their own. It seemed that both of his mother's bequests had been destroyed with Jane's death.

His father, already a strict taskmaster, now became both solitary and silent and completely unprepared to care for the young children—and unwilling to let Hershel do so. Each one, therefore, was farmed out to Jeremiah's sisters or sisters-in-law, seeing their father only on Sunday, when he insisted on taking them to church. Leonard, Virgil, and Debbie would slowly lose track of whose family they belonged to, mingling with numerous cousins and forgetting their mother and Jane, as well as the grief-stricken twelve-year-old boy, Hershel. Jeremiah and Hershel, though they lived in the same house, seemed to see each other best through the work in the mine, walking there together each morning and back again each evening.

By this unusual winter morning of his fifteenth birthday, Hershel seemed to be coming out of a trance, remembering happy times with the whole family together instead of dwelling only on death and sorrow. It would surely turn back into winter tomorrow, but he looked on this brief January thaw as a birthday present—from his mother, from Jane? Never did he suspect that his father would appear late in the afternoon with a most unexpected gift: his own pair of ice skates, though they were a hand-me-down. The West Fork River might be a sewer for the towns and mines along its path, but in winter, it froze over hard enough for skating, and he had long dreamed of the freedom of gliding across its surface. For a boy who had worked for seven years now in the blackness of a coal mine, the thought of sailing through a white wilderness seemed like heaven itself.

1905

Seventeen years old and already nine years in the mine, Hershel felt that life was passing him by. What could he do, he wondered, that would give him something new to think about? One day, that something new was just dumped in his lap.

"Hersh, how about you watching out for Lucy while I'm gone?" His brother Charlie had joined the army and was about to be sent off to Texas for his training. Charlie was a big, strapping fellow who loved to drink and dance, and he had met Lucy, who loved the same things, at the local roadhouse. They were "promised," but not yet engaged, because Charlie couldn't afford to marry until he'd saved up some money.

"I'm not sure what you mean, Charlie."

"Aw, you know, go some places with her and remind her of me every now and then. I won't be gone long this time around, and after that, we'll be married and she'll have a house and maybe some kids to take up her time."

"I don't know, Charlie; I never know what to say to people."

"Well, you don't have to worry about that. Lucy talks enough for three or four people. You'll just have to listen a lot."

"How about I just think about it awhile? You're not leaving yet, are you?"

"No, but you'll need to get used to her before I do leave. Come on out with us tonight, and put on your dancing shoes."

Hershel didn't have, nor did he think he'd ever have, any dancing shoes. Still, he agreed to go, and he found listening to Lucy to be almost like listening to his sister Jane. *Girls must be pretty much alike,* he thought. The trouble started after Charlie had gone to Texas.

Lucy and Hershel often found themselves at the roadhouse after work. Her father and brothers were miners, and she was a clerk at the company store. He'd never been inside the roadhouse until that night with her and Charlie, but he liked listening to the music. As a ten-year-old, he had signed the Women's Christian Temperance Union pledge never to allow alcohol to touch his lips, and he'd stuck to it up till now. He had his coffee, which he'd had to bring from home, while Lucy had her beer, which was all right with him as long as she didn't tempt him to have beer as well. She'd finally given up trying to persuade him to dance with her, but she still teased him about being so straitlaced. He just smiled.

One Saturday night, she asked what he would be doing the next day.

"Well," he said, thinking she would suppose he was crazy, "I'm going to ice skate to Fairmont."

"Fairmont! But, Hershel, that's miles and miles away."

"Not by river," he said.

"My land, I never thought of you as an adventurer."

"I've never seen you among the skaters, even when you were younger—not that you're so old now." He coughed. "And besides, it's not an adventure as much as it's just fun. And it's free."

"I like the free part, but it looks more like work than fun. Fairmont?"

"If you want to go with me to the river tomorrow, I'll just stay around here and go to Fairmont next time by myself."

"But I don't have any skates, and besides, I don't know how."

"Okay, just meet me at Big Elm at noon, and I'll see if we can borrow skates from somebody. Much as you love to dance, you should be a snap at skating."

Next morning, an icy-cold day with the threat of snow in the air, Hershel went all through the coal camp asking about skates, but he could find only some clamp-ons that would be way too big for Lucy's shoes. Still, she could try them. As she came up the road riding her father's mule, she waved hello to everyone along the riverbank, her face glowing red from the cold. Some sat on logs and stumps putting on their skates; some huddled around the fire they'd built, while others gathered more brush and limbs to keep it going. Coffee and rye whiskey were flowing freely. Not many women skated; it was a man's game. Still, Lucy wanted a lark, and learning to skate might be just the thing.

Spotting Hershel loading wood on the fire, Lucy tied up the mule and ran over to meet him. "Did you find me any skates?"

Looking sheepish and disappointed in himself, Hershel showed her what he'd been able to come up with. At first, she frowned; then she smiled and said, "They'll have to do. Let's try them out."

They sat on a log placed close to the edge of the ice, and he helped her turn the key on each clamp that would hold the blades to her shoes. Then, putting on his shoe-skates, he said, "Please don't hurt yourself; Charlie would never forgive me."

Feeling quite put out by this reminder that she was promised to Charlie, and having gotten used to being so free while he was gone,

Lucy said, "Don't you worry about me. I'll be fine with a little practice. It can't be that hard." And down she went with her first step onto the ice.

After a few more false starts, she gave it up entirely and contented herself with sitting by the fire, drinking a little toddy, watching Hershel skating in circles so free and easy, and making herself dizzy with the watching and the whiskey. Out there on the ice, he seemed a different person—not the closed-up, silent figure sitting with her night after night, on guard for Charlie. Here, he held up his face to the white sky and swung his arms to gain speed and then turned in a large arc. Coming back to the bank and turning the skates sideways to come to a stop, he sprayed ice onto anyone in his path. Sometimes, another skater would chase him back out across the river, but none could catch him, and eventually, the game turned into a grand snowball fight—grown men, day laborers in the coal mine, playing in the snow like children.

Hershel gave up his opportunity to skate to Fairmont that day and many a day after that. Lucy never again tried to learn the skill of skating, but she did seem to love going to the river to watch Hershel practice the art. They rode the mule together to her home, and then he walked the rest of the way to his. He grew accustomed to being needed again, as his younger brothers and sister had once needed him. He loved to feel her arms around him and her head resting on his back as she slept her way home on the mule. He knew she would marry Charlie and he tried to treat her like a sister, but this closeness still felt like dangerous territory.

CHAPTER 4

1905

Neither Jeremiah nor Hershel had ever received a telegram, and neither could read what it said. Jeremiah had asked the delivery boy to read it for them, but he had resisted, saying, "I just deliver 'em; I'm not s'posed to read 'em." When Hershel took it to the company store where Lucy worked, she said it must be bad news as soon as she saw the envelope. Then she read the last line, signed *Charlie*.

"Oh, God, Hershel, it's from Charlie—he's coming home. The army is sending him by train as far as Parkersburg, and he'll hitch rides from there."

"Why do you look so scared? I thought you'd be happy to see him."

"Well, he may not be the same person who left here, and I may not be the same person he left."

"How could that be true? He's only been gone a little while."

"Well, he's done more and seen more than either one of us, so I'm afraid of what's become of him. He started out writing letters, but I haven't heard from him lately at all."

Lucy looked forlorn and Hershel wanted to comfort her, but here they were in the middle of the company store amid the stares and the tsk-tsk's of their neighbors. He chose instead to flee the scene—out the door, down the steps, and off into the snowy afternoon headed for home. Charlie could take care of the comforting when he got back.

Saturday afternoon and there was Charlie, bursting through the door, shouting his joy at being home, and startling Jeremiah, who had been dozing by the fire.

"Here now, what's all this?"

"It's me, Dad; I'm home and happy to be in these hills. Texas was okay, but it was flat and dusty, and it seemed like you could see to the end of the earth. To tell the truth, I felt kinda lost in it all."

"How long you been on the road, son?"

"Well, the train took four days, and I was two days hitching rides from Parkersburg. This uniform got me lots of rides, but I'm ready to shed the olive drab, for a while, at least."

"So, you're done with the army?"

"No, Dad, that's not how it works. I'll be home for a couple of weeks, and then I'm off to Alaska."

"Alaska—where's that?"

"Oh, it's way out west and way far north, and I've signed up for duty there."

The sound of feet stamping off snow on the porch ended this explanation. Hershel opened the door, not expecting Charlie to be there yet, but Charlie grabbed his brother and swung him around in circles until they both collapsed in laughter.

Later that night, when Jeremiah had gone to bed, Charlie and Hershel sat at the kitchen table drinking coffee—Charlie telling tales and Hershel listening, as usual.

"So, are you taking Lucy with you to Alaska?" asked Hershel.

"Are you crazy? You can't take women with you to the army."

"So is she just s'posed to wait for you?"

"Ah, Hersh, I've met a lot of other women now, and she's nothing special."

"So when will you break the news that you're no longer engaged, or promised, or whatever else?"

"I guess when I'm damn good and ready, little brother. What business is it of yours, anyway?"

"It became my business when you asked me to look out for her, which I have, and which I enjoyed, by the way."

"Then you can have her, and good riddance."

Hershel puzzled through this situation over and over, wishing he knew what to do. In their time together, he had come to see a possible life with Lucy, and now that Charlie was out of the way … But she had always said she didn't want to spend her life here "in this godforsaken place"—that she wanted to go to a big city, like Chicago or New York, and find a job. He always wondered where Charlie had fit into that picture. Sure, Charlie didn't want to stay there and mine coal either, but would he ever have gone to live in a city?

Hershel and Charlie spoke as little as possible for the rest of Charlie's leave, and Hershel never knew when or even if the situation with Lucy was settled. What he did know was that he hated seeing her sad, and he worried about her cough that seemed to be getting worse, rather than better, as the winter wound down to spring. The river thawed, so he could no longer invite her to the ice-skating parties on weekends. He still found her most nights sitting alone at the roadhouse, nursing a rye and smoking a cigarette—her new habit—so he would make some coffee and join her there in the dark. One such evening, he asked about the cough.

"Oh, it's just what's left of the winter, Hershel. My old Irish granny says to mix a little whiskey with a little sugar and that should fix me right up."

"I sure hope it works, Lucy. Now, what are you doin' about Charlie?"

"Charlie's gone, and I don't care if he never comes back. It turned out just like I thought—he wasn't the same, and neither am I."

She could not have said anything that would have made him happier, but there was still the question that hung over him: Would she pack up and leave anytime soon?

Hershel sought out the opinion of his friend, Orie, who had married Lucy's sister Bessie.

"Orie, Charlie and Lucy have called it quits, and I need to know if she still plans to leave here to get a job someplace."

"Well, why don't you just ask her?"

"She'll want to know why I'm asking, and then I'll be stuck."

"What do you mean 'stuck?' Why do you want to know, as if I didn't already know?" teased Orie.

"Come on, now, this is serious business."

"Okay, I'll ask Bessie what she knows about it."

Bessie knew what Orie thought of Hershel, and now she knew what her sister thought of him, too. It seemed that Lucy's fear of Charlie coming home was connected to her growing love for Hershel—his patience, his kindness, his concern for her, his love of the natural world. She could still see him whirling on the ice, seemingly free of the everyday fears that surely must plague those who worked in the dark underground. She had concluded that with no family anywhere but there, no references except maybe one from the company-store manager, her chances of success anywhere else were small. She'd be just another dime-a-dozen girl with no education out there struggling.

Though love was never mentioned, Bessie managed to convey that the plans to leave had been cancelled. The next night at the roadhouse, Hershel said, "So are you through with ideas of marriage and family?"

"Marriage and family with Charlie?" she wondered.

"Well, marriage and family with anyone?"

"Oh, I don't know. I guess it could happen if the right guy came along."

"You could marry me, if you wanted to."

"Hershel, are you proposing?"

"I guess I might be. It's always been hard for me to talk to people, but we're friends and I like being with you, and besides, you usually do all the talking anyway."

"Well, I guess if you might be proposing, I might be saying yes."

Lucy and Hershel were married in the spring, and Hershel began to surround their small company house with wildflowers he dug from the sunny hillsides, tall black-eyed Susans and Queen Anne's lace, the blue chicory that bloomed each morning and then closed up for the rest of the day. He saved the woods flowers for the shady side of the house.

Never one to speak of his love for Lucy, he could only show it through his work, which led him to a lifelong interest in the intricacies of digging and planting, weeding and watering. A ladies' garden club in Fairmont occasionally brought rooted cuttings from their flower beds to give to the miners' families in Monongah, and Lucy took great pleasure in carrying home as many little pots of these as she could as a surprise for Hershel. He, in turn, laid out small beds in diamond patterns, perhaps to take the place of the ring he could never afford. One day, she would at least have a gold band, he thought.

Lucy worked at making a home, surprising herself by sewing curtains and slipcovers by hand, saving chicken feathers for pillows, and learning to cook and bake—skills she'd never practiced as a girl. She had been going to have a career, of course, not a houseful of kids. Her sister Bessie was always pestering her to learn to make a pie—"Never saw a man didn't like pie," Bessie said. When Lucy asked Hershel for his opinion, he blinked hard and said he guessed he missed his mother's blackberry pie. So she finally asked Bessie for a lesson.

"Okay, now take this dough and divide it in two, and roll out both pieces for the crusts." Try as she might, Lucy's pie dough kept cracking and splitting so that she had no pieces big enough for a crust, top or bottom.

"Here, just put a little water on it and stick it back together," said Bessie.

"Okay, I'll try it again." Over and over, she failed.

Bessie finally said, "Just mash it all together again and we'll make a cobbler." They poured the honey-sweetened berries into the pie pan, pinched off pieces of dough, laid them on top of the berries, and put the pan in the oven.

Hershel came home that night to the smell of baking blackberries. Although the "crust" on top was a little burnt, they ate Lucy's first pie, laughing about the process, but loving the outcome. "Can you do that with apples?" he wondered.

"Now that I've conquered the berries, nothing can stop me," she bragged.

Together, Lucy and Hershel learned to can tomatoes and blackberries for winter suppers and to wrap the cabbages and potatoes he grew in straw and bury them deep in the ground, where they would keep till spring. They tied the onion leaves together and hung them under the porch rafters to dry, making a game to see who could who could dodge the mud daubers and hang the most onions the quickest. Once the red wasp nests were disturbed, the game was over, but not before Lucy had to make a paste of water and soda to soothe two stings on Hershel's wrist and elbow.

Without the winter pall of coal dust in the cold air, Lucy's health seemed to improve. On his day off each week, Lucy and Hershel walked the woods together looking for flowers; then they lay on their backs looking up at all the shades of green in the canopy overhead. If the day was sunny, they would walk through fields of broom sage and tall grass that smelled of summer. They both loved to watch thunderstorms off in the distance and listen to the rumble that said, "Better head for home." Running and laughing through the first raindrops, hoping to beat the deluge, they enjoyed their one day of life each week. The other six days were filled with backbreaking work and the burdensome and ever-present worry of life in a coal camp.

As summer turned to fall, Lucy's cough grew worse again. They tried to keep up their woods walks since she loved the changing colors of the oak and maple leaves, but when she began coughing up blood, those days were over. Though she had long given up smoking, her drinking grew worse, as she increased her dose of whiskey and reduced her dose of sugar. Granny's recipe had failed. By 4:00 in the afternoon, when Hershel came out of the mine to the darkness of winter, he often found Lucy sprawled across their bed, sound asleep. As her illness worsened, she seemed unable to do anything but drink and cough and sleep.

"Lucy, you've got to let me take you to the doctor. You're not getting any better."

"I'm not going to any doctor. You know what they do with people who cough too much? They lock 'em up in hospitals and don't let 'em out. No, that's not for me. I just won't do it."

Never one to use force, he let her have her way. He tried to talk about it with his brother-in-law, Orie, as they worked together in the mine.

"She refuses to go to the doctor, and I don't know what to do."

"Well, Bessie's stubborn, too. I guess it runs in the family."

"She's gonna die, Orie, maybe if she goes to the doctor or not. She says she won't be locked up in the hospital, but I can't just let her go. She's my life."

"Well, damn, Hershel. Maybe you could get her on the streetcar to Fairmont with some excuse, and when you get there, you just walk her right to the doctor before she knows what's happening."

"She'd know, but even if she gets mad, I can try."

Before any plan could be tried, she grew thin and weak, unable to ride the streetcar or walk anywhere. Hershel tore squares of cloth from old clothes to catch the blood from her coughing and piled them by the bed, but eventually, she couldn't even reach for one. When it seemed to him that the whole world, outside of the mine itself, was covered in blood, Lucy died. She had tuberculosis. She left him with memories of her lovely face and a company house he no longer needed. They'd had seven months together.

Hershel had suffered loss before—his mother, his sister, the younger children taken away from him, but this was different. He had thought he would spend his life with Lucy, that they would work and play together, that they would eventually have children to love, and that one day, he would be able to provide the life she deserved. Now she was gone. Was it his fault? Could he have changed the course of her illness? Never loud or carefree, he had always just laughed at her games and smiled at her joys, but now he became morose, the saddest he'd ever been, unable to take pleasure wherever it might be offered.

As the anger he tried to control boiled up and spilled over, he found himself on his knees, pounding at the dirt piled up on her gravesite until he collapsed in bitter tears. Orie found him sprawled there and tried to help him up, but he fought off his friend. Only when Jeremiah called his name and said, "Come on now, son. This ain't doin' no good," did he come to his senses. He knew he should just go home and face the truth that his life now consisted only of work.

CHAPTER 5

Lucy's sister, Bessie, took in boarders. She and Orie and their two small children, Ivy and Orie, Jr., had a company house with one spare room, and she brought in extra money washing clothes and feeding miners who didn't mind sleeping four to a room on pallets on the floor. Jeremiah had moved in with Bessie and Orie shortly after Hershel and Lucy took their own place. Now Hershel needed not only a home, but also the comfort of a family, so he arrived a few days after the funeral with his meager belongings and the food he and Lucy had put by for the future. With this invitation, he once again had small and lively children in his life and a happy family, though not his own, around the dinner table each night.

Bessie and Orie had married and started their family early. She remembered his proposal well.

"Bessie, I think I need a wife," he'd said as they sat on her porch steps.

"Oh, do you now?" she'd replied.

"Yes, I do. Would you know anyone willing to take on that job?"

"A job, you say."

"Yes, the duties would include cooking, cleaning, and mothering my children. But the most important part would be putting up with my wicked ways and having lots of fun doing it. Might you apply?"

"Well, I'm very good at cooking, but I hate cleaning. Mothering sounds like fun, and I already know about your wicked ways. So, any other applicants?"

"No others, so, it's settled then?"

"Settled!"

She, a tiny woman compared with her large and boisterous husband, loved to sing and loved to laugh, and he joined in the fun, never complaining if dinner was late because she was in the yard throwing a ball with the children. Bessie could read and she could play the piano, picking out the chords that accompanied the hymns and old-time songs she taught the children. People said she played by ear, and she supposed that would serve as well as any other explanation. Though they had no piano of their own, she was free to play the one in the nearby Evangelical United Brethren Church she attended every now and then. Bessie was a believer, but she never insisted that anyone else join in her belief. "Each one finds the truth in his own way," she would say, and that freedom was applied to her children as well as her husband. Orie practiced kindness and humility as his virtues, and the Golden Rule served as his motto. He and Bessie were, indeed, a matched pair.

Hershel and Orie worked together in the mine, Monongah number eight, its name a shortened version of Monongahela, the river that joined with the Allegheny to form the Ohio at Pittsburgh. Two Monongah mines, number six and number eight, were joined together underground, a mining practice outlawed in other states because of the danger that an explosion in one mine would expand outward to engulf the other as well.

Hershel, Orie, Jeremiah, and two other miners, Clemente and Domenic, brothers recently arrived from Italy, walked to work as usual each morning and returned home each night to the plain but filling supper Bessie prepared as best she could. Little meat was ever available, but dried beans were cheap even at the company store, and berries were free for the picking on the hillsides above the mines. Clemente and Domenic were accustomed to hard work in Italy. They had been recruited, along with ten other young men, by a *padrone,* an immigrant from the village of Duronia who was sent back home to bring others to America.

"Come on, Missus Bessie, let us show you how our mother uses these scraps," said Clemente one evening after supper as Bessie was about to throw away the peelings from the potatoes, carrots, onions, and tomatoes she had cooked for their meal.

Not wanting to hurt his feelings, she reluctantly agreed, and she watched as he carefully washed and picked over the scraps, discarding anything that was discolored but keeping everything else.

"Now we just need some boiling water for the broth, okay?" he said.

Again, she let this cheerful boy take over her kitchen, though she doubted any good would come of it.

"We had so little to eat at home, we never could waste anything, even scraps, so our mother said when we came to America, we should always remember her lessons."

After Bessie tasted the concoction they made that night, she decided to ask them what else they had to offer, and she subsequently learned to make a wonderful tomato sauce. When the tomatoes came in, they seemed all to be ready at once, so the excess had to be used up in some way.

"Let us help you with the peeling and chopping, okay?" asked Clemente. He always seemed to be asking a question, but he was really making a suggestion. Bessie thought that wasn't much of a language problem between them. Since it was a Sunday, they were home with nothing especially to do. Orie and Hershel had gone off squirrel hunting and wouldn't be back till dinnertime. Just being outdoors, even in the end-of-July heat, meant that even if they killed no game, the day would be a wonder for these two who spent their days in dark, cramped spaces underground.

Preserving a bushel of tomatoes required so much time and hand work that she gladly accepted the brothers' help. Domenic rarely had anything to say, but he smiled as he held the beautiful red tomatoes that reminded him, perhaps, of home. Together, Clemente and Domenic sang Italian songs as they worked, while Bessie tapped her foot in time, though she had no idea what the music meant. *Where—or what—is Sorrento?* she wondered.

"Now, Missus Bessie, you must cook the tomatoes for a long time with just a little water, so they must be stirred often in the pot. Then you must crush them and cook some more. We are here and can do that for you if you will let us."

Bessie agreed and went on her way, taking Ivy and Orie for an outing. When she returned, the house was filled with an intense aroma she had never experienced before and with the celebration of these two Italian boys who had felt the touch of their home and their mama from that aroma. The thick, beautiful tomato sauce went immediately into canning jars so that they could all have summer in January.

The nearest neighbor, elderly Mrs. Ola from Poland, joined Bessie for coffee each morning after the men had gone to work, saying that they should rest "just a little" before starting their own day's work that didn't end till bedtime. The resting consisted of sharing their troubles and their joys as they had their coffee and perhaps a bit of sweet bread Mrs. Ola brought along. Her boarders, Polish miners, spoke her language and helped her care for her husband, Papa, himself crushed in a rock fall years before in the old country. Having no small grandchildren of her own, Mrs. Ola lavished trinkets, pieces of broken jewelry or a marble here and there, on Ivy and little Orie, who seemed to have less trouble understanding her than most adults. She taught Bessie the art of tatting so she could make antimacassars to keep her chairs free of hair oil.

"Bessie, do you think Hershel will be all right without his Lucy? He never looks up to see who is really there, but he just looks off, like he sees something in the distance."

"I hope he's remembering the good times they had and not those last few months. She was such a carefree girl for so long; it's hard to accept she's gone. I miss her so much—we were children together, the two oldest."

"I thought she would marry Charlie and settle down, but he's gone, and now Hershel has the sorrow," said Mrs. Ola.

"Yes, Hershel has had more sorrow than you know. His twin sister died before you moved here, and their mother had died before that, so he's had much to bear. I think having the children around is helping a little. He never mentions Lucy, but he doesn't talk much anyway."

This day, they were sitting in Mrs. Ola's tidy, but crowded, sitting room. Bessie looked around at the statues of saints, at icons and a Saint Christopher's medal, thinking of the comfort these objects must bring, though nothing like them existed in her sparse evangelical upbringing. What did exist was duty, and it was time to see to it.

"Well, I've got a pile of clothes to wash, so I'd better get started," said Bessie. "Sometimes I think it's easier to birth a baby than to do a day's wash."

Washing the bedclothes proved the most frustrating of the jobs of these coal camp women because no matter how hard they scrubbed, everything hanging on the clothesline was soon stained with coal dust, so they didn't look like they'd been washed at all. Bessie had to pump water from the well, heat it over an open fire for the wash tub, and then scrub the work clothes with lye soap, rinse them in a second tub of cold water, and hang them to dry. She had no wringer but her hands, and on winter days, if the shirts and trousers froze before they dried, she brought them inside to hang on lines strung across the front room, where they steamed and dripped.

On this particular winter day, Friday, December 6, 1907, Bessie worried about Hershel and Jeremiah. She had seen the two of them off on the early streetcar to Fairmont where they would see a doctor to be tested for tuberculosis. Anyone who lived with a tuberculosis victim had to take the test, and Jeremiah had lived with Lucy and Hershel for a little while before Lucy had become so sick.

The test only required a saliva sample, but it was the potential results that were so frightening. The waiting room was crowded with potential tuberculosis patients, some coughing, some spitting into handkerchiefs tinged with red, some trying to keep from breathing in what the others were breathing out. As they waited, Jeremiah grew angrier and Hershel grew more anxious.

"I don't know why we have to go through this," Jeremiah complained.

"Well, we'll know why if the tests show we have what she had," said Hershel. "God knows she wouldn't have wanted us to suffer as she did."

"I know, son, and I'm sorry for her and for you, but we haven't been coughing, have we?"

"It doesn't always start out that way, so they have to check."

They were called in one at a time, so neither knew what the other was experiencing. When Hershel's name was called, he reluctantly entered the examining room and was told to spit into a bowl. Spit and splutter he did, over and over, until the doctor was satisfied he had a good sample for the test. Jeremiah was called next, and when he came back out, they were free to go. They would have to wait two weeks for the results. As they passed a little shop on the way to the streetcar station, Jeremiah offered to buy them a cup of coffee, which Hershel gladly accepted, since they had not eaten at all that morning. They finished their coffee and a doughnut just as the car arrived at the station. Preparing to step aboard, they heard a muffled roar from far off. Puzzled, they sat down for the short ride home, soon learning of the disaster that had occurred in their brief, but fortunate, absence.

CHAPTER 6

Hershel and Jeremiah arrived, of course, to chaos, entered the mine as rescuers, and finally found Orie's seemingly untouched body. In the days that followed, conversation around the supper table remained subdued, with even the children reflecting the solemnity of their lives now. Once the bodies had all been found, wooden caskets filled, and funerals held, the practical concerns of life emerged once more. Would they be able to keep the company house? Would Hershel, Jeremiah, and Clemente ever be paid for the recovery and cleanup work they had done, or would payday only come after a month of loading coal? Bessie had put up her vegetables and berries, but she still needed at least flour and coffee from the company store. Rumors flew through the coal camp that money was being collected and would be distributed in time for Christmas.

"Did you hear anything about any money coming from the owners?" asked Bessie.

"Them sons-a-bitches won't give us nothing, and we all know it," said Jeremiah. "They're trying to blame the explosion on some poor miner, so they won't have to do anything a'tall."

"I don't know how that could have happened. Do you?"

"They say a careless shot got blowed out, settin' off the dust."

Hershel shifted uneasily in his chair, never willing to contradict his father, but wishing to change the subject as the children's eyes glistened with tears. Glancing at Bessie, he offered to carry them to bed, and she quickly agreed. *No tears tonight,* she prayed.

Later in the evening, as the men sat around the table, the talk turned again to the causes of the disaster.

"Looks like we'll never know," Hershel said. "We do know that back in number eight, the coal dust was piling up, even though the inspectors said it wasn't. And I know for a fact that the gas was always there in pockets, even though the inspectors said it wasn't. Clem, you 'member when we saw that feller, George what's-his-name, fell out just as he went around a corner and we had to drag him back by his boots to where there was some air?"

"Oh, yes, I remember. What a day that was."

"First they tried to blame it on a trapper playing a prank," said Jeremiah. "Now it's a blowed-out shot. Anything but gas and dust. Anything but the operators and their smart guys connecting two mines so the fire goes both ways. Any fool would know that was a bad idea."

"What about a union? Would that help?" asked Clemente.

"They'd run off any organizer dared show his face around here. Besides, if they called a strike, there you'd be. Stuck without a job or a house or a piece of ground to live on."

Until any relief money came, each family had to make do with what they had set aside for the winter. The pipe in the community well froze, so Bessie had to melt snow for water. If she didn't get the snow as soon as it fell, it would quickly be covered with coal dust and soot. That year, a short-lived January thaw was followed closely by a February blizzard. Bessie hurried over to Mrs. Ola's to see if she would mind the children so she could climb the hill and try to dig out some of her buried vegetables, hoping to miss the worst of the storm.

"I hate to burden you, but could Ivy and Orie stay with you a little while this afternoon?" asked Bessie.

"You know, my dear, that I love these children as my own, but what are you doing going out in this weather?"

"I've run short of potatoes and cabbage. I'll get some for you, too."

"Yes, that would be very good. I've been hoping to go up to the root cellar, but I can't take the cold like I used to. Papa can't do it, and the only boarder we have left gets home way after dark. If you find any apples, I'd love to make a kuchen for supper."

Bessie hugged the children good-bye and set off with an ax to break open the frozen ground and a bucket to carry her treasures home in. Sometimes it did seem like digging for treasure, especially if the things she'd buried back in the fall were still in good shape. The root cellar they shared with Grandma and Papa Ola had been dug into the hillside about a quarter of a mile from their houses, across the road marking the boundary of company land. The clouds seemed to be lowering and the sky darkening, even though it was early afternoon. This land had been timbered and cleared long ago, so there were no real landmarks, but she'd been living here for three years and knew where she was going.

Bessie searched along the edge of the hill that was rapidly covering with snow until she found the wooden slats that closed off the root cellar. Scraping off the snow with her ax, she found that the slats were frozen together, so she chopped a couple in two so she could wedge her arm inside and try to force this makeshift door open. After several minutes, she decided to chop a hole in the slats big enough for her to slip through. They could fix the door later. The hole in the door let in enough light for Bessie to see the clay pots that held her precious bounty. She gathered enough potatoes to last awhile and added two cabbages, some turnips, and two carrots—not many of those left, she noticed. Re-covering the pots with straw, Bessie searched for apples, but she didn't know on which side of the cellar they'd been stored. She couldn't go home empty-handed, so she spent too many minutes searching.

"Ah, there they are," she said to herself. "Grandma Ola will be so pleased."

As Bessie climbed out of the cellar, she was shocked to see nothing but white. The snow was coming down sideways and she couldn't see any houses, any chimney smoke, any signs of the dirt road she'd crossed on her way to the root cellar. Grabbing up her bucket and ax, she began wading through drifts that were getting deeper and wider. The snow that now contained little pellets of sleet burned her eyes. Squinting, turning first one way, then another, Bessie felt real panic that her babies who had just lost their father would soon lose their mother, too. She decided to walk to the right for one hundred steps, but she still saw nothing to go toward. She turned around and walked two hundred steps to the left, but still nothing. Maybe walking forward would help, so she tried that, but still nothing. Walking through the deepening snow was so hard that she sat down to rest for a minute.

Startling awake, Bessie knew she must find her way home, but how? When she'd left home earlier, she had walked to the right up a rise, across the road, and then on to the right up the hill to nearly the top where the root cellar lay. Reasoning that if she'd come out from home to the right, she'd now need to go to the left, or would it be to the right since she was going the opposite way back? Of all the trips she'd made to the root cellar last fall, surely she could remember which way was home.

"Oh, God, let it be to the right," she pleaded.

All of a sudden, she floundered deeper in the snow, so she scrambled up a bank and found herself on level ground. Surely, this was the road and across it she would find another ditch. Falling in on the other side, she climbed out and continued on to the right. As the day grew darker, in the distance, she saw a dim light and wisps of black smoke across the white sky, so she hurried on. She made it back to the company houses, coming out three doors from her own home, two doors from Mrs. Ola's, where her beloved children sat in front of the coal fire eating the last few crumbs of the Polish cookies Grandma Ola had shared with them.

Bessie opened a jar of boysenberries and mixed up a cobbler crust of flour, salt, and lard, putting it in the oven to fill the house with sweetness when the men arrived for supper. Beans and cabbage would fill them up, but cobbler would make them happy.

Every night since the explosion, there had been nothing but sadness in this house, and that wouldn't change for a long time, she knew. The ache she felt thinking of Orie sitting there so peacefully in the mine waiting for rescue turned into a throbbing nightmare when she tried to sleep. The dream found her alone in the house, unable to move, unable to scream, trying to speak—though no one was there to speak to—capable only of a whimper. As she awakened with her heart pounding, when she did move, there were her children in the bed beside her, peaceful, like their father had been.

Hershel and Clemente arrived first, having made a path home for Jeremiah through the deep snow. Stamping their feet and shaking the snow off their shoulders on the porch, in they came red-faced from the cold, bringing news from the mine.

"They've finally come up with some figures on how much each family will get from the relief fund. The company still hasn't made any decisions," Hershel announced.

"I hate to even think about it all in terms of money, but we sure could use some," said Bessie. "Christmas came and went with no help from anybody, and the three dollars a week I've got since January for me and the children didn't go far, so I guess it's about time."

"We heard that each widow will have $200, plus $174 for each child."

Bessie added up the numbers on the back of Orie's last pay stub.

"Okay, four and four is eight, seven and seven is fourteen, carry the one, one and one and one and two is five, so that means my husband's life was worth exactly $548." At that, she sank to the table, her hands over her face, tears streaming.

Jeremiah came grumbling into the house, worn out from his day's work and his trek home in the snow. Hershel seized the moment to help his father off with his coat and offer to put supper on the table. Bessie recovered herself enough to wash the children's hands and take her place at the table. They were not a family to pray at their meals, but Jeremiah was heard to mutter to himself, "Thank God for berry pie."

Bessie had already filled out form after form for the relief committee. Now, she supposed, she could go to their offices and collect her money. The chatter in the coal camp had been around the need to put your funds in a bank so that it could make more money—a wonderful idea, Bessie thought. Hershel's brother Bill, who worked in the mine office as a bookkeeper, had confirmed that this was possible. She was soon to learn, however, that the committee was sure that some women couldn't manage their own or their children's money, so they would hand it out in small amounts at a time.

"I'm Bessie Morris," she said to the clerk behind a desk, "and I've come to see about my relief money."

"You'll have to wait while I find your file, Mrs. Morris. The waiting area is back the way you came."

Yes, Bessie had noticed a roomful of women on her way in, but the only empty chair was next to a squalling two-year-old who had dirty hands and a dirty diaper. The iron potbelly coal stove in the corner roared with flames and overheated the room to the extent that Bessie felt dizzy, so she chose to wait out on the porch steps. She'd heard these processes could take a long time. To embroider the piece she'd brought along to pass the time, she would have to take off her gloves, so instead, she made mental notes of some of the things she would be able to buy now that she'd have more than three dollars a week. She had seen a copy of the Sears and Roebuck catalog and hoped to get a store-bought dress for Ivy and a toy truck for Orie.

Women came out one at a time, some looking quite cheerful, others with frowns and puckered lips as if they wanted to either scream or cry. At last, Bessie's turn came.

"Well, Mrs. Morris, I have news for you. In total, you will eventually receive $548 from the relief fund, but your payments will be stretched out over a two-year period. Thus, you will receive $22.33 each month starting in April of 1908," said the clerk.

"Why can't I have my money now? I want to put it in the bank and earn—what do they call it?—yes, interest."

"Let me look at the notes in your file. Just a minute."

"Who would make us wait for this money that was freely given by people all over this country?"

"Mrs. Morris, let me assure you that these decisions were not taken lightly, but it seems that your funds are being held back for several reasons. First, you are young and unaccustomed to handling such a large sum of money. But, foremost, it is noted here that there is a moral issue of concern."

"Moral issue? What does that mean?"

"Well, before your husband died, you and he took in boarders, among them a young Italian immigrant. He and two others still live with you, now yourself a young, widowed woman."

"But the other two are family. Hershel was married to my sister, and Jeremiah is his father. Besides, I have invited my mother to live with us. My father was killed in this very mine in 1903."

"I'm sorry, Mrs. Morris, but there's nothing I can do about this decision."

"We'll see about that," said Bessie as she hurried out of the office.

CHAPTER 7

If there was one thing Bessie knew how to do, it was how to save. She saved food; she saved old clothes; she saved the scrip her husband had received for his work until spending it was absolutely necessary; she saved what little money came her way. The very idea that she couldn't handle the relief funds her family deserved so infuriated her that she ran all the way home and burst in on Hershel, who was off work with back problems that day.

"Hershel, you'll never believe what I just learned at the Relief Committee office. They want to give me twenty-two dollars a month for two years instead of the whole thing now!" shouted Bessie.

"I heard about them doing that to some women but never thought it would be you, since you always managed the money just like my Lucy did."

"Well, there's more to it than that. They said I was living with three men and not married to any of them. Sounded like they meant 'living in sin.'"

"Oh, Bessie, that can't be right. We're family, all except for Clemente, and he's just a kid."

"I couldn't throw him out, even if I wanted to, and I don't. He's lost his brother, just as we've lost Orie. There may never be any money paid to him or his mother for the loss of Dominic."

"Tell you what, let's ask Bill to come and help you figure out what you can do. It wouldn't do to talk to him at the mine office. I'll get Dad to invite him to supper, if that's all right.

"Oh, yes, that's fine."

As it turned out, Bill couldn't come to supper that night or the next, but he arrived on Wednesday, explaining that there were lots of company meetings to attend these days. One of the main concerns was the distribution of this relief money, though it was supposed to be in the hands of the committee and not the company.

"How's the back, Hersh? How'd it happen?" asked Bill.

"Oh, a few days' rest fixed me right up, so I went back in this morning. Don't know about you, but I never had such a thing before—every time I put my foot down, I got a shooting pain down my leg. We had a car go off the track inside the mine, and me and another guy tried to lift it back right. Soon as I lifted, I heard a pop, and then I couldn't stand up straight. Thought I'd never get home."

"No, I've never had a back problem, though sitting hunched over a desk all day can't be good for you. Still, don't you be trying to move a coal car anymore."

Bessie brought in a dried apple pie, interrupting the conversation, but nobody minded. It was time to talk business.

"So, Bill, what do you know about these stretched-out relief payments?" asked Bessie. "They want to pay me a little amount over a long time, so that I can't get any of that interest you told me about."

"What reason did they give?" asked Bill.

"Well they said I was young and that I was living here with three men and no husband."

Bill began to laugh, yet no one else chimed in.

"What the hell's so funny about that?" roared Jeremiah, his eyes flashing with anger.

"Yeah, at our first meeting, they said that some folks would have their money delayed for moral reasons, and you've just shown me what 'moral reasons' means. Of all the people in this coal camp, to think of you as immoral is just ridiculous," said Bill.

"Well I'll not have bad things said about Bessie. By God, we have to do something about this," swore Jeremiah.

"I understand that some of the women have appealed this decision, and there've been rumors about pickets at the mine," said Bill.

"I'd be happy to join a picket line," said Bessie, "but then Hershel and Jeremiah would have to cross that line to get to work."

"Maybe it won't come to that. Let me see what I can learn in the next few days. In the meantime, don't get yourself in trouble," counseled Bill.

"I'll try, Bill, but if it takes too long, there won't be anything left anyway. They'll take the three dollars a week I've been getting out of the sum I'm supposed to get, so it's growing smaller by the week."

"Maybe I should check on the babies," said Hershel, "while you fix our pie. It sure smelled good when I got off work today."

Bessie wrote out her appeal, showing that the men living in her house were a brother-in-law and his father and an immigrant who had been with her and her now-deceased husband Orie for over two years. She mentioned that she had invited her mother, herself the widow of a miner killed in the Monongah mine four years earlier, to come and live with them. Her last argument was that if she had no boarder who worked in the mine, she would lose her company house. Once again, she made her way to the offices of the Relief Committee, and once again, she sat outside waiting her turn. Finally, the clerk read her letter and said that she could do nothing personally, but would pass the appeal on to the committee. In the meantime, Bessie's mother, Belle Murphy, agreed to come back to Monongah from her daughter Ada Maude's home in Ohio and live with Bessie and her boarders.

Belle Murphy had given birth to nine children, all of whom would live into adulthood. Bessie was her first child, born in 1883, and Wilbert, born in early May 1903, was her last. Her husband, Jacob, lived only twenty-five days beyond the birth of this last son. The Monongah mines, like all others, had been taking lives one by one, and on that day, May 30, three had been killed by a slate fall, just before the end of the day shift. Others tried to dig them out, but with the slate came the release of toxic methane, so the rescue was abandoned. Four of her children were married, and three middle daughters, ages fifteen, twelve, and ten, begged to stay in Ohio. That left two boys, ages seven and five, to try to fit into the small company house in Monongah.

Bessie would, of course, share her bed with Belle. Hershel, always handy with carpenters' tools, quickly put together a small bed for the two smallest children and a little larger one for the two little boys, Russell and Wilbert, due any day from Ohio. Scrap lumber was always available at the mine, and a straw tick could be fashioned from old clothes and held up with rope stretched tight. Clemente had always slept on a pallet on the floor, as had Hershel until the day of his back injury. Now Hershel either had to share the bed with his father or sleep on the davenport in the front room, so he chose the latter. Jeremiah had a loud snore that Clemente could sleep through, but Hershel thought it could wake the dead.

Belle and the children would be arriving in Fairmont by train and would then take the streetcar to Monongah. Hershel welcomed Belle, the mother of his beloved Lucy, back into the family and hoped she would be happy enough there to stay. She was known to be a strong woman with a hot temper to match, and she'd spit in the eye of anyone who dared to cross her. Hershel wondered what she'd think about the "moral issue" that hovered over their home.

As the streetcar eased to a stop, Bessie waved her handkerchief to identify herself in the milling crowd anxious to climb aboard themselves. Belle wasted no time getting herself and the boys off the car along with her large carpetbag.

"Why are you waving that silly thing? Don't you think I know my own daughter?" Belle huffed.

Not wishing to start off on the wrong foot, Bessie ignored the words and took the carpetbag in hand to carry home. Orie and Ivy were with Mrs. Ola, so Bessie just fussed over Russell and Wilbert, telling them how much they'd grown since she saw them last, patting their cheeks and telling them she had hot cocoa waiting for them at home.

Belle said, "Now, you're not to spoil these two. They're not used to such petting and won't be the better for it."

Bessie just gave her mother a hug and said, "Let's go."

The only way supper could be managed was to feed the children first, so Bessie set the table for four and called them in from the game of horseshoes they were playing in the yard. Orie was too small to lift and throw the heavy horseshoe, so Russell, now the biggest kid, took a turn for him. They resisted coming in since the game was tied, but they relented when Belle said they could go back out after supper if they cleaned their plates. The men were just arriving home from the mine as the children finished their meal, so the table could quickly be re-set and supper served again. Bessie and Belle worked well together in the kitchen, since Belle had long ago taught her what she knew about cooking.

Hershel thought how different it would be if Lucy and Belle were trying to work together in this crowded kitchen. Lucy had refused her mother's efforts to turn her thoughts away from moving to some big city and concentrate instead on being somebody's wife who could cook and sew and make quilts and raise a garden. She had, however, learned most of those things in her short life when, as his wife, they had done them together and had filled those chores with laughter. Only at the end had she lost her spirit.

"Hey, daydreamer, come to supper," said Clemente, bringing Hershel back from his thoughts of those days with Lucy.

The rest of the evening was spent clearing up the kitchen and getting the children, faces washed, ready for bed. Clemente hauled inside the trunk that had arrived on the late streetcar. Unpacking it would have to wait. Belle turned in early, and Bessie joined the men at the table, where talk turned to the ever-present "moral issue."

"Missus Bessie, I can find somewhere else to stay, if that would help," offered Clemente.

"No, I won't hear of it," she replied. "We'll wait a little longer, and then I'll make another appeal."

"You know, I bet if you added the fact that the two boys and their mother are here now onto your first appeal, it might make a difference. I'm their brother-in-law, and she's my mother-in-law," reasoned Hershel.

"Well, they make three more mouths to feed, so we need more than twenty-two dollars a month. Mom takes in sewing and ironing, but people will have to learn that she's here and willing to work before we can count on that," said Bessie.

The next morning, Bessie sat at the kitchen table writing out her second appeal. Belle joined her with a cup of coffee and asked what all the secrecy was about.

"I heard you talking last night, so what's going on that I don't know about?"

"Well, there's a fund of money to be given out to the widows of Monongah, and because I'm young and living here with three men, they want to give me just a little bit at a time and stretch it out over two years."

"Why on earth—"

"Because they think that makes me, uh … incompetent … yes, that's the word … incompetent to handle the money."

"Oh, Bessie, that ain't right," insisted Belle.

"No, it's not, and that's why I'm making this appeal. Now that you're here with the boys, surely they'll change their mind. I'm taking this to the office today."

"Well, not without me, you won't. I'll give them a piece of my mind they won't never forget."

As they walked to the center of town, Bessie worried that her mother would only make things worse if she insulted the clerk at the relief office. Belle had a way of talking sometimes that made Bessie blush with shame. All her life, she had feared her mother's outbursts that were usually followed by stone-cold silences and a stare that could crack a mirror. It had been common knowledge in Monongah that no one trifled with Belle Murphy, but she'd been gone for a few years now and those memories may have faded away. Bessie's hand shook as she reached to open the door for her mother. What came next could not have been more stunning.

"Why there's little Mary June Calabrese sittin' there bein' a perfect secretary," gushed Belle.

"Mrs. Murphy, can that be you? I haven't seen you in years. And I'm now not a secretary, but a clerk for the Relief Committee."

"Bessie," Belle said, "this is Mary June who lived next door to us when she was a little girl, and now she's got herself a job and everything."

"Hello again," said Bessie. "I've brought you a new appeal letter for the committee. My mother is living with us now, so that should make a difference."

The coal in the stove shifted and flared up. The widows lining the chairs around the wall, the clerk, Bessie, and Belle—everyone in the room paused and took a deep breath.

"Yes," said Belle, now becoming serious, "there seemed to be some problem with Bessie's money—something about not being able to take good care of the money, something about living in her home with her brother-in-law and his father and a boarder—none of which made any sense to me. Bessie always was careful with money. Since there was so little, it could only go so far. So you can just put that worry behind you." Changing her tone again, she said, "When do you expect we can hear from you?"

"Uh, Mrs. Murphy, it's not up to me, but I'll certainly give this letter to the committee and put in a good word."

"Well just see that you do that, Mary June. I'll be back tomorrow if we haven't had word by then," promised Belle.

As they walked home, Belle confided that she liked to start out with a little sugar, but then she had plenty of piss and vinegar to apply if necessary. Bessie had never seen a lot of sugar from her Mother, but she'd certainly been on the receiving end of the vinegar.

The Relief Committee still met daily since there were so many widows and children to process. At nine the next morning, Mary June Calabrese knocked timidly on the meeting-room door. Besides the committee members, there were two coal-company executives sitting around a large oval table. She quickly handed Bessie's newest appeal to the company man serving as chairman, said, "One request has been revised, sir," and hurried out the door.

"This won't amount to much," he said, "so I may as well take a look before we start the meeting." When he got to the part where Bessie said,

"My mother, Belle Murphy, and my two small brothers now live with us," he began to laugh. The others looked at each other, puzzled by his behavior.

"What's so funny?" said the other coal operator, impatient to be done with these proceedings and, indeed, with all that had to be done before they could just get back to hauling coal.

"Well, we've got ourselves a little problem here, Jim," said the chairman. "You see, we had decided to award our relief money a little at a time to one Bessie Morris for several reasons. Now she's invited her mother and two little brothers to live with them, and she's asking us to reconsider."

"I don't see the problem," said Jim.

"The problem is her mother, Belle Murphy. You remember the cat fit she had a few years ago when her husband, Jacob, got killed in a slate fall and we had nothing for her, with a new baby and all?"

"Well, we couldn't be responsible for every baby of every miner who got hurt. Coal mining is a tough business, and they sign up for it voluntarily, don't they?"

"Yes, they do. But if Belle Murphy's back in Monongah, it'll be the devil to pay if we don't nip this in the bud. What do you say we just go on and give Bessie her money and let her waste it if she's of a mind to? I seem to remember we finally gave Belle train fare for herself and several children so they could go to Ohio, and good riddance. Don't you remember her? She's the one who, after screamin' and hollerin', just sat herself down in the mine office day after day, looking so prim and proper doing her tatting, or whatever the hell it was, saying that she'd never move from there. We finally had to carry her out bodily."

"Oh, God, yes, I remember now. We can't have any of that this time. The newspapers would be all over it."

"Now, if we just release Bessie's funds, we won't have to deal with her mother or any of the rest of that family. How many of them are working for us now?"

"Let's see—there's Jeremiah Martin and his son Hershel and one Italian boarder. Bessie's husband, Orie Morris, and the Italian's brother,

Domenic Giancetta, both died in the explosions, but she also has two small children at home."

"And now her mother and two brothers—all living in a four-room house? Well, I say let's give her the money and let the devil take the hindmost." With that, the matter was concluded.

When the check arrived a few days later, only Jeremiah knew what had happened to change the minds of the Relief Committee. He remembered what Belle had done when Jacob was killed. *How can such a pretty woman be such a hellcat?* he wondered, smiling to himself.

CHAPTER 8

Hershel, only twenty years old, had worked in the mines for twelve years and knew every job to be had by now, everything from loading the explosives and tamping the charge to running the automatic cutting machine, but his favorite job had been apprenticing under the lead electrician. Every supervisor knew he could count on Hershel to learn quickly, do the job right, and get along with everyone else. Perhaps his most valued trait was his ability to keep his head in emergencies, no panic, no shouting, just a calm study of what needed to be done and a quick completion of it.

Hershel had been in the mine the day Lucy and Bessie's father was covered up in the slate fall. All day, he had worried when he heard the roof talking. Every sort of sound meant something different, and he had reported what he heard it saying, but no one listened at that point to a sixteen-year-old boy. Now he questioned whether it was wise to keep working at Monongah, where the explosion in one mine instantly spread to the other, killing more than five hundred men and boys. He knew better than the official coroner's jury report that said it was only less than four hundred. What about all those little fellas coming to work with their dads who were not on the clock? How could there be any record of them?

Maybe I should make a change, he thought, *but what?* He mulled his choices over and over. He had heard there were still some logging jobs farther south in the mountains. Hereabouts, the hills had been clear-cut almost to nothing, but mines and railroads needed roof supports and cross ties. He knew he could handle the team of mules used to drag the logs out, and he and Jeremiah had cut up some trees that fell across the road, but he had no experience in a sawmill. He'd be out in the daylight, but then he'd heard so many stories about men being killed in the log woods. Besides, he felt sorrow at the death of the trees that made the hillsides look like bald men all hunched together, the soil washing clear away when it rained. His true calling might have been farming, but he had no land. Watching seedlings sprout in their small garden and carrying posies of flowers into the house gave him a sense of peace and contentment. What could he do that felt right and didn't chance death every single day? Of course, his first duty was to earn a living.

A possible answer came with the call for experienced men at the newly expanded mine at Riverview south of Monongah on the West Fork River. They had all gone to the nearby town of Shinnston for the annual Fourth of July parade and found flyers posted everywhere announcing: "Jobs at the new mine at Riverview. Apply now!" Bessie read the words to Hershel and saw his eyes light up. She began to wonder if it would ever be possible to leave the sorrow of Monongah behind and start over somewhere else.

"Hey, Bessie, want to ride over to Riverview on the streetcar? Remember, they got jobs for hire, and I hear the company houses there are bigger," said Hershel the next Sunday morning.

"Now, Hershel, are you thinking of moving?"

"Well, this mine and this place give me the willies, so if there's someplace we could all go, it might be a good idea," he replied.

"Oh, I would love to live somewhere else. I keep seeing Orie everywhere I turn. Every day you three go to work, I think about who might not come home. Let me just see if Mom wants to go. She's got a say in everything now, too. And what about your dad?"

"He's getting his Sunday afternoon rest, so let's just leave him be for now."

Cool air blew in the open windows as the streetcar rolled its slow way along the West Fork River. The only reason they had this transportation was for the convenience of the coal operators. The Interurban Traction Company line from Clarksburg to Fairmont brought miners to work and took them home again and also allowed other company employees to coordinate the business dealings of the many mines scattered along this river. Bessie chatted all the way with first her mother, who barely responded, and then with Hershel, who only nodded in agreement. Bessie's voice had returned since the disaster, and now she seemed to be making up for lost time.

As they got off the streetcar, they noticed the coke ovens, black holes gouged out of the hillside. Though they weren't lit up on Sunday, Hershel could imagine that on weeknights, they would be a sight to see. Maybe he could learn to run a coke oven. That, at least, would get him out in the open air.

"What's all that, Hershel?" Bessie asked.

"They're coke ovens that burn coal to put together with iron to make steel. We don't have 'em in Monongah."

"It's pretty quiet around here now. Wonder what it sounds like when they're goin,'" said Belle. "I hate noise at night. Don't seem right, somehow."

"This mine don't run twenty-four hours, so I reckon the coke ovens don't either, but I bet they put out a nice glow," said Hershel.

Their walk along the gravel path toward the mine revealed six- and eight-room company houses with good-size gardens in the back. Some stood empty, just waiting for them, Hershel wished. Today, in the sunshine, they looked welcoming. *Wonder what they'd look like on a winter's day under an overcast sky,* he thought. The builders had left some old trees standing here and there, maples mostly, and Hershel could imagine them turning all colors in the fall. Here along the river where logging would have been difficult, there were still red oaks and pine trees that would no doubt show up as giants looming out of the fog that was bound to happen in this valley. Hershel had always liked fog. It seemed ghostly and haunting, appearing and disappearing suddenly, only to appear again just a few steps farther along.

"Look at that house, Mom," said Bessie. "Wouldn't you love to live in a house that big with a front porch and a swing?"

"I'm not sure we could ever have such a place, Bessie, but it would be nice." Belle had given up even hoping for things like bigger houses and bigger garden plots. Life had given her the hardship of nine children and a dead husband, so her chances, she felt, were slim.

Since the mine itself was closed on Sunday, Hershel couldn't go in for a look around, but he noticed signs with lists on them hanging under a little roof by the mine office door. "Bessie," he said, "can you read what these say?"

"Well, let's see. It looks like the jobs that are open and hiring, and it says that to apply, you should come to this office weekdays from 8:00 to 4:00 to fill out paperwork."

"I'll be working those hours, but could you come and get the paperwork and we could fill it out at home? How 'bout it?"

Bessie never wanted to refuse to help Hershel, but she wondered if these men would allow her to do what he asked. The biggest surprise in her life had been when the Relief Committee had granted her request, and she was sure it hadn't been because of anything she had done, but instead was her mother's doing. Bessie wasn't at all shy with people like herself, but she grew afraid of men in suit clothes. After a pause, she agreed to come back in the morning and see what she could do.

Once again, Bessie was confronted with a clerk behind a desk handing out sheets of paper.

"Good morning," she said. "May I have three work applications?"

"And who would those be for?" said the clerk.

"My brother-in-law, his father, and our boarder, who all have lots of experience," replied Bessie. "They're all at work right now or they would have come themselves."

"From Monongah, I guess?"

"Yes, ma'am."

"We sure have had lots of applicants from Monongah. I suppose that's to be expected, what with the disaster."

Trying to put on a cheerful expression, Bessie said, "Yes, but this looks like a good little town, and the company houses are much bigger than where we live."

"Yes, I've lived here all my life, and I wouldn't trade it. There aren't many houses left, though, so tell these men to get their papers in quick."

Later on, after supper, Bessie and the three men sat at the kitchen table talking about what might lie ahead. Clemente was eager to get away from memories of his brother, one of the miners whose body had never been fully recovered. He had nightmares of turning a corner in the mine and seeing Domenic lying in pieces on the track. His mother had written a letter begging him to come home, but he felt he had a future in America, since he made forty or fifty cents a day in the mine and had only made ten cents a day as a farm laborer in Italy. He still sent half of his pay to his mother, but he just put off answering her plea. Jeremiah, on the other hand, had already changed mines over and over through strikes and layoffs and just wanted to stay put.

"Dad, let's just ask Bessie to fill out papers for all of us and we'll see who gets hired," suggested Hershel.

"Have it your way," grumbled Jeremiah, as he turned toward the porch for a smoke. "They prob'ly won't have me anyway—been on this earth too long."

When she got to the "job skills" question, Bessie had to ask what to write for each. Clemente had little to offer but asked her to say that he "learned quick." Jeremiah had begun work when all they had was black powder and a shovel, both of which he had to buy with his own money. He had been there when the automatic cutting machines came along, so he knew how to operate those. Otherwise, there was nothing much to say. Hershel had always sought out new experiences, so he named over the list of jobs he'd held and asked Bessie to say that he had already been an apprentice electrician and was well suited to that job.

Bessie hopped on the streetcar the next morning to deliver the applications to the clerk, hoping for a fast response and a chance at one of those houses. As she waited her turn, she went over plans for moving in her mind. Fall was coming on, and she could pick the corn and tomatoes and dig the potatoes in her garden in time to move, if only they got an answer soon. The root cellar had been mostly emptied out in the spring, just before a powerful shot in the mine below had caused it to cave in, burying some precious jars of berries she'd put there, she'd thought, for safekeeping. She might even be able to gather some mid-summer apples that had fallen from the tremors.

The clerk said that since they didn't have a telephone, Bessie would need to come back the next day and the next, and perhaps several more, before any hiring decisions had been made. She got in the routine of catching the streetcar early every morning to scan the lists of new hires posted outside the mine office. Although it was only twenty minutes to Riverview and twenty minutes back, the trip started her day off late. Her mother was there with the children, but the preparation of food for winter was underway, and she had so much to do that she almost gave up hoping for the best—her usual approach to life. In the middle of the third week, however, there was good news and bad. Hershel's wish for the job of electrician had come true, and Clemente was hired as a loader, the same backbreaking job he had at Monongah. Jeremiah had not been hired as a machine operator. When Bessie inquired if any jobs were left, the clerk said there was a weighman's job left at the tipple. Surely, Bessie thought, Jeremiah could run the scale and give credit for the coal loaded by each miner, but she didn't know if he could count or not, if he recognized numbers, if he could cipher.

Bessie fed the children their supper and quickly sent them out to play in the late-summer sunlight. She loved to sit out in the evening and ponder the long shadows, but this night was going to change their lives—for better or worse, she didn't know. The men came home, tired and hungry as usual, so she waited till they were finished to tell the news.

"We finally have some answers," she said, "and they're not all good."

Belle turned from clearing away the dishes, and all eyes focused on Bessie. "So, what did you find out today?" said Hershel.

"Well, you'll be glad to know that they think you can be an electrician and that you, Clem, can be a loader, just like now." Both

Hershel and Clemente were delighted with this news, but both could see that something else was coming and it wouldn't be good, so they stifled any celebration.

"Jeremiah, they didn't hire you, but maybe there's still a chance. What do you know about the job of a weighman? That's still open."

Jeremiah looked down at his feet, sighed a deep breath, and said, "Don't think I could do it, Bessie."

Hershel quickly said, "Why not, Dad?"

"You know I didn't go to school."

Bessie interrupted with her own question. "Jeremiah, can you count?"

"Well, sure, I can count to a hundred."

"Can you write numbers?"

"Yes, but I couldn't match up the names and the numbers, 'cause I never learned to read. Them letters don't mean a thing to me."

"But if you only had to match the weight on the scale with each man's check number on the coal car, could you do that?"

"Don't know, Bessie, but, look here, if I quit this job and then couldn't do that one, I'd be out of work, so no. I'll say no more about it."

At that moment, a cloud passed over the setting sun, casting a shadow over the land to match the pall that had settled over the family still seated around the table. Jeremiah retreated to his pipe on the porch. Bessie and Belle cleared away the supper dishes and called the children in for bed. Hershel and Clemente spoke in quiet voices about their hopes for the future. The young men and young woman chased different dreams; the older man and older woman had seen too many dreams denied to chase anything at all. *Still, it never hurt to hope, did it?* thought Belle.

"Jeremiah, surely there's something we can do to keep this family together," said Belle, joining him on the porch.

"If you're thinking I could learn to read and take that job, you're crazier than I thought you were," he replied.

"No, I reckon you're too old a dog to learn any new tricks," she said.

"Well, now, I ain't that old. Speak for yourself."

"Just how old are you?" she asked.

"I'll be fifty-six on my next birthday. How old are you?"

"I just turned forty-six and counting. I just think we should all stick together. It's us and them in this world."

"You're right about that. I been wonderin' just how such a handsome woman as yourself got to be such a hell-raiser."

"Go on with you, Jeremiah. Handsome is as handsome does, and if it takes a little hell raisin,' so be it," she said. And with that, she slammed the screen door behind her.

CHAPTER 9

Bessie rode the streetcar once again the next morning to say that both Hershel and Clemente would accept the jobs offered at Riverview. "When would they start?" she asked. According to the clerk, the new crew would not begin work for two weeks, which gave a chance for Hershel and Clem to give their notice. Never knew when they might need to return to Monongah, or if they might ever work under some superintendent they'd had before. Couldn't take any more chances than needed—this work gave enough over to chance. The problem now was what to do about Jeremiah. They couldn't leave him all on his own, but could they take him along? He could make the twenty-minute ride to work morning and night, or he could stay and board with some other family.

The little town of Monongah had begun the long, slow process of accepting its loss. Winter had turned to spring and spring to summer. Nearly every family had faced the absence of someone dear, whether he had been a husband or father or an immigrant boarder. Each one was deeply felt, and in the churches, prayers were still being offered up for their souls' rest. The violence and suddenness of the disaster took away the chance for last rites, for repentance and forgiveness, for what was thought a good death. Besides that heartbreak, now arose the question of the company houses, an issue the company had let lie till now.

Two of Mrs. Ola's three Polish boarders had been killed in the explosion; the third had recently gone back home, and her husband,

Papa, was too old to start over mining coal. Their sons had moved on to the great open West long ago and would not be returning. Word of the disaster had spread across southern Europe and the flow of immigrants to Monongah had dwindled, so she could not be sure of any more young men knocking on her door inquiring after rooms to rent.

"What will become of us?" said Mrs. Ola to Belle, who had taken to visiting every morning along with Bessie. "They're telling me that we must move out of our home since we have no miners living here."

"Won't they give you a little more time?" asked Belle. "Surely they're not that hard-hearted."

"They said we have two weeks."

Bessie's thoughts had turned lately to their move to Riverview, and now, perhaps, there could be an answer to Jeremiah's need to stay in Monongah. "Mrs. Ola, could you possibly put up with Hershel's father as a new boarder? He's a little grumpy, but then, who's not sometimes? Hershel and Clem will be taking new jobs at Riverview, but Jeremiah refuses to go."

Mrs. Ola looked somewhat startled at this suggestion. "Well, he sometimes sits out in the evenings smoking with Papa, talking about the old days. Do you think he would eat the kinds of food I cook?"

"Well he's never complained about what I've given him, and I'm not the cook you are, after all. One thing he does like is sweets, and you're the best at those dainty little cookies and cakes. The most I can do is pie," said Bessie.

"Oh, do you think he would agree?" said Mrs. Ola, clapping her hands and smiling for the first time in many days.

"Let us take care of that," said Belle, rising to put their coffee cups in the sink. "I think we can convince him, don't you, Bessie?"

"It would be a prayer answered, and a way for us to still be friends," said Bessie, hugging Mrs. Ola. "We could visit Jeremiah and you at the same time, and I know Orie and Ivy will want to visit. They think of you as their second grandmother—no offense, Mom."

"Ah, but I also have come to love the two new little boys, your sons, Belle. And I will miss all of you, so please try to win Jeremiah over to our plan."

All day, Bessie and Belle packed boxes, filling them with clothes and bed clothes, leaving just enough to get by before the move. The kitchen items would be boxed up last, along with the remaining food. On moving day, they would eat cornbread with milk for the children and coffee for the grown-ups. Tonight, they would seek Jeremiah's approval. Bessie thought he would agree—Belle thought he should agree—but it was his decision. He might just stomp out the door, giving no answer at all.

After supper, Hershel grinned as Bessie whispered the plan and asked him to approach his father with the question. "Bessie, I think you should be the one to ask him," said Hershel.

"Why? He's your father," she said.

"Well, that's why. He might not even look at me, but he likes you, so go ask him right now, while he's still in a good mood from supper. He'll just think I'm trying to tell him what to do."

Belle, overhearing the conversation, shooed her daughter out the door. "Just go on now; it'll be all right," she said.

Jeremiah sat leaning his back against the wall, smoking in peace, but he looked around as Bessie came out onto the porch. "I thought you'd be longing for your bed. It's been a long time since you fixed my buckwheat cakes this morning," he said.

"Well, it's such a pretty night, and I've got something to ask you," she replied.

"Oh, what's that?"

"Now … you know we're just about to move away … and Mom and I had a talk with Mrs. Ola this morning. Seems she's about to be put out of her house, with no miners living there. What would you think about boarding with the Olas? That way, you could just move next door, and they could keep their house. You wouldn't have to live in Riverview and ride the streetcar to work every day."

No words were spoken for a long few seconds. Then Jeremiah growled, "Looks like you've worked it all out."

"Oh, it's not like we don't want you living with us anymore! It just looked like we could kill two birds with one rock," she cried.

"Well, I ain't no bird and I ain't killed, but … maybe it's not such a bad idea."

"So you're not mad at me, are you? Please don't be mad," she coaxed.

"No, I guess I ain't mad. I'll think on it."

Hershel had borrowed a mule and wagon for the move to Riverview, hoping to make it in one trip. He had never unpacked most of his belongings from his home with Lucy, so those could go in the wagon first. Jeremiah had indeed thought about it and decided to stay in Monongah with Grandma and Papa Ola. He'd already moved his sparse possessions the night before, shocking the old couple with his sudden appearance at their door. Once he'd made his mind up, he wanted it done. He still slept at home that night, though, and now began carrying out items of furniture to load onto the wagon.

Off over the hill and down the road a racket started up that seemed to be coming toward them. The sound came not from the direction of the mine, as had the explosions, but from the small town. The children stopped, wide-eyed, wondering if they should run to their mamas. Hershel stood with his hand shielding his eyes from the morning sun when a large black shape topped the rise and came fully into view. Although he'd never seen such a contraption up close, he'd heard that one of the mine operators had purchased himself an automobile—a Packard, it was called. The closer it came, the more beautiful it seemed to him, sunshine glinting off the shiny surfaces, the wheels perfectly clean and black with white circles in the center, the running boards smooth and the interior dark and shaded. The only person he could see was a driver sitting alone in the front behind a clear glass windscreen. Smoked glass rose behind the driver, concealing those being carried in such style. *They're headed to the mine to show it off,* he thought. *Someday, I'll have one of those for myself.*

They'd managed to get a two-story company house at Riverview with a good-size garden plot in back. The front porch was under roof and had room for a swing that Hershel could build as a place for the children to be lulled into their naps and their daydreams. Ivy and Orie were still put to bed in the afternoons, though Russell and Wilbert were allowed to play quietly, building forts and pretending to be soldiers. No shouting and no fighting in the house were the rules Belle laid down for these two and strictly enforced. She was also set on the idea that they would never work in the mine, seeing to it that they attended school and did their sums at the kitchen table after supper. Belle had tried to impose her will on all of her children, and Bessie had lasted through eighth grade, so there was a model before these boys.

"Let's set up the kitchen first, Mom," said Bessie. "We can worry about the other things later. I want our first supper in this new house to be special."

"I'll get Clem to start us a fire in the cookstove, so we can stew some of your canned tomatoes. We have cornbread left over from breakfast, and we can boil a few ears of corn and have a feast," said Belle. "I noticed that the pump is right close to the back door. Now, where is that big pot?"

Bessie and Belle put supper on the table while Clemente and Hershel carried in the larger things and the children helped out with small boxes and odds and ends. A neighbor came over with a welcome gift of apples from a windfall and was introduced all around. Her tiny daughter clung to her skirt, peeking around at Ivy, but not saying a word. There would be plenty of time for friendship, thought Bessie, glad to see another little girl among all those boys. Everyone went to bed exhausted that night. The new twelve-hour days would begin at 6:00 a.m., with breakfast and the lunch buckets packed at 5:00. The mine itself was only about a mile away, a quick walk for young men.

The little community of Riverview stretched a good ways along the West Fork River. In summer and fall, everyone stayed as far away from its foul, sulfur-smelling water as they could, and this September day would be no exception. The mine tipple loomed over the railroad tracks running through the middle of town and over the one paved street. Side streets leading to the company houses were just dirt roads that were either dusty or muddy, depending on the time of year. Hershel's house was among the last to be built and the farthest away from the town.

The company store had been constructed on the main street near the tipple, and a hotel had opened up across from the store. The streetcar ran between Clarksburg to the south and Fairmont to the north, with Shinnston in between. Just north of Shinnston lay the tiny communities of Riverview, Enterprise, and Viropa, each one constructed as new or extended mines opened up.

Hershel and Clemente arrived early that first morning and were happy to see some familiar faces on the work crew. This mine had a man-trip ready to carry some of them back to their assigned places for the day. "Beats the hell out of walking," said Hershel. "I wonder when Monongah will get one of these now that they got themselves an auto-mo-bile," he said with a laugh.

"See you at home," Clemente said, boarding the car and waving good-bye. His job as coal loader would take him deep inside the mine, while Hershel's as second electrician began outside in a meeting with the head electrician and his helper. The two men looked suspiciously at Hershel and he looked right back, intending to get off to a good start the first day. He stuck out his hand and the older of the two shook it and said, "Let's get to work."

"Suits me," said Hershel, wondering why they both looked like they could bite a nail in two—maybe he'd gotten the job the younger one had his hopes set on. Maybe he was the older one's son, or his brother. Guess he'd learn soon enough.

As they walked toward the electrical shop, the older one finally introduced himself. "I'm Jack Warden, and this here's Tommaso, but we just call him Tommy. He's my helper and he'll be yours, too, if a two-man job comes up and you need him. Most of the time, he's running wire and finding parts, you know, the sort of stuff a helper does."

"Well, I can't say as I've ever had a helper before, but I've been one. I was mighty happy to be hired on as second electrician, Mr. Warden, and I'm prepared to do whatever it is a second electrician does," said Hershel. "They only had one electrician and a helper at Monongah."

"It's Jack, Hershel. We're a bigger operation than they have at Monongah. I heard you were there. Awful shame, that was."

"Yes, it was. I lost my brother-in-law that day."

"Guess it's time to get down to business," said Jack. "Just one thing, though. I thought you'd be much older when I said I'd have you working with me. Said you had lots of experience."

"Well, sir, I started as a trapper. I was eight years old, and I've been at it for twelve years."

"All right, I guess that answers my questions, then. I'll be expecting a lot from you. We're wiring one section at a time, starting with the newer works first. No use doing anything to the old works, as they'll be closed off soon anyway."

"Will there be lights inside?" asked Hershel.

"No, there's no money for lights, just for running electricity to the cutting machines and the motors that haul the men in and the coal out," said Jack. "The wires run along the ceiling, so it's a good thing we have a nice, high coal seam here. If men were already working on their knees and kneeling down in water, it would be awful hard to electrify a mine."

"The first place I worked was just like that," said Hershel. "This mine looks mighty fine."

"Just be ready to start hanging wire first thing in the morning," said Jack at the end of the shift.

"Yes, sir."

Hershel was satisfied with his first day on the new job, although he'd spent most of it following Jack around. Maybe they'd given him hard looks that morning because of his age. He'd just have to work harder than most to prove his worth. He knew he wasn't just a kid, but they'd have to be shown.

CHAPTER 10

1910

The three years since the Monongah disaster had been marked by change. Jeremiah had suffered broken ribs in a rock fall and had come to Riverview to be nursed by Bessie and Belle. Old Mr. Morris, Orie's father, arrived unannounced one day, but he was welcomed into the household, where he sat by the kitchen stove on cold days and on the porch in fair weather. His heart had been broken with the death of his youngest son, but Orie's two children brought joy once again. Clemente had saved his pennies and gone home to Italy, only to return with a new bride named Bonita. They would move into their own small company house, if ever one was vacant.

"Mom, don't you envy the lovebirds?" asked Bessie one day not long after their arrival.

"No, I don't. They've got a long, hard road ahead of them," said Belle.

"But they seem so happy. I miss those carefree, happy times with Orie. We had such fun together—and then he was gone."

"Now, Bessie, don't go feeling sorry for yourself. You're young. You can be happy again."

"It seems like all I ever do is scrub and clean and cook. And worry. I want more than that; don't you?"

"Bessie, I've had nine children, and two aren't even grown yet. What else is there but taking care of your family? And speaking of family—there's a perfectly good young man right here in your house, if it's love you're looking for."

"Oh, Mom, I can't believe you said that. He was Lucy's husband, and Orie was mine."

"Bessie, Lucy is dead. Orie is dead. There's no need for the two of you to live with the dead any longer. I've seen the way he looks at you, especially when you're busy with your sewing and humming a little song like you do."

Bessie blushed pink and refused to talk about it anymore, but she couldn't help thinking back over the last few months. Ivy and Orie had begun calling Hershel Daddy when he took over helping them with their letters and numbers after supper. He couldn't put the letters together, but he could teach them how to make each one in the right order and in tiny, very precise, fashion, so they looked like little drawings. Numbers came easier to him, and he had a basic knowledge of adding and subtracting.

Hershel came home from work one evening complaining about the teasing he took from the other men. "I have to get somebody to be a witness when I sign my name with an *X*," he said. "I'm sick of it."

"Well, why don't you just learn to write your name?" Bessie said.

"I was done with school a long time ago, Bessie, and I don't plan on going back."

"I could show you how," she said. "Sit down here, and I'll write it on this paper poke and you can copy it off."

"No. I've tried before and couldn't do it."

Ignoring his protest, Bessie wrote out *Hershel Martin* and said, "There's your whole name. Is that the way you want it to look?"

"Well, my first name is Clarence," he said.

"That's a lot to write. You could just use letters. That would make it C H Martin. Sounds sort of official that way. What do you think?"

"Let me try." Gripping the pencil, he made each letter individually: *c h m a r t i n* "I can print it like that, but it doesn't look like yours," he said.

"That's because I wrote it and you printed it. See if you can just draw out the writing," she urged.

He soon filled the space around her signature with his copies of it. Over and over, he drew the signature, until he had perfected it. Finally, he put the work aside to see if he could make the signature without looking at hers. When she saw that he could, indeed, she clapped her hands and danced around the kitchen, saying, "Well, there you are, the new Mr. C. H. Martin." Never a dancer, he rose from the table and grabbed her for a hug, thanking her with a rare smile.

Hershel thought about that hug as he tried, with no luck, to go to sleep that night. Throwing off the covers, he sat up on the side of his bed and worried that Bessie would think he had been too forward. Here they'd lived under the same roof all these years—surely she knew he'd never hurt her, and besides, she hadn't pulled away from that hug. She'd just laughed and continued her dance till Orie and Ivy ran in to see what the fun was all about. She proudly showed off Hershel's new writing skill and offered to teach each of them to write their names, too. *Maybe it will be all right,* he thought.

After his restless night, Hershel awoke late to the wonderful smell of buckwheat cakes and coffee perking on the stove. Forgetting that it was Sunday, he hurried into his work clothes and rushed into the kitchen and came face to face with Bessie, who was likewise hurrying to get the children to the table for breakfast. "Oh, there you are," she said. "I was about to give up on you this beautiful Sunday morning, sleepyhead. Let me just call the kids, and then I'll finish your breakfast."

"No hurry. I'll just have some coffee first." He took his coffee out onto the porch to enjoy the rare sunny day. It was late summer, the season of yellow wildflowers and spiderwebs. He hated to miss days like this and thought about how to make the most of his day of rest. Maybe they could have a picnic up on the hillside, away from the river. His father and Mr. Morris would be going to church with Belle and her two boys. Clemente and Bonita would go to mass at noon. Bessie would take Ivy and Orie to Sunday school and come back home mid-morning, leaving the afternoon free. Now, how could he go about suggesting a picnic without looking too forward? Forward, *there's that word again,* he thought.

"Ooh-hoo! Come and eat," Bessie called. She had rolled up a fried egg in a buckwheat cake—his favorite—and added a link of sausage and a sliced tomato to his plate. "Surprise!" she said. "I took some of the money I've been saving to buy a piece of sausage for each of us. And while I was there, I asked if they needed anyone to work a few hours a week at the company store. Would you believe they said yes, they'd been looking for someone to work from 9:00 to noon Monday through Friday? Mom said she'd mind the children, so I'm going start a week from tomorrow. What do you think?"

"Gosh, Bessie, I never thought you'd be happy doing that sort of thing," Hershel said. "You love to cook and sew and can and garden, don't you?"

"Yes, but I also would like a little extra money, and this will make me some. I've never touched a penny I got for Orie's death, and I want to save it as long as I can. It's making interest, you know."

"Not sure what that is."

"It's money you make while the bank's using your money to make money. That's my understanding of it, anyway."

"What I think is that you should do whatever you want to do, Bessie. If you want to work at the store, then you should just do it. And if you want to put the money together with that interest money, then do that, too."

"Now that Jeremiah's up and walking again and Bonita can help Mom around the house, I'm ready to do something new. Mr. Morris is no trouble, and Mom says four kids are no harder to look after than two. I guess we'll see about that."

"I guess we will. I was just thinking—could we have a picnic up on the hill today? We could celebrate your new job."

"What a good idea!" replied Bessie. "I'd love to do that. We'll see who wants to go."

As it turned out, neither Jeremiah, nor Mr. Morris, nor Belle had any interest in leaving the house that afternoon. Bessie offered to take all the children, so she packed enough simple food them and for herself and Hershel, too. Clemente and Bonita were meeting some of their friends from Italy for the afternoon.

Russell and Wilbert ran ahead of the slow-moving smaller children, promising to find just the right spot to put down the quilt in the tall grass. Hershel carried the basket of food and the jug of water, and Bessie carried the quilt, looking back from time to time to be sure Ivy and Orie were still in sight. Once settled, Hershel offered to play a game of catch with the boys while Bessie and the younger ones played jacks on a large slab of flat rock they'd found. Soon, they were trying to see who could throw the ball highest in the air and wearing themselves out. When everyone was good and tired, Bessie put out the picnic lunch and quiet was restored.

After lunch, the little ones napped, and the bigger ones ran off to climb one of the few remaining trees on the hilltop. Bessie and Hershel sat listening to the wind in the grass and a bird calling and calling with no reply.

"That's a sad sound," said Hershel. "Seems like its mate won't answer."

"Or maybe something's happened to its mate," said Bessie. "That's even sadder."

"Yes, it is."

"Something happened to our mates," mused Bessie. "Mom says it's time we stopped living with the dead, Hershel."

"I guess I never thought of it that way, but she's probably right. Looks like that's what we've been doing for years now."

"I truly loved Orie, but he's gone."

"And you know I loved Lucy, but she's gone, too. But how do we move past those deaths? I have to tell you, I worried all night about hugging you, for fear you'd think I was being forward or taking advantage or something awful."

"Oh, Hershel, I loved being hugged. It's been a long time since anyone but a small child hugged me, and it felt good. I think I know you well enough to tell the difference between affection and something, as you say, awful."

"I thank you kindly for teaching me how to write my name and especially for not taking offense last night. And I'll be interested every day to hear all about your new job."

"And I thank you for letting my children call you Daddy and for taking his place in so many kind ways."

Ivy walked back home holding her mother's hand. Hershel carried little Orie on his shoulders, and the two older boys played leap frog down the hill, tumbling over one another, laughing all the way.

CHAPTER 11

Bessie loved her new job. She was learning the intricacies of taking both scrip and cash for goods and thinking all the while about how she could get the most for her money as a buyer of those goods. The scrip came in denominations like cash, with the smallest at one cent and the largest at one dollar. She was taught to put the money and the scrip in the till, which rang a bell to alert the manager that a sale had been made. Most of the time, though, she kept busy finding things for the customers and keeping the merchandise clean and neat. She especially enjoyed scooping up the bulk items like dried beans and weighing them on the big scale. Each morning, she made sure the scale weighed right by putting on a ten-pound box of nails to see if it came out as ten pounds.

The company store had more things to buy than anyone had money for, she thought. There were barrels of apples and barrels of pickles, barrels of flour and barrels of salt. There were bolts of gingham and spools of thread in the colors of the rainbow. There were blasting caps and shovels, even small ones for small boys. The very thought of those small shovels made her sad, thinking that both Orie and Hershel had used them as children. She'd better not get used to thinking her pay would let her have more than she could afford. Still, she'd never lingered long enough in the company store to see just how much there was. She soon learned, however, that her pay would be in scrip, not cash, and that it could only be used in that store. Her dream of putting it in the bank was not to be.

"Good morning, Bessie," said Mr. Humphrey, the store manager. "I've been away for a little while and haven't had the chance to say hello to our newest employee."

"Good morning, Mr. Humphrey," replied Bessie.

"Please, call me James. We don't need to be so formal."

"Oh, I couldn't do that, Mr. Humphrey, you being the boss and all."

"I insist. I may be the manager, but we can still be friends," he insisted, patting her on the shoulder.

"Friends—all right, but you're still Mr. Humphrey to me," she said. Bessie hurried on to her work with a little frown that she couldn't seem to control. Something didn't seem right.

All during the morning, Bessie noticed that Mr. Humphrey kept finding reasons to be at the cash register if she was ringing up a sale, or wandering among the dry goods if she was there straightening up, or inspecting the mining equipment if she was dusting in that part of the store. If she looked up from her work, he would be looking at her with a little smile on his face, so she quickly looked away and wished the hands of the clock would move just a little faster so she could go home. The jangling bell above the door startled her from these thoughts, and she was happy to see her mother coming in.

"Hi, Mom, what brings you here this morning?"

"Oh, I was just taking a stroll on this wonderful fall day and thought I'd walk home with you. You're just about finished, aren't you?"

Mr. Humphrey sidled over to be introduced, as if he had a right to know anyone Bessie might speak to. "May I help you?" he said.

"Mr. Humphrey, this is my mother, Belle Murphy. She came by to walk me home."

"How do you do, Mrs. Murphy? I'm glad to meet Bessie's mother, since she's making us such a fine employee."

"Happy to meet you, Mr. Humphrey, and glad to know Bessie's working out. She's a hard worker, and I'd be disappointed to hear otherwise," said Belle.

"Well, Bessie, you may as well run along since it's ten till twelve. I'll see you in the morning," said Mr. Humphrey.

"Oh, no, I'll certainly finish my shift."

"Indeed, she will," said Belle. "I'll just wait out in the fresh air."

"Very well," said Mr. Humphrey.

Bessie's little frown came back as she walked along home. "What's the matter, Bessie?" asked Belle. "You don't seem like yourself today." The rumbling coal cars pulling onto the siding made it hard to talk. Once the train came to a stop amid screeching brakes, backed up about a foot, and stopped again, Bessie had thought about her answer.

"It's Mr. Humphrey, Mom. He makes me nervous."

"Why on earth, Bessie?"

"This morning, first thing, he asked me to call him by his first name, and, of course, I couldn't do that. Then he just seemed to be watching me all morning as I went about my work. I don't know if he thinks I might steal something or what."

"Oh, Bessie, surely he wouldn't think that. You never stole anything in your life."

"Well, what could it be? Everywhere I went, he went. And he had this funny little smile—I guess it was a smile—on his face. He was out of the store for the last two weeks—the same two weeks I've been there, so maybe he just doesn't trust me to do my job right."

"Maybe he's like that with all new employees, especially ones that start in his absence. Give it a little time and things will be fine, I'm sure."

After supper, Bessie sat on the porch in the twilight while the children played hide and seek. Ivy had been chosen as "it," so she stood leaning her head against the house counting, *1-2-3-4-5-6-7-8-9-10*. She called out, "I'm coming," and ran to all the familiar hiding places, but she didn't find anyone but Orie, who had run to hide behind his mother. He loved to play but was too little to be it. Circling the house, Ivy spotted Wilbert and ran as fast as she could to tag him before he reached home. "Gotcha!" she shouted. "You're it."

"Ollie, Ollie, in free," finished Ivy's turn being it.

Hershel came out to see what all the yelling was about and sat down on the porch steps. "Hershel," said Bessie, "can I tell you something?"

"What is it? What's wrong?" he replied, seeing a frowning face instead of her usual smiling one.

"Well, it's about my work at the company store."

"Have they said something to you about your work?"

"No, no, nothing like that. It's just Mr. Humphrey, the boss. He asked me to call him James, which I wouldn't think of doing. Then he just seemed to be underfoot all morning, smiling. Seemed like he didn't trust me to just do my work. I couldn't wait for it to be noon so I could go home."

Hershel didn't say a word for a long time, but then he said something shocking to Bessie. "Maybe he's just sweet on you."

"Hershel, don't talk crazy. He doesn't even know me."

"He doesn't need to know you. All he needs to do is look at you—a young, pretty woman to work with every morning. I bet that's it."

Now it was Bessie's turn to pause; she blushed a lively pink and looked down. Hershel had never spoken to her in such a personal way before, and she didn't know what to make of it. Two men confusing her in the same day, one a stranger and the other her dear friend. "Well, I don't like it one bit," she said, and called the children in for bed.

Hershel sat thinking about their conversation and its abrupt ending. The calls of the cicadas filled up the night as a train whistle blew long and low across the valley, a lonesome sound so familiar in the coal camp. He wondered why it bothered him so much that this unknown man might be interested in Bessie. Might come along and steal her away from their home. Might take not only Bessie, but her children, who he had come to love as his own. She didn't seem to like the fella, but who knew what a woman might do? A store manager could do far more for her than he could ever do.

Next morning, Bessie walked to the store a little anxious about what she might find. Mr. Humphrey was nowhere to be seen, but in his place was the older woman, Mrs. Serilla, whom Bessie had worked with the previous two weeks. Relaxing into her morning's work, Bessie wondered why she had been so concerned the day before. It must have been her imagination, she decided. "What's become of Mr. Humphrey?" she asked.

Mrs. Serilla, who loved to gossip, came quickly to Bessie's side and whispered, "He had to rush home to Pittsburgh. His wife had a baby, you know, two weeks ago, and suddenly she needed him back, it seems."

"Oh, I hope nothing's wrong," said Bessie, perplexed at this news. She felt both relief that Hershel's opinion had to be wrong since Mr. Humphrey had both a wife and a new baby, and fear that one or both had taken ill.

The bell above the door rang often that morning, since it was the end of the month and payday had come at last. Families had charged merchandise all month with the hope of having something left at the end. This mine paid by the day, and this month had twenty-five workdays at $2.25 a day. That earned Hershel, now the chief wage earner in their household, a total of $56.25. Items taken out of his pay that month took up $41: $6.50 for rent, $32 for merchandise, $1.50 for coal, and a dollar for the doctor who looked at Ivy's throat and said, to everyone's relief, that she didn't have diphtheria. The $15.25 that remained came as scrip, so it would have to be used for necessities that could only be purchased at the company store.

Miners who couldn't read brought their monthly statements into the store to ask what their pay had bought and what they had left. One young man who worked second shift had been in every day for the past two weeks to buy just one piece of penny candy. *He must have a real sweet tooth,* Bessie thought. *At least it won't take much out of his pay.*

"Hello again, Miss Morris," said the young man. "I'm Ronnie Logan, and I'm here for my candy."

"Good morning, Mr. Logan. Which kind would you like today?"

"Red's always good," he said, his face taking on the color of the candy.

"Fine, I'll mark it down on your account, or are you ready to settle up today?"

Ronnie dug his pay slip out of his dungaree pocket and handed it over. "I'm not sure how much I have left," he said.

Ronnie was a boarder who paid for his rent and food out of his pay, but he had no other expenses that month, so he had thirty dollars left over. "Well, Mr. Logan, it looks like you have quite enough to have more than just one piece of candy," Bessie said, smiling up at him. "You actually have thirty dollars worth of credit at the store."

"Well, gosh, that's wonderful. Can I buy you a present with all that money?"

Flustered, Bessie took her turn at feeling her face turn red and said, "Why, no, you can't, but thank you anyway. Now, is there anything else I can do for you today?"

"Well, ma'am, you can let me come and call on you this Sunday."

"Oh, no, I'm afraid that's not possible. There's always so much to do on my days off. No, I'm sorry. It's out of the question."

"Well, then, you just think about it, and don't forget I asked."

Bessie walked home in a daze. She never thought that working out in the public would be so confusing. First she'd imagined her boss didn't trust her, and now this boy wanted to call on her at home. Maybe her mother would have some advice for her. This was not a topic to be discussed with Hershel.

Belle and Bonita were just emptying the rinse water and shaking out the clothes to hang on the line when Bessie got home. No time to discuss silly young men. She hurried in to feed Ivy and Orie their lunch. Russell and Wilbert had started school, and Belle had packed their lunches the night before—bread and cheese with some dried apple slices was all she could manage, but they seemed satisfied. The school gave each child a small bottle of milk provided by the coal company, so that was something to be thankful for. With a bite of bread to tide her over, Bessie put the children to bed for their naps and ran down the porch steps to help with the wash.

"Bessie, we're about done here, so how about putting on the kettle for tea?" said Belle. "Come on, Bonita, let's go sit down. I'm worn down to a frazzle."

Bonita, looking puzzled, picked up the clothesbasket and followed Belle to the porch. "What you mean, 'frazzle?'" she said.

"Oh, it just means I'm tired," said Belle, collapsing onto the rocker, worn down also with explaining.

"I go help Bessie," said Bonita, slamming the screen door behind her.

"I swear," said Belle to herself, "that girl will be the death of me."

Bonita had decided to join the children in a nap, leaving Bessie and Belle drinking tea on the porch. "Mom, I had another strange thing happen this morning," said Bessie.

"Not your boss again, I hope."

"No, no, I learned that he's gone home to Pittsburgh to be with his wife and new baby. It was one of the customers—"

"So, out with it."

"Well, this Ronnie, he had considerable money left from his pay, and first he asked if he could buy me a present with it, and then he asked if he could call on me on Sunday!"

"My stars, girl, what did you say?"

"Well, of course, I said no to both questions."

"But did you say *hell* no? Sometimes you have to be real plain with people."

"You know I don't say those words, Mom. And besides, I don't know what to think. I feel like I have a bull's eye on my forehead and people just keep taking aim at it."

"Bessie, you've been sheltered too long. You need to grow up and learn to take care of yourself. You married Orie too young, and he could always be the big, scary one in the family. If you continue to work outside of the house, you've got to expect men to be like men, and that means being interested in you. Does this man know you have two kids?"

"I don't know what he knows, but he did call me Miss Morris. And he's not really a man at all; he's a boy."

"Well, man or boy, if he comes sniffin' around here, I'll be happy to send him packin.'" Which is just what she did on Sunday afternoon.

Spotting Belle on the front porch, Ronnie said, "Hello, ma'am. Is Miss Morris at home?"

"You must be the young fella asking after my daughter."

"Yes, Mrs. Morris. I'm Ronnie."

"Well, Ronnie, you've got quite the nerve coming here unasked. Now, listen to me. I'm Mrs. Murphy, and I have a daughter whose name is *Mrs.* Morris, and she is the mother of two small children. So you'd just better be one your way."

"Oh, yes, ma'am. I will. I'm so sorry," he said, and he hightailed it back the way he came.

CHAPTER 12

The screen door screeched as Hershel came out onto the porch, cup of coffee in his hand. "Guess I need to oil those hinges, Belle. Who was that guy? I never saw him around here before."

"Another suitor for our Bessie," replied Belle. "Never know who's gonna turn up next."

"Another suitor? How many are there?"

"Well, son, the number's growing by the day. You better speak up soon or somebody's liable to snatch her up, you know."

"I'm not sure what you mean."

"Oh, I think you do. As I told Bessie, you two must stop living with the dead."

"Is that what we're doing? I thought we were just letting enough time pass to mourn the dead and get on with life."

"To my mind, you've mourned enough in your years to last you a lifetime. Now it's time to let go of Lucy and help Bessie let go of Orie and just live and breathe and be happy for a change. Mark my words; someone will strike her fancy if you don't hurry up."

Hershel, ever thoughtful, oiled the door hinges, wondering how to strike her fancy himself.

Bessie finished cleaning up after supper, put the children to bed, and decided to sit out on the porch as the day cooled to evening. It had been a hard day at work, with Mr. Humphrey once again dogging her footsteps.

Apparently, his wife and baby would have no effect on his behavior, and Bessie had worried and puzzled over it all day. As she stepped to the door, she saw Hershel sitting there in the twilight, twirling a leaf to attract the attention of the two stray kittens that had taken to begging each evening for food scraps.

These two seemed desperate for food, but they would never come close while anyone was on the porch. Instead, they waited and watched and then grabbed whatever she put out and then ran off. Hershel seemed intent on taming them, which she found oddly sweet. As she watched, the kittens crept up one step after another, following the twig of leaves Hershel dragged just out of their reach. *How strange,* she thought, *that he cares so much for these little wild things.* His patience seemed endless, but to what purpose? she wondered. Something to love, she supposed, but, of course, he would never say. She would leave him to it and decided to check on Ivy, who could be heard mumbling in her sleep—not another nightmare, Bessie hoped.

As Bessie walked to work the next morning, she thought about what she could say to Mr. Humphrey or what she could do that might change the situation. She needed this job, so she couldn't take a chance on making him angry. Her mother had not given her any advice that she thought she could actually use. To say, "Get the hell away from me and go home to your wife," would never do.

Arriving a little early, Bessie noticed a shadow cross the threshold of Mr. Humphrey's office and realized that he was there before her and that no one else had come in as yet. As she hurried back toward the front door, he came out of the office and said, "Why, Bessie, where are you going?"

"Oh, Mr. Humphrey, I thought I'd just wait on the porch till Mrs. Serilla got here. It's such a pretty morning."

Taking her by the arm, he led her back into the store and said, "Perhaps we can get a little better acquainted while we wait for time to open. Come into my office and sit down."

Pulling a chair up beside her, he said, "Now, Bessie, I understand that your husband was killed at Monongah and that you have two small children to care for. It must be very difficult to manage under those circumstances."

"Yes, sir, that's right."

"Oh, let's not have any *sir* or *madam* here. Please, do call me James."

"It just wouldn't seem right, sir, calling you by your Christian name."

"I'd like for us to be more than employer and employee, Bessie. I'd like for us to be friends."

At that moment, the front door closed, and in bustled Mrs. Serilla, a few minutes late. "Oh, Mr. Humphrey, I'm sorry, but that coal train blocked my way this morning."

"Well, maybe you should start a little earlier next time," he grumbled. Turning to Bessie, he smiled, winked, and said, "Don't forget our little talk."

Her face scarlet, her hands trembling, Bessie tied on her apron and began her morning ritual of checking the stock, dusting the shelves, and counting the hours till she could go home. Ivy had come crying to her during the night with another nightmare, and now this. Although Mr. Humphrey hadn't done or said anything out of the way, Bessie felt that something just wasn't right.

At ten o'clock, Mr. Humphrey left the store for a company meeting at the mine office, giving Bessie a chance to speak to Mrs. Serilla.

"I'm sorry to bother you, but can I ask you something?"

"Why, yes, Bessie, what is it?"

"Well, I've noticed that Mr. Humphrey seems always to be where I'm working, as if he doesn't trust me to do my job properly. I don't know what to make of it, and I thought with your experience here, you might be able to help me figure it out."

Mrs. Serilla, looked down at her shoes and said in a quiet voice, "I don't think I can be of any help to you. This will be your problem to solve. Just do your work and try to keep out of his way." As the screen door slammed shut, she said, "Ah, here's a customer coming in—looks like that Jimmy here to buy his penny candy."

Bessie was hanging up her apron and gathering her things for her walk home when she heard a car pull up. Mr. Humphrey waved and motioned for her to come over to the car, a shiny new Ford, she noticed. "How do you like it? It's a Model T called a 'Tin Lizzie.' Let me give you a ride home and we'll call it a Tin Bessie," he said, ushering her toward the passenger seat and giving her no chance to refuse.

"Oh, Mr. Humphrey, it's beautiful, but I have just a short walk, so I'll be on my way."

"Not on your life," he said. "I won't take no for an answer, so in you go. In fact, let's just go for a little ride on this wonderful afternoon. I've just forked over $900 for this little beauty, and I want to show it off. No better way to show off than to have a pretty girl in the passenger seat."

Completely at a loss, Bessie sat with her hands folded, looking only out the window, but never at Mr. Humphrey. She'd never been in such a predicament in her life. Her mother had been right. Orie had protected her, and now she was on her own. She'd never had to scream or faint, never had to say no to anyone, never had anyone force her to do something she desperately didn't want to do. What did other women do when faced with determined men who wished them harm? And it was harm she was sure he meant, though here, he was being jolly and cheerful, all the while taking her farther from home.

They drove along the river for a while, and then he pulled off the road under a tree and cut the engine. "Now, Bessie," he said, "we can continue this morning's conversation without being interrupted. As I said then, I know you're having trouble making ends meet. I just want to help you, if you'll let me. A little kindness from me to you, a little kindness from you to me, and we'll get along very well. What do you think of that?"

Finally finding her voice, Bessie said, "I'm not sure what you mean by 'a little kindness from me to you,' Mr. Humphrey, and I'm not sure I like the sound of it."

"Let's start the other way around, then," he said. "I've seen you admiring the pretty things for ladies in the store—the dresses, the petticoats, the hats. I can give you all those things. Besides, I don't know why we even stock them; they go to waste here in the coal camp. But they'd look very fine on you. In return, you could start by calling me James, and we could go from there."

"Mr. Humphrey, there's nowhere to go from there. You have a wife and a new baby in Pittsburgh, and I have my two children at home. That should be enough for both of us, don't you think?"

"No, it's not. It doesn't have to be. My wife refuses to come here to live, and yet this is where my job is located at the present. I can't take off and go home whenever I please, so I need someone here to, well … you know … to take her place." The last few words came out sheepishly. Recovering himself, he said, "And isn't having a ride in this new car better than going home to two squalling brats this afternoon? You can do better for yourself, Bessie."

At the words *squalling brats,* Bessie found her courage. "No, indeed, to all of your questions, Mr. Humphrey. I love my children dearly—they're all I have left of their father, who I also loved dearly. As to you and your wife, you can all go straight to hell!" She got out of the car as swiftly as possible and started walking back the way they had come. Yelling back, she said, "And you can't fire me, because I quit!"

Behind her, she heard him trying to crank the engine, which coughed and spluttered. Over and over he turned the crank, cursing and spluttering himself, and eventually, it started. He pulled the car alongside and said, "Get in the car; you can't walk all the way home."

"I can do anything I damn well please," she said.

"All right, have it your own way. You may as well not tell anyone about this, because no one would believe someone like you anyway."

With that, he drove off, leaving her in the dusty road with miles to go. She knew her mother would worry, but there was nothing she could do about that. As for herself, she felt stronger than she had in the days leading up to this, so she just put one foot in front of the other. She had most of the afternoon left to make her way home, and she had the river to guide her. As she walked, she thought about his words, *someone like you.* Who was "someone like her?" She knew she had been loved by her husband. She knew she loved her children. But how did someone like her go forward in this life? Where would she go, and what would she do? Her sister, Lucy, had always dreamed of going to the city, but that life had never appealed to Bessie. What she cherished was a happy family, kids and a dog, a garden and a porch swing. She still had Orie's money safely put away in the bank, so she wouldn't starve, even though she'd just given up the only job she'd ever had. The price to keep it would have been way too high.

Trudging along as the sun moved lower in the sky, Bessie thought about the words she'd thrown at Mr. Humphrey. Her mother must be rubbing off on her, she mused. *Hell* and *damn* were nothing new for Belle, but Bessie had never let them slip from her mouth. Her feelings of strength and triumph faded as the road stretched out in front of her. She was not a coarse woman, and she certainly was not a loose woman, as Mr. Humphrey seemed to think. The small wages she'd received had allowed her to buy things for her children never before possible. Now they would have to make do with less, as she would have to do. *Oh, why does life have to be so hard?* she thought as she rounded a turn in the road and the company houses began to come into view. Running now, she saw her mother and Hershel standing in the yard, and she felt a great rush of gratitude. Here were two people worrying about her, waiting for her. Both would be gruff, she knew, until they knew what had happened, and then they would be angry. Her job now would be to prevent either of them from confronting Mr. Humphrey, making matters worse. Hershel, she hoped, would listen and do as she asked. His job probably depended on it, but her mother was another story.

The next morning, Belle could wake the dead, Bessie thought, crashing around the kitchen in her anger. "Bessie, I can't forgive a man like that for making such suggestions to you and then making you walk home, to top it off."

"Oh, Mom, he would have brought me home, but I wouldn't have got back in that car for anything on this earth."

"Well, I just want to go down to that store and give him a good piece of my mind. The very idea of treating my daughter like a common tramp makes my blood boil."

"Please don't do that, Mom. Somebody from this family will still have to shop at that store, since we can't buy things anywhere else with the scrip I earned. So please don't make an enemy of the man in charge. I just hope he won't hold a grudge against me and make life harder than ever."

"Bessie, he's the one in the wrong here. Don't you ever begin to think that you did anything to be sorry for. I knew from the beginning when he watched you all the time that he was up to no good. Men like that take advantage of young women any chance they get, and you just happened to be there, available."

"I just don't want any more trouble. I had time to think as I walked home yesterday, and there doesn't seem to be any answer to how a widow can live in this world. I don't know how you've managed all these years since Dad died in the mine."

"I've lived from hand to mouth many a time, but, as I'm doing now, I've lived with my children more often than not. I've taken in boarders, as you have done. I've done washing and ironing; I've done knitting and tatting and quilting. I've done without. I've watched my sons go into the mines, all but these last two, and I'll be damned if they go in. The only thing I haven't done is turn myself into the kind of woman Mr. Humphrey wanted to make out of you, Bessie."

"But what does it say about me that we're living off of Hershel's good graces, here in his house?"

"It says that you have the good sense to accept favor for favor. You took him in when Lucy died, and he took you in when Orie died. Enough said."

Late that afternoon, a step on the porch alerted Bessie that she had a visitor. To her great surprise, there stood Mrs. Serilla, looking over her shoulder as if someone might be watching.

"My goodness, how unexpected!" cried Bessie. "Come in, please."

"I almost felt that I needed to make you an apology, Bessie, after yesterday."

"Why, what would you have to apologize for?"

"That I put you off when you asked about Mr. Humphrey. I should have just told you what was happening before my own eyes. He was just up to his old tricks."

"His old tricks?"

"Yes, the only reason there was an opening at the store was that the previous young woman had quit as abruptly as you. And the one before that."

Bessie felt such relief that she was speechless for a moment. "Oh, I'm so glad to know that it wasn't my fault."

"Your fault? No, never your fault. He's a playboy from Pittsburgh, and his father got him this job to try to settle him down. Seemed to think a little time in a coal camp would make him take life more seriously. Instead, he just throws his money around, trying to impress people, when all that does is make them lose respect for him. He's a sad case, really."

"But isn't it worse that he has so much power?"

"Yes, and that's why I felt I needed to come see you. He told me he fired you for thievery, but I knew that couldn't be true. He said he was confiding in me and that no one else needed to know. Mark my words, he'll tell that same story to everyone he knows, spreading it like a fever. I've just come to give you fair warning. I must go now."

"I thank you kindly for coming, Mrs. Serilla. Just one question: Who were the other two women he employed? They may be my only chance of avoiding such shame in this community."

"Neither one lives here any longer. They both just moved away. One, Jamie Lee, went back to Monongah, and the other, Betty Coffman, moved to Clarksburg."

"Oh, I remember Jamie. Surely I can find her. I really can't thank you enough for coming here. I hope you get into no trouble on my account."

"I think I'll be all right. Mr. Humphrey always says he needs to hire people who are 'adequately old,' to use his big word, and 'adequately poor,' and I meet both of those employment requirements."

CHAPTER 13

The next morning, Bessie caught the early streetcar to Monongah, hoping to find Jamie Lee. She dreaded the sight of the mine, but she thought it would surely be easier to find someone in this little town than in the city of Clarksburg. She inquired first at the post office but was told that they could not give out information. Retracing her steps, she went next to the company store, and there behind the counter was her old friend, Jamie. She had to bide her time because the store was crowded with customers, but a quick word brought agreement that Jamie would speak with her at her lunch break. Now it seemed that she would have time on her hands until noon, so she began walking to Grandma Ola's house. The familiar path brought back so many memories of her life with Orie—of their courtship and marriage, of the birth of their children, of the tragic days that seemed endless at the time but seemed long ago now. Passing by her old house, she noticed that someone had applied a new coat of whitewash and that the garden was flourishing.

The Ola house had not fared so well. The front porch sagged away from its foundation, and weeds filled the yard. Of course, she knew that the old couple would be unable to do much, especially on the outside of the house, but she wondered at Jeremiah's failure to help them. He had recovered from his broken ribs and had gone back to work three months ago, so surely he could be more helpful. Papa greeted her at the door calling, "Mama, Mama, look who's come to see us."

"Bessie, come in, child, and see what has become of us. Here's your Jeremiah with his broken leg. Ach, I don't know what we will do now."

Bessie took in the astounding scene. There lay Jeremiah with his leg in a cast and lifted into the air with a sort of pulley. There sat Papa in his rocker, looking helpless. There stood Grandma, wringing her hands and looking about to cry.

"When did this happen, Jeremiah, and why didn't you let us know?"

"It's been three weeks now since the slate fall," he said, "and I didn't want to burden you with my troubles again so soon."

"But Jeremiah, you're our family, and we would have come much quicker. I've been working in the company store and Hershel's been doing double shifts for the past month, but that doesn't excuse our tardiness. I'm so sorry. Now, Mrs. Ola, tell me what I can do today."

"Just come in the kitchen with me and sit down for a cup of tea, and we'll think on it."

Bessie knew that the Olas were dependent on Jeremiah's board for their living, and now that he wasn't working, she despaired over their future—over the future of all three of them. Maybe they could find another boarder until Jeremiah could go back to work, but the supply of labor at Monongah had not yet recovered from the shock of the disaster two and a half years ago. She was reminded of her own needs as a widow in a coal camp, and yet the needs of this elderly couple far exceeded her own. She was young and strong, but they might never regain any sort of comfort in this life.

Sipping her tea, Bessie asked, "What kinds of food have you run out of? What can I bring when I come back? Hershel and I will be able to help out on Sunday, so let's make a list."

Mrs. Ola opened her pantry to very little but empty shelves. She did have tea, flour and lard, salt, and some molasses, half a dozen eggs from her chickens, and a little milk brought over by her neighbor. She said, "I sometimes dream of killing a chicken to roast, but then I wouldn't have enough eggs. Before the mines exploded, I had enough to make little sweets for Papa, but those days are gone. Those poor boys killed that day were always so generous and so grateful, and we were so content; it's hard to think we'll never have that again."

List in hand, Bessie said good-bye and rushed back to the store, tears rolling down her face, hoping she hadn't missed Jamie's lunch break. Her friend was just tying on her apron when Bessie hurried in the door. "I have a couple minutes left, Bessie, now what is so serious?"

"It's Mr. Humphrey. He is no gentleman, and I've had to quit my job in the company store because of that. Now he's spreading the word that I'm a thief. I understand that you once worked for him and that you quit as abruptly as I did."

"Oh, I'm so sorry to hear this. It's true that I couldn't continue working there with him after me all the time. But I don't know what you want from me."

"I guess I just want to know you would be willing to stand by me if it comes down to that. I have no idea what might happen, and I'm frightened."

"I can't do anything that could threaten my job here, Bessie, though I feel very sorry for you. I don't know what he said about me when I left, but I moved back home to be on the safe side. I just can't get involved."

"Yes, I see. I'll have to work it out some other way, then. I'll let you get back to work. One more thing, though—I've just been with the Olas, who are in serious trouble. Hershel's father, Jeremiah, broke his leg in a slate fall and can't work, but he's their only boarder. Could you ask around about anyone else who might want to live there? Mrs. Ola is a wonderful cook and housekeeper, so you'd be doing a favor to anyone who needs a place to stay."

Jamie touched Bessie's shoulder as she turned to leave and said, "Of course, I'll see if I can find someone. About Mr. Humphrey, though, I'm so very sorry, but I can't take a chance."

Bessie arrived home to find Bonita in charge of the children and her mother nowhere in sight. Mr. Morris sat in his usual spot on the porch. "Bessie," he said, "your mother left here in a high temper awhile ago."

"Where did she go?"

Bonita joined the conversation and said, "She go to the company store and give somebody peace of mind."

Oh, no, thought Bessie, it wouldn't be peace of mind he'd get, but a good tongue-lashing. What more would go wrong today? She decided just to start their supper and let her hands take over from her thoughts. She loved to cook, and while the coal stove heated, she would take an inventory of her own pantry to see what she could spare.

Belle marched into the house, head held high and color in her cheeks. "Bessie, you shouldn't be hearing any more from that scoundrel."

"Oh, Mom, I asked you to let it be, and now you've gone and made things worse."

"No, indeed, things are better, not worse. I just marched into his office and shut the door. I told him that he'd been seen driving off with you and coming back alone, leaving you stranded way out at Big Elm. I got right up in his face and said that if I heard any more talk about my daughter, there would be hell to pay, because I knew the source of such lies and gossip."

"What did he say to that?"

"He just got sort of pale around the gills and said he didn't know what I was talking about. I just laughed at him, and then I whispered that I had given him fair warning and that he should mark my words."

"What did he say to that?"

"Not one word."

After supper, they all talked about the Olas and Jeremiah's misfortune. Of course, on Sunday, Hershel's only day off, they would go to Monongah to take food and discuss what should be done. It would be hard, if not impossible, to move Jeremiah with his leg broken, but physical repairs to their house needed to be done, and Hershel could do all of that. The matter of the loss of income to the Olas was a harder problem to tackle. If Jamie Lee couldn't help with Mr. Humphrey, maybe she could try to scour up a boarder or two in Monongah. Bessie could only hope that her mother's solution would work, but now she had others besides herself to worry about, which was a sort of relief.

On Sunday morning, Bessie watched the wires spark above the slowing streetcar. They had several bundles to haul aboard, but the conductor didn't hurry them along on this lazy day. Hershel, Belle, Wilbert, and Russell had all come along to help with the cleanup, and Bessie had nearly emptied her kitchen of things Mrs. Ola lacked—dried apples and her own canned beans and tomatoes, plus what little sugar she had. Hershel had found some whitewash and nails at the mine and had brought his own sparse set of tools, so they all spent the day with their old neighbors and Hershel's father, working and laughing and telling all the old stories once more.

They caught the last streetcar back to Riverview late that afternoon. Bessie was so exhausted from both work and worry that she felt her head nodding as they rolled along. She startled awake as the car stopped, embarrassed and apologetic to find her head resting on Hershel's shoulder.

"No need to be sorry, Bessie," he said. "It was no trouble at all. It felt kind of natural."

She just smiled and hurried to catch up with her mother.

Five days later, Bessie received a letter from Jamie Lee, who had gone to the Olas' home to ask what she could do to help. Jamie was met with the news that the county authorities had presented the elderly couple with an order to report to the county poorhouse in two weeks. They were, of course, behind on their rent and had exhausted their credit at the company store. Now considered paupers, they were at the mercy of the local superintendent in charge of the poorhouse. Jeremiah would be forced to go, too, unless other arrangements could be made.

With Hershel at work, there was nothing to be done, so Bessie walked the floor wringing her hands all day, while Belle fumed and cursed and stomped her feet at the injustice of it all. A way must be found to bring Jeremiah home, but a horse and wagon would be needed. He couldn't ride the streetcar with his cast that had to be elevated. They could go and get him on Sunday, but that left Grandma and Papa Ola with nowhere to turn. They had worthless but treasured heirlooms they had brought from the old country, but would these be safe in the poorhouse, where they took in not only old and helpless people, but all sorts of criminals, Bessie had heard? Would it be clean? Would it be warm enough in the winter? Would it be stifling and filled with flies in summer? Would there be enough food? Would Papa ever again have the little sweet morsels that he craved?

All these questions kept swirling round and round Bessie's head, and cooking supper provided no relief this time. She thought of taking out Orie's money and paying off their debts, but with no income, the money would soon be gone, with no way to get it back. With paydays came only scrip, not real money, so no one in the coal camp had any funds they could borrow. There was no way to get ahead—ever. They all simply worked and lived from day to day, with no hope for the future.

Hershel bartered for a horse and wagon for the day by promising to help build a stable for the horse, a scruffy mare that didn't live up to her name of Pretty Girl. He felt quite silly saying, "Gitty up, there, pretty girl," but that's what his neighbor said he had to do to persuade her to move at all. Belle had asked around for empty boxes, so they had enough to bring home Jeremiah's possessions, as well as anything Grandma Ola wanted them to keep safe for her. Once more, Hershel, Bessie, Belle, and her two boys, plus Clemente, set out for Monongah. This time, they found Grandma in tears, Papa resigned and silent, and Jeremiah in a fury. His helpless state only compounded his anger.

All day, they packed things that Bessie had never seen before—handmade quilts and tablecloths, embroidered pieces from Grandma's mother—as well as the ordinary objects of life: a tea kettle, mixing bowls, a rolling pin. The former would go home with Bessie for safekeeping; the latter to the poorhouse, just in case Grandma would be allowed to do her own cooking. Grandma took the set of four tea glasses covered in fine silver filigree with her because they reminded her of home—home in Poland and home in Monongah. Finally, when the sorting and packing were done, at dark, Hershel and Clemente lifted a barely conscious Jeremiah into the bed of straw they'd made for him in the wagon and carefully propped up his leg. Bessie and Hershel would ride home in the wagon with Belle in the back with Jeremiah, while Clemente took the boys home on the streetcar to Riverview.

As they reached the river road connecting the two towns, a dense fog caused a fine mist to begin to fall, and although it was still autumn, the air cooled, and those in the wagon became chilled and miserable. Stopping to dig out covers, Bessie said, "What can I get for you, Hershel?"

"Just your good company will do," he said. "Find something for yourself."

Belle covered herself and Jeremiah as best she could with blankets and a tarp they'd thought to bring along. There wasn't much she could do to help him, but just another soul for comfort might be enough, she thought as she, too, dozed off.

He awoke with a start and said, "Belle, what the hell are you doing in this wagon? Why didn't you take the streetcar?

"Well, you old codger, I thought you might need some company. So much for a thank you."

CHAPTER 14

Hershel spent a restless night, concerned about his father but at a complete loss over the fate of the Olas. Mrs. Ola had been so kind to Lucy as she sank into despair over her illness. Whereas he had demanded that Lucy fight her tuberculosis, she had quietly comforted his wife with soft words and cups of tea, sitting by her bedside during the long hours Hershel was at work. Now it seemed he had no comfort to give back. He had no money to see them through this crisis. Lucy's illness had wiped away what little he'd managed to save doing handyman chores for those who actually had money. His earnings could only be used to buy goods at the company store, so no matter how many hours he worked, he could never get ahead. The only bright spot in his life was Bessie.

Now there was a thought—Bessie. She had been so happy with her job. She was earning money for the first time in her life. Even scrip was better than nothing, and she had seemed to enjoy picking out little odds and ends to bring home to Ivy and Orie. Now that was all in the past. Even thinking about her treatment at the hands of the manager made him seethe with rage, but Bessie was right; he should not confront the man or even speak to him. His job was at stake, and he knew better than to challenge the company on anything. He and Clemente were now the only wage earners in the household, and even Clemente would eventually move on to his own place with Bonita.

Hershel knew that Bessie was not like her sister Lucy. Bessie loved home and family. Lucy had longed for adventure. Bessie held to some religious beliefs, but Lucy would have none of it. Bessie seemed rather shy and retiring. Lucy, before her illness, was more like their mother, Belle. She was quick to anger and didn't mind it spilling over for all to see. When he thought about it, he tried to practice more of Bessie's traits than Lucy's, in that he generally kept himself to himself. He'd loved Lucy for all of her qualities, but they wouldn't be right on Bessie. Maybe he was beginning to love Bessie for her own qualities.

Hershel's morning passed quickly because they were planning out the next phase of wiring the mine. By the time he sat down with his lunch bucket, however, the events of the previous day began to wear on him, and he looked forward to the end of the shift. Never admitting that he couldn't read, he'd managed to learn enough about the drawings and diagrams to understand what was needed from him as an electrician. He worked hard, no matter the job, and he hoped to be promoted on that basis.

Hershel's boss, Jack, started back to work and noticed Hershel finishing off the last of his coffee. "You all right, Hersh?" he said. "You usually beat me back after lunch."

"I'm just a little tired from moving my father back home yesterday. He was boarding with some of our old neighbors in Monongah, but he broke a leg in a slate fall, and now they have no boarders and no income. It just makes me sick that they're having to go to the poorhouse and there's nothing to be done about it."

"I heard they're moving all the 'dead weight'—yeah, that's what they're callin' 'em—out of the company houses in Monongah to make room for another batch of immigrant workers they've brought over."

"For God's sake, some of those workers would have been lucky to live with Mrs. Ola. She's a great cook, and her house was always clean and smelled like gingerbread. What a waste."

Walking home from the mine, Hershel began to wonder if anything actually could be done for the Olas. He would talk it over with Bessie after supper. Looking up, he noticed an automobile parked in front of their house, and, panic setting in, he began to run. Was it that lousy guy from the company store? Taking the porch steps two at a time, he opened the door to see a man in a black suit bending over his father. "What's happening here?" he said.

Bessie rushed around the man and said, "Oh, Hershel, your father's taken a bad turn, and this is the doctor come to see about him. He's been in a lot of pain this afternoon."

"Hello, I'm Dr. Franklin," the man said. "The part of your father's leg that I can see above the cast is quite inflamed, so I'm going to remove the cast and examine his lower leg where he has a compound fracture." Noting the puzzled looks on their faces, he said to Bessie and Hershel, "That means the injury was complicated by the fact that the bone broke and splintered, breaking through the skin."

"What can you do for him?" asked Bessie.

"I won't know that till I take a look, so let me get to work. Please close the door and take yourselves and your children out of earshot."

Jeremiah was in one of the front rooms, so everyone, including Belle and Mr. Morris, went out to the backyard and pretended to busy themselves in the garden, noting which beans would be ready to pick soon, which tomatoes would be ripe by the morning, coaxing the children to come farther and farther from the house. Hershel brought chairs from the kitchen, not knowing how long they might remain in the yard, but not a sound was heard, not even one, "Goddamn, son of a bitch," from Jeremiah.

Eventually, the doctor joined them and remarked that although his patient was one tough old bird, the leg would have to come off above the knee. Infection had set in, and there was nothing to do but remove it. He had given Jeremiah morphine and said that he would sleep through the night, but he would have to go to the miners' hospital in Clarksburg in the morning. He would arrange for transport to be paid for by the coal company, but someone would need to go along. Bessie volunteered, although she wasn't next of kin. The doctor said he supposed that would do if Hershel would write out a note saying she could act on his behalf. Bessie quickly agreed that they would certainly get that done, and the doctor went on his way.

"Bessie, you know I can't write a note," Hershel said.

"No, but I can, and you can just sign your name. You remember our lessons, don't you?"

"I've never had to do it, but if you'll let me practice it again, maybe it will work."

So she wrote out his signature, and he went over and over it until they thought it was good enough. She wrote the note, he signed it, and after checking on Jeremiah once more, they went out to the front porch for a breath of air to end this day. They sat in the swing and listened to the soft clink of the chain as they rocked back and forth. After a few minutes of silence, they said at once, "What a day." They both laughed quietly and then stopped, wondering how there could be anything to laugh about. "I'm so sorry about your father, Hershel," she said. At that same moment, he said, "I'm so sorry we're such trouble, Bessie." Instead of laughing this time, they just stopped and looked at each other. When he reached for her, she reached back, and they sat holding each other for the longest time without saying another word. They both found comfort in the gentle movement of the swing and the warm embrace neither had expected to find ever again.

The sounds of cicadas filled the night, seeming to grow louder and blend with the bullfrog chorus echoing from the banks of the river. The sun had set two hours ago, so the sky would be lit up now with stars. "Let's see if we can find the Big Dipper, Bessie," Hershel said, helping her up from the swing.

"I wouldn't know it if I saw it," she said.

"Well, then, let's have a lesson. You taught me to write my name, so I'll teach you about the sky. My mother loved the stars, and she taught me and my sister Jane all she knew about them. She loved the clouds, too, even though she didn't know their names. She knew which clouds brought rain and snow and which sunset foretold bad weather. I can't match her for that, but I love to look at them just the same. Guess I've spent too much time underground to know much about the daytime."

"So where is this Dipper?"

Taking her by the hand, Hershel scanned the sky and settled on the North Star at the tip of the dipper's handle. "There it is—look where

I'm pointing. See that real bright star? Now think of a dipping gourd and look for the outline of its handle, starting with the bright star. Then you'll see the cup of the dipper at the bottom of the handle."

"Oh, I don't see anything like that," she said, disappointed.

"Here, sit down and look just above that treetop. Now do you see it?"

"No, I don't see it."

"Can you see the bright star?"

"Yes, but where do I go from there?"

"Let your eyes just move down from that star in a sort of curve and imagine holding a dipper in your hand."

"Oh, Hershel, there it is! How wonderful. A drawing in the sky."

"Yes, that's what it is. One day, I'll find my mother's sketchbook and show you her drawings. She made little pictures of stars and flowers and animals."

"Yes, I want to see it. We can show it to Jeremiah to cheer him up." In her enthusiasm, Bessie began dancing around, grabbing hold of Hershel and taking him with her. The dance ended with a hug just as the screen door screeched open and Belle emerged from the house.

"What's going on out here, I'd like to know?" Spotting the embrace, she said, "Well, it's about time."

Hershel and Bessie jumped apart, looking guilty, but came back together at Belle's last remark. Maybe it was about time.

Jeremiah had his first night of rest in weeks but woke in pain, his forehead hot to Bessie's touch. He refused anything but coffee, even though she begged him to try to eat just a little, saying, "You never know what you'll get in that hospital."

"I hope I can keep this coffee down, Bessie, so can't take a chance on anything else."

"Here's the doctor now with some sort of contraption to get you to the hospital." The contraption was a flat wagon with a roof on it pulled by a mule that would take Jeremiah the long miles to Clarksburg. Dr. Franklin called it an ambulance, but it looked more like a hearse to Bessie.

"Now, Mr. Martin, you'll need to stay as still as possible. I'm sorry to say the road won't be very smooth, but at least it's been dry lately, so there won't be any mud to hinder your trip. We'll wedge you in as best we can. I'll give you something to blunt the pain, and perhaps you can rest awhile as you go."

Bessie sat up with the driver, thinking they would never get to the hospital. She hoped he knew where they were going, because she sure didn't. She'd never been any farther away than Shinnston, the small town a mile or so from Riverview where they'd gone for the July Fourth parade. She'd brought along a few things in case they'd let her stay over. Surely someone would need to stay with Jeremiah for a day or two, and Hershel could take her place on Sunday. Hershel—now there was a thought. She smiled to herself, thinking about their lesson on the stars. Her mother had said any number of times lately what a good man Hershel was and that she ought to think seriously about that. Of course she'd always known that about him—look how he had cared for Lucy. The question was, what did he think about her?

When they arrived, the staff hustled Jeremiah off to the operating room and settled Bessie in the waiting room after taking Hershel's note and filling out some papers. Luckily, she had thought to bring along a piece of needlework, which kept her occupied as the afternoon dragged on into evening. Family members of other patients came and went, and when she was finally alone, she hurriedly ate the apple and cheese she'd brought. No one said she couldn't have it, but she'd never eaten in a public place before, so she didn't know the rules. A water cooler in the hall provided her a drink in a paper cup—another new experience. The clock on the wall said it was 9:00 when they finally came to tell her that Jeremiah's surgery had been completed and he was resting in room number 238.

"He'll only be in that room until morning, and then he'll be moved to the ward once he's recovered from the chloroform," the attendant said.

"I can stay with him tonight, though, can't I?" asked Bessie.

"Yes, he'll need a family member with him until he wakes up. Are you his daughter?

"No, not his daughter."

"Oh, well, daughter-in-law, then?"

"No, not exactly."

"Well, who are you, then?"

"All right, you see, he was my sister's father-in-law, but she died, and his son works in the mine at Riverview."

"That's too complicated for me, but if you say you're a family member, I guess you can stay."

When Bessie arrived at room 238, she could see that Jeremiah was sleeping, but when she looked around, she was dismayed that there was only one straight wooden chair for her. The waiting room chairs had been bad enough, but this one was worse. She hadn't slept sitting up since her babies were small, but that was what she was in for now, if any sleep was to be had. As the night wore on and Jeremiah began to toss and moan, guilt took the place of discomfort for Bessie. Here she was, thinking only of herself, while he was suffering. Toward morning, she slipped out to find the ladies room, feeling relief just to be moving about. On the way back, she ran into the woman who had questioned her the night before and was surprised to be offered a hot cup of coffee. Though Bessie was a tea drinker, she accepted this gift and asked only for a little milk to tone it down. *Such a harsh taste,* she thought, but by the last sip, she wished for more.

When the doctor arrived for morning rounds, Jeremiah was awake but in pain, so he was given a sedative to ease him through the bandage change. Bessie sat in the waiting room, wondering what she should do. They had said she could stay only that first night and that no one could stay with a patient in the ward. She certainly couldn't afford to stay in a hotel, so she would plan to stay for the day and go home on the streetcar in the evening.

Bessie was one of many passengers aboard the streetcar to Riverview, arriving at sundown after several stops along the way. Walking home with the news that Jeremiah had survived the surgery felt good, so she hurried along. In the distance, she saw Hershel coming toward her, looking worried and sort of lost. Running now, she yelled out, "He's all right! Your father's all right."

"Bessie, how can I ever thank you for going with him? He's really all right?"

"Yes, they let me stay in his room, but today they moved him to a ward, and no one can stay with patients in a ward. That's why I came home."

"They took off his leg?"

"Yes, the doctor explained that it would never heal and the poison from it would spread all over his body, so there was no other choice. He's going to have lots of pain, but at least he'll be alive. They said he might have to stay awhile. When I asked how long, they said that would depend."

"Depend on what?"

"On how well he does with the healing, and they won't know till it happens."

Putting his arm around her shoulders, Hershel said, "Thank you for buying me some time. I'll be able to visit him on Sunday."

Slipping her arm around his waist, she said, "You're welcome. I'll come, too, if you don't mind."

So it was settled.

CHAPTER 15

After eleven days in the hospital, Jeremiah returned to Riverview. The hospital provided a pushchair to get him to the end of the long hall, but Hershel and Bessie had to help him use his new crutches to reach the waiting taxi, for the first taxi ride of their lives. At the station, they waited for what seemed like forever for the next streetcar to arrive. Finally onboard, Jeremiah collapsed against the window and stared out at the countryside going slowly by. "I thought I'd never see that sight again—thought I'd die in that place," he said.

"Aw, Dad, everything will look better once we get you home," said Hershel. "It's been a big day and you're just tired out."

"Tired out and missing a leg that still aches. The nurse said that was normal, but it seems mighty strange to me that something you don't have can hurt just like it did before. I don't intend to talk about it because people will say it's my imagination, or I've lost my mind, or I'm just plain crazy."

"All right, Dad, we won't say a word."

"That's right, Jeremiah, we won't say a word," said Bessie.

Bessie was awakened at 2:00 a.m. by the cries of five-year-old Ivy, obviously in the midst of another nightmare. Taking the child in her arms, Bessie rocked and whispered, "Now, now, there's nothing to be afraid of." She'd heard you should never wake a person from a nightmare, but she couldn't just let her suffer, could she?

"Mama, I keep seeing a face in the dark, and I don't know who it is. Who is it—who can it be?"

"I don't know, Ivy, but there's no one in this room but you and me and Orie, so there's no need to be afraid."

"But, Mama, wasn't there someone else whose name was Orie? Where did he go?"

"Yes, child, that was your daddy, but he got killed in the mine, so he hasn't been here in a long time. Do you remember him?"

"I remember a big man who used to sit at the supper table. But, Mama, we already have a daddy who lives here now."

"Yes, Ivy, that's Hershel, and he's as kind to you as your daddy was. Is that who you're seeing in your dream?"

"No, Mama, I see the big man, and he reaches out for me and scares me."

"He loved you very much, Ivy, so you don't need to be afraid of him. I think it must be just a memory you're thinking about. He used to carry you around on his shoulders and jiggle you up and down until you giggled, so maybe you can try to remember that and not be so scared. Now, let's go back to sleep."

"All right, Mama, I'll try."

Next morning, Hershel said, "I heard Ivy crying in the night. What's wrong?"

"She had another bad dream, but this time she calmed down enough to tell me about it. She said a big man was reaching out for her, and I think she's remembering Orie. When I explained that he was her daddy, she said we already had a daddy. That would be you, of course."

"I hope you don't mind her thinking that way."

"Mind? Why would I ever mind? That's just what they both needed when Orie was taken so early. I thank you every day for letting them think of you that way. I've wondered if we weren't an awful burden on you. Here we are, living in your house and keeping you from any other life you might want to live."

Rising from the breakfast table and taking her hands in his, Hershel said, "Bessie, let me tell you what a burden would be: if you ever left this house and took these children from me. I feel like I am their daddy. You know I lost my sister and my mother about the same time. Then my father doled out the smaller children to the relatives, so I never got to see them grow up. Our mother would have hated to know that her family was split apart, but that's the way it was. I don't want to lose anybody else." Grabbing his lunch bucket, Hershel rushed out the door just before the whistle blew for the shift change.

All day, as Hershel worked on wiring and switches, he thought about their early-morning conversation. The thought of Bessie leaving with the children was an idea he had pushed out of his mind for too long. He knew he loved Ivy and Orie, but did he love Bessie? He loved her ways—that was for sure. Except for times of real trouble, she was more happy than not. She played games inside and out with Orie and Ivy, usually resulting in laughter, even from Mr. Morris and Jeremiah, to whom laughter was a stranger. She was kind to these two old men, making them take their medicine and giving them their favorite food when they could afford little treats. She dodged the sharp tongue of her mother, never talking back but still doing things her own way. She was easy to talk to, even for such a quiet person as himself.

What might their life together be like? he wondered. Their first job would be to raise these two children. So far, that had been easy, since they had fully accepted him as their father. He hadn't been sure of that till this morning. Surely, they would have children of their own someday. They would save up to buy some land, so they could raise a garden and plant fruit trees. They would always have enough to eat. He'd had these dreams with Lucy, but she was gone. Bessie had probably had the same dreams with Orie, but he was gone. As Belle had said, it was now up to them to make new lives for themselves.

As she washed bedsheets for the whole family, Bessie thought about their early-morning conversation. Her hands weren't as raw as they would be when winter washdays came, but when she had hung the last sheet to dry, she worked some salve into the driest places and sat down for a cup of tea with her mother.

"You and Hershel sounded awful serious just before he ran out the door this morning," said Belle.

"I guess you heard Ivy crying last night," said Bessie.

"Yes, what's got into that child?"

"She dreams about a big man reaching for her, and when I told her it was just probably a memory of her daddy who had died, she informed me that she already had a daddy right here."

"Ah, I see. And you told Hershel that."

"Yes, and I said I was afraid we were a burden. His answer was that the worst burden would be to take the children and go away."

"Bessie, don't you see that he loves them and wants to really be their daddy?"

"Oh, I guess so, Mom, but it's all so complicated."

"That's all in your head, Bessie; just let go and be happy."

"It's just that Lucy was his true love, just as Orie was mine, and I don't think either of us wants to be second best."

"Bessie, you can't hang on to what's gone. First love, true love, or just plain love, what difference does it make? If he cares for you and you care for him, and if he will take good care of your two babies, then let him. He knows what he's doing."

Hershel and Bessie felt a chill in the air as they took their places once more in the porch swing after supper. At first, she chattered away about nothing more than the weather, but at last she, too, lapsed into silence. It had been an exceptionally warm fall, and now, in November, their evenings on the porch were coming to an end.

"Bessie, come out in the yard and let me show you something."

"All right, but what is it?"

"Remember when we looked at the stars and found the Big Dipper?"

"Yes, there it is."

"Well, tonight, we're looking for something else. It doesn't come up till winter, and we'll be lucky if we can just barely see it. By Christmas, it will be real plain."

"What's it called?"

"It's Orion the Hunter, but some folks call it 'three buttons on a shirt.'"

"Orion?"

"Yes, Bessie, your Orie will always be up there in the winter sky if you need to see him. Now look to the east, you know, where the sun rises, and find three bright stars in a row, one above the other."

Tears running down her face, Bessie looked where he pointed but still couldn't see anything. "Oh, Hershel, where is it? I don't see it."

"Just be patient," he said. "It's just barely visible. We'll stay here till you see it. Remember that as the days get shorter, these stars will get brighter and farther up in the sky. This was my mother's favorite set of stars, even better than the Dipper, she thought."

Hershel ran to the front hall to get Bessie's sweater, as she'd begun to shiver in the cold. One star seemed to wink at her, and there, above and below it, two more appeared. "There it is!" she cried. "Why did you want to show it to me tonight?"

Taking a deep breath, Hershel said, "Bessie, I've been thinking for a while that we might ought to take your mother's advice about giving up the past. I wanted to show you that I'll always respect your love for Orie, but that there might be a future for us, too. Would you think about spending your life with me?"

"I've thought about it a lot."

"And?"

"I have no way to show my respect for your love for Lucy, but I do. She was my favorite sister, and I loved her dearly. I think we'll have to work hard to keep them from coming between us, but I'm willing to try."

As they drew together for their first real embrace, sealing the bargain with a kiss, both wondered if they were doing the right thing. No words of love had been spoken, but perhaps those would come with time.

Belle, looking out the window, said, "I think there's a wedding in our future."

"Well, it's about damn time," grumbled Jeremiah.

CHAPTER 16

Hershel's first thought about the wedding was that it would be a simple trip to the courthouse in Clarksburg, to take place sometime between Thanksgiving and Christmas. Bessie and Belle, however, had a different idea. Why not make it a party and invite their old friends from Monongah to celebrate their marriage? He didn't object, thinking the only ones invited would be those he knew well. Hershel had always felt uncomfortable with strangers, and he simply refused to make small talk. "I do" would probably be the only public words he would speak.

When they went to get their license, they learned that a new law required a blood test for both of them to make sure they didn't have any diseases that would prevent their marriage. "I wonder what that's all about," said Bessie.

"It's not for TB, because that one's not a blood test," said Hershel. "You have to spit in a cup for that one."

"Where can we get this test done?" Bessie asked the clerk.

"Oh, your local doctor can do that," he said.

"So we go back home, get the test, and then come back for the license?"

"Yes, ma'am, you'll get a certificate from the doctor that you'll bring back to me."

So they turned around and prepared to start over. Once the test was done, there would be a waiting period of three days and then the license could be purchased. The date of Sunday, December 18, was chosen for the marriage to take place at their home, with the local Evangelical United Brethren preacher doing the honors.

Bessie had written to Jamie Lee in Monongah to invite her to the wedding, and not only did she agree, but she also offered to try to bring Grandma and Papa Ola along with her. She would call at the poorhouse to see if they could attend and would pay their streetcar fare to Riverview. Hershel's brother Bill still worked in the coal company office at Monongah, and he would bring their younger sister Debbie. Bessie's sisters had moved off to Ohio, so they wouldn't be coming. The one person Bessie worried about inviting was Hershel's friend, Bobby Anderson. Orie, Bobby, and Hershel had started out as trapper boys together years ago, and Bobby had been the one who always made jokes and played pranks at the expense of the other two. She wondered if he had changed at all and whether he would take their day seriously enough. Hershel made light of her concerns, so Bobby would receive an invitation and whether he showed up or not would be up to him.

The cold had really set in by late November, and snow was predicted by the look of the clouds that had raced across the sky all day. No more evenings on the porch till spring. Hershel had taken all the double shifts to be had trying to have enough scrip built up at the company store to afford extras for the wedding party. People would bring covered dishes, Bessie said, but he wanted to be able to get enough sugar for the cake Belle planned to bake, along with coffee and punch for the guests.

The Sunday before the wedding, Hershel's brother Bill came, bringing along a suitcase.

"Mornin', Bill, are you movin' in or takin' a trip?"

"Neither one, Hershel. I've brought a suit to loan you for your wedding. Coal miner's clothes won't do for the big day."

"Is it yours? Do you think it'll fit me?"

"Well, we're about the same height. I've got a little weight on you, but if you button the jacket, no one will ever know."

"I'm much obliged, Bill. Bessie will be so pleased."

"Now, how about a cup of coffee, little brother."

They entered the warm kitchen that smelled of baking bread. "You'll stay for dinner, won't you, Bill?"

"I could make a meal of that smell alone. Thanks, I'd love to stay."

The sewing of Bessie's wedding dress was well underway. It turned out that Clemente's wife, Bonita, was a fine seamstress, so she took charge, telling Belle and Bessie to "leave it to me." The company store, it seemed, had bolts of material suitable for the current style in dresses, and Bessie was relieved that Bonita and Belle took care of those purchases. She hesitated ever going to the store, fearing that Mr. Humphrey would be there. Trying it on for the final time, Bessie was delighted with the formality of the dress—ivory-color sateen with a high, white collar that made her seem so grown-up. For her marriage to Orie, she'd worn a flowered summer dress, and the ceremony itself had taken place at the courthouse. Bonita was making a little girl dress for Ivy from Bessie's scrap material, and Orie would have a new shirt and pants from the store. For all of this, Bessie nearly used up the last of her earnings from the store.

Their wedding day dawned bright and sunny, but bitter cold. Guests hurried into the house seeking relief from the wind, laughing and hugging each other. Bill had picked up Grandma Ola and Jamie in his new automobile, so they wouldn't have to come by streetcar. Papa, it seemed, was too feeble to attempt the trip. The preacher arrived out of breath and red in the face, but ready for the simple ceremony he had conducted so many times before. Jamie sought out Bessie for a special present—a small bouquet of tiny pink roses she'd bought at a florist shop in Fairmont.

"Oh, Jamie, how wonderful. I can't thank you enough," said Bessie.

"Bessie, I couldn't let my friend get married without a few little flowers, now, could I? Your dress is perfect. You look like you just stepped out of a magazine. I'm looking forward to meeting your new fellow."

"Well, he's not exactly new. Remember my sister Lucy's husband?"

"Oh, yes. Tall and thin and quiet. I admired the way he took care of her before she died."

"Tall and thin and quiet he still is—and soon to be my husband."

"I'm so happy for you, Bessie. You deserve to be happy."

"Thanks, Jamie. Remind me to tell you about my adventure getting away from Mr. Humphrey."

Belle bustled into the room and said, "It's time, Bessie."

Jamie said, "I'll do that, but no need to think about bad people on a good day."

As Bessie followed Ivy out into the front room, she noticed a handsome man in a dark-colored suit standing next to the preacher. He smiled at her, and all at once, she realized it was Hershel who looked altogether different in his finery. The assembled guests sang, "Here comes the bride," and she blushed a delicate pink. Hershel turned to stand beside her and the preacher began with the words, "We are gathered here today …"

Hershel, meanwhile, thought that Bessie was as lovely a vision as he had ever seen in her homemade wedding dress with her pink roses that matched her glowing face. He determined then and there to match all his actions to the vows he made to love, honor, and cherish for all the days of his life. Everyone applauded at the conclusion of, "You may kiss the bride," which he did with great pleasure.

Belle said, "Let's eat before all this wonderful food goes to ruin." She had noticed Bobby Anderson lurking around in the kitchen during the ceremony, but thought little of it. Most everyone wanted either coffee or tea on this cold day, so the punch was barely touched. Belle saw Bobby take Hershel aside and insist that he taste the punch.

"Come on, buddy; it's good. We'll have a toast to your happiness."

"I'd really rather have coffee, Bobby, but I reckon one taste won't hurt."

"Here's to you and your bride. May you have a long and happy life. Now, drink up."

Hershel drank from the cup, and before he could set it down, Bobby was filling it again. "Now, isn't that good? Let's have one more."

It really doesn't taste that bad, thought Hershel. Maybe he'd have a little more.

The women all gathered around Bessie as she opened the gifts they'd brought, mostly items specially homemade. The most beautiful and treasured gift, however, was from Grandma Ola. Two of the silver filigreed tea glasses that Bessie had packed so carefully for Grandma's move to the poorhouse now sat sparkling on her kitchen table.

"Oh, Grandma, you can't give me these."

"Yes, Bessie, I brought those over from the old country and never broke a one. But two have already been broken in our new home. People are so careless. I know you will take good care of them, and it is my wish that you have them."

"Thank you, yes, I will keep them safe for you."

The guests began to put on coats and scarves, preparing for the cold. Belle, who found herself thirsty, let out a shriek. "Somebody has spiked this punch!" Bobby, sitting in a corner talking with Hershel, looked away, but she could see the little smirk on his face. Conversations flowed among the guests.

"Surely not, Belle."

"Here, let me try some."

"Don't you dare. We're going home right now."

"Bobby, you son of a bitch, did you do this?" Fortunately, the preacher had gone home before Belle asked this question.

"Hershel, are you all right? You don't look so good."

The combination of excitement, exhaustion, and punch had taken their toll on the nondrinker. Following Bessie's suggestion that he lie down for a little while, Hershel awoke early the following morning just in time to drink some coffee and grab his lunch bucket before the shift change whistle blew. *What have I done?* he thought. *How will I ever make this up to Bessie?*

"Well, there you are," said Belle, standing at the stove stirring a pot of vegetable soup. Hershel's long day of work had not helped answer those questions, and he dreaded getting home. "Wipe that hangdog look off your face and come on in here. Bessie's been worried about you all day, so go tell her you're all right."

He found her sitting in what was to be their bedroom, polishing the silver glasses.

"Bessie, what can I say to make this be better? I can only promise it will never happen again. I've never been one to drink hard liquor, or even beer, since I've seen too much of that in the coal camp. My brother Charlie made a bad example, you know."

"Hershel, I've been so worried that you'd made yourself too sick to work today, but there you went off like lightning this morning. Are you well now?"

Sitting down on the floor by her side, Hershel said, "I'm just fine if you're just fine, too. I never got the chance to say how beautiful you looked yesterday. First the women took you away, and then Bobby took me away, and then it was all over. I never even got to eat any of the wedding cake. My head was spinning and my stomach was aching all at the same time. I'm just sorry I made such a fool of myself. Remind me never to speak to Bobby again." He grinned.

"Remind me never to invite him again. I didn't think he'd do such a thing to you on your wedding day."

"He'll do any damn fool thing he can think of, and we gave him the perfect chance for mischief. But can you forgive me for falling into the trap?"

"There's nothing to forgive. I never got the chance to tell you how handsome you looked in your good clothes yesterday. You'll have to dress up more often."

"I'll have to get some good clothes of my own, then, since they made such a good impression."

"Indeed, you will. Let's go tell Mom we can all eat supper now."

CHAPTER 17

With Christmas upon them, the four children in the house began writing their letters to Santa.

"Now, don't you kids get carried away. Here, Russell, help Orie get his ready," urged Belle.

Bessie was determined that every person in the household should have one gift, whether it was handmade or store-bought. The two oldest members of the family would be happy with a plug of tobacco each, she thought. Belle had been busy knitting mittens for Orie and Ivy and caps for Russell and Wilbert, but they still needed something special each. Orie should have a set of jacks, and Ivy wanted a jump rope. The two older boys had both asked for a penknife, and there were some small ones at the company store. Bessie had long ago added some tatting around the edges of handkerchiefs for Belle and Bonita and had gotten a small harmonica for Clemente, who loved music, especially the old Italian songs he'd learned as a child. Now that left only Hershel. How could she possibly know what he would like? He never said. The expression of a wish for any sort of object was as foreign to him as it would have been to the cat that sat dozing on the rag rug by the hearth. They both seemed to hold contentment within themselves.

She'd been too busy with the wedding to think about Christmas till it was too late to order anything from the Sears Roebuck catalog. Still, she could page through it looking for things she might have seen at the company store. Some folks called it the "wish book," but she always thought everything was too expensive for her to even wish for. The clothing, especially, was all beautiful, the waists, the gowns, the street skirts, and the men's suits were very smart-looking but far out of reach. One day, she would buy Hershel something nice from the catalog if she could find a way to earn actual cash money. Back in the middle of the book, she came upon ladies' purses, and there was a small selection of men's billfolds. The combination coin purse and billfold was forty-six cents in the catalog, so it would probably be two dollars at the store, but if they had one, that would be just the thing. Maybe her remaining earnings would be enough.

Deciding to beard the lion in his den, Bessie marched off to the store that afternoon but was relieved to find that Mr. Humphrey was not there. Thinking at first that he might be in the office, she whispered to Mrs. Serilla, "Can you tell me how much credit I still have from my work?"

"Yes, Bessie, but why are you whispering?"

Cutting her eyes toward the office door, she said, "I'd as soon not see him."

"You're not to worry, dear; he's gone."

"Gone?"

"Yes, every young woman who has worked here has quit on the spot, so the company finally decided to give him what they called a 'transfer.' He now must confine himself to working with men in the mine office at Dola."

"Oh, I'm so glad. I've hated the thought of ever seeing him again."

"One thing, though. He tried to punish those who spurned him by canceling the credit they had built up from their wages—yours included. Let me look. Yes, it says zero by your name."

"What can I do? I needed that credit for Christmas. That's why I'm here today."

"Bessie, you know how the place runs. Mind the customers while I go over to the mine office to see what they say."

"Oh, yes, I can do that." Bessie hung up her coat and replaced it with an apron. The store had certainly suffered from neglect in the months since she'd been here. Everything needed a good dusting, but there was no time, since a shift change had brought several miners into the store for last-minute shopping. There were no other clerks, which seemed odd. Usually, there was at least one other person working—one extra in the morning and one in the afternoon. She'd helped three people before Mrs. Serilla got back.

"Bessie, do you still want to work?"

"Oh, yes, I surely do."

"Well, then, knowing the circumstances of your departure, they want to take you back, starting today. As you've probably noticed, we're quite shorthanded."

Both anxious and relieved, Bessie said, "I'll need to run home to make sure my mother can care for the children the rest of the day before I can say yes or no."

"All right, fine, run along, and come back as soon as you can."

Turning back from the door, Bessie said, "Will I be working mornings or afternoons? Mornings are really best for me."

"Mornings will be fine, Bessie. I'm here full-time and I think they've found an afternoon girl, but I need you to fill in today."

"I'll be back directly," she said.

Running home, Bessie couldn't believe her good luck. If she hadn't taken a chance on seeing Mr. Humphrey today, they might have hired someone else. She couldn't wait to tell her mother and Hershel the good news. Working in the store this afternoon would help pass the time till he got home from the mine, so she just hugged her mother and rushed back to work. Work—*what a wonderful word,* she thought.

Mrs. Serilla had more good news when Bessie returned to the store. The company restored three dollars worth of scrip to her account, and while she was off from work, they had begun a policy of allowing store employees to trade scrip for cash, at a reduced rate, however. At the 50 percent reduction, her three dollars was worth a dollar and a half. Still, if she saved enough, in time, she could order from the Sears catalog or the Montgomery Ward catalog, where prices were much better. During her ten-minute break that afternoon, Bessie found no men's wallets, but she did find a model car—not a toy, but a real model of the Packard she'd heard Hershel speak of so highly. She asked Mrs. Serilla to put this item aside for her, along with those for the children so that with what she would earn between now and Christmas, she could take them all home.

Hershel had saved as much of his pay as possible while still paying the rent and providing food for the ever-growing number of people living in their company house. Jeremiah and Orie's father asked for so little; he welcomed them both. Belle helped out with her tatting and quilting, and her two boys were great help with gathering coal along the tracks and working in the garden. Clemente and Bonita paid their share or even more. The two little ones needed milk, so he had managed to barter his labor on a local farm for a cow, which then needed a shed for winter. The shed was built, but he would be working off his debt till spring. Now, though, he had his heart set on two things: candy for the children's Christmas Eve and a ring for Bessie.

No big snows had yet fallen this year, but on Christmas Eve, fat, fluffy flakes began whirling slowly down, coating tree limbs and filling the rutted lanes of Riverview. Bessie had worked during the morning and on into the afternoon taking care of the last-minute shoppers who filled the store. A shipment of oranges had come in on the morning train, and she planned to carry home four of the precious fruits for the children's stockings. In her lifetime, Bessie had always been lucky enough to have an orange for Christmas, and the smell of them brought back lovely memories of both her childhood and her years with Orie. It seemed that Hershel had never eaten anything so strange.

Hurrying home through the twilight, Bessie determined to think only of Hershel and not let the past catch up to her again. She'd learned to look up on clear nights to see Orion now that the winter sky loomed so bright overhead. Her new husband had no constellation of his own, but he had given her this one, and she loved him for it. There seemed to be no jealousy or envy in him, so she could remember Orie without guilt. Still, Orie was now as distant as those stars, and she could see him fading as time passed. Perhaps she should adopt Jeremiah's way of dealing with things he couldn't change: "It's all in the past, and we'll speak no more of it."

Christmas plans had been underway for several weeks as they tried to honor the traditions of their Italian friends. On December 6, St. Nicholas Day, for instance, Clemente and Bonita would customarily eat fava beans, but there were no such beans to be had, so the whole family ate dried butter beans, already a favorite. For Christmas Eve, Italian families had what they called the Feast of the Seven Fishes. Clemente searched for fish without success until he found a small store in Fairmont that sold codfish, which he proudly brought home.

"Now, what do I do with that smelly stuff?" asked Belle.

"Please let me worry about that, Missus Belle," cried Bonita, "I know how to make a delicious fish for us."

"Well, I'm cooking potatoes and cabbage. Will that go with your fish?"

"Oh, yes, just let me have some tomatoes to cook with the fish and we'll truly have our feast."

After dinner, the families all gathered in the living room to set up Bonita's miniature ceppo she had brought from Italy and Belle's manger set her father had carved for her many years before. The pyramid-shaped ceppo held the same tiny holy family as the manger set, but the children had cut out paper animals to add to each and an angel to fasten to the eve of the manger. Hershel slipped quietly from the room as Bonita told the story of La Befana, the witch who brought gifts to good children and pieces of coal to bad ones.

"Sounds like Santa Claus to me," said Russell. "I got ashes and switches once."

"Mama, will the witch come to our house?" asked six-year-old Ivy, her eyes growing wide at such a thought.

"Well, if you've been a good girl, you won't have anything to fear," said Bessie, smiling at her daughter.

Hershel, who had re-entered the room unnoticed, said, "Did you hear anything back in the bedrooms just now? I'm not sure what it was, but let's go see."

The bigger boys, now nine and seven, leading the way, they crept through the dark rooms. Ivy took Hershel's hand, while four-year-old Orie stayed behind with his mother.

"I don't see anything at all. It must have been nothing," said Russell.

"Let's let our eyes get used to the dark," said Hershel. "Wait—what's this on the windowsill? Ivy, reach up there and see what it is."

Standing on her tiptoes, Ivy felt along the high sill. Nothing was there. All of a sudden, her hand touched something smooth and round far over in the corner. Taking it down, she discovered a piece of candy in a shiny wrapper twisted at both ends.

"Where did it come from, Daddy?" she said.

"It must have been Santa's elves, Ivy. They come around on Christmas Eve watching little boys and girls to see if Santa should come after all. Looks like you passed the test."

Meanwhile, the two older boys found their own treats, and Bessie brought Orie along to find his. Thus began a tradition to be passed along through the years that would make darkened windowsills magic places on Christmas Eve.

Bonita and Clemente dressed in their finest for midnight mass, joining their friends singing their way to the Italian church, and the rest of the household settled in for the night. Hershel and Bessie sat together in front of the coal fire listening to the children whispering their hopes for Santa Claus.

"How kind of you, Hershel, to make Christmas Eve special for the children," said Bessie.

"It made it special for me, too, Bessie. That's just what my mother always did. Sometimes she had candy and sometimes just a walnut or a piece of dried apple, but there was always something for us to find. She loved to play games with us and tell stories. I've never been any good at stories, but I can play games."

"You told me a wonderful story about Orion the Hunter, and he's up there tonight sparkling clear. I wish I had something as nice to give you."

"At this moment, Bessie, I don't want for anything. I have four precious children in this house, and I have you. No words can say how much all of you mean to me." Reaching into his pocket and taking out a small box, Hershel said, "Maybe this will help me say what's in my heart."

Bessie took the box, and there inside was a thin silver ring with one tiny, blue stone. "Why, Hershel, it's beautiful. What's it called?"

"I got it at the jewelry store in Fairmont. They said it's a small sapphire and it's meant to bring you peace and love. Since it's also your September birthstone, I thought you might like it."

"Oh, I love it! And I love you for thinking of it. I never thought to have anything so fine."

"I went looking for a diamond, but they were all too big and expensive. One day, you'll have one, though, Bessie."

Hugging him close, she said, "And one day, you'll have that Packard, too, Hershel. Mark my words." Retrieving a package from the mantle, she said, "For now, this will have to do."

CHAPTER 18

After Christmas, winter hardened into gray and endless days of snow that piled up along the railroad tracks, covering any spilled coal that could have warmed the houses of the Riverview miners. There would be no saving and no trading scrip for cash, since coal had to be purchased from the company at elevated rates. The previous summer, Russell and Wilbert had mastered the art of timing the passing of the coal trains and then running along with gunnysacks, especially along curves where coal was likely to fall from the cars, trying to be first on the scene. Now snowdrifts made it impossible to run, and smaller pieces of coal quickly sank into the snow piles. The two boys and Ivy trudged off to school each morning as Bessie made her way to work. Hershel had had his breakfast at 5:30 so he could be at the mine when the six o'clock whistle blew.

For his twenty-third birthday at the end of January, Bessie baked Hershel a cake decorated with small candles, the first of his life. As birthday presents, each child wrote him a letter that Bessie had helped them compose, though they could say whatever they wished. "Dear Daddy," wrote Ivy, "thank you for teaching me my letters and numbers. My teacher says I write them very well." Little Orie just said, "Happy birthday," while Russell and Wilbert said the same, but also that they hoped he would take them deer hunting when they got old enough. Hershel's wish as he blew out the candles was that every member of the family would be there again for his twenty-fourth birthday and beyond.

There was no January thaw that year, but spring came early, pausing first for locust winter, then dogwood winter, and finally blackberry winter before settling in for warm days and cool nights. Pretty Girl was once again bartered for, in order to plow up the garden spot. The whole family pulled weeds from the big clods, hoed them down to size, and planted onion sets, the saved potato pieces that each contained one eye, and the cabbage, radish, and carrot seeds. Tomato seedlings, currently lining the windowsills, would be set out later after the danger of frost was past.

Clemente and Bonita had finally found a home of their own and welcomed their first "American" child, a healthy boy, Dominic, named for the lost brother. Bonita's mama had come from Italy for the birth and stayed on to help out. The loss of Clemente's income had been a blow to the family finances, but the house had begun to bulge at the seams. Bessie missed Bonita's help, especially on washdays.

On a rainy Saturday evening in April, Bessie opened one of her last jars of blackberries for the children's bedtime treat. There they sat under the clotheslines strung across the front room, hoping no drips landed on their heads, blackberries bobbing and peeking out of the surface of bowls of milk.

"Look how dark the berries are," said Ivy. "I love the sound of the seeds crunching, don't you, Russell?"

"Don't guess I paid any attention to that, but I just love blackberries. They were making flowers up on the hill yesterday, so in a while, we'll be able to eat them right off the bush. That's the best way."

Laughter erupted as a drop of water from the pants hanging upside down over his head landed on Wilbert's forehead and began running down his cheek.

"Look at the crybaby," teased Russell.

"I am not a crybaby; that's water off these dang dungarees," said Wilbert.

At that moment, several drops fell on Russell's head, and one splattered in his milk. "Now who's a crybaby?" said Wilbert.

Hearing the uproar, Belle arrived in time to hurry them up and send them off to bed. Talk around the supper table this night was not for their ears. The mine whistle had shrieked out at 1:00 in the afternoon with news that there had been an accident, the nature of which was unknown at the time. Bessie had just gotten home from work, so she ran to the mine entrance, dreading what she might find this time. There seemed to be no fire or smoke, no explosions, no earth tremors. Second-shift workers came running from the company houses, carrying shovels and picks. An announcement soon came that there had been a roof fall and several miners were farther back behind the debris. No one knew yet how many lay under the slate or how many were safe but trapped. The fall had formed a solid barrier, so time would be running short to dig through so that air could be directed beyond the fall.

Hershel was nowhere in sight, and with nothing to do but wait, Bessie ran home to tell the family what she knew. Her mother had started the washing that morning and had clothes hung on the line when it had started to cloud up. Not feeling able to wring out the heavy work clothes again with her sore, chapped hands, Belle had started taking them down to re-hang in the house. Just then, the whistle blew.

When Bessie got home, Belle and Mr. Morris were struggling to get the clothesline up in the front room. Jeremiah just grumbled and fretted, since he couldn't be of any help. Bessie's word that men were trapped under and behind a roof fall brought their work to a standstill, but Bessie quickly said, "Let's just get this done, and I'll go right back." Her father had been killed in a roof fall; her husband had been killed in an explosion; now her new husband was somewhere in this mine. They all depended on him for their living and their home itself. What would she do if he was hurt, if he was dead?

Bessie had endured great hardship in her life. Still, she had grown up, had grown strong since Orie's death at Monongah. She now promised herself that she wouldn't cry or scream or collapse this time. She would stand in the now-pouring rain with the other women and repeat to herself over and over, "He's alive; he's alive; he's alive," till he came walking out. Three hours later, he appeared, having helped with the digging out of twenty-three living miners and five who'd been under the rubble.

As they walked home together, she, soaked through and through, and he, stained from the coal he'd been digging and wet from the rain, she said, "Hershel, I kept telling myself you were alive until there you were—alive."

"I'm sorry I couldn't get any word to you. We had to work fast before they ran out of air."

"Oh, yes, I know, but you'd think the operators could make announcements from time to time instead of just letting the families wait and wait and wait with no word at all."

"Bessie, sometimes I think they don't care how many lives are taken, just so they get their coal mined."

After supper, Bessie and Belle were clearing away the dishes when they heard a clatter on the porch. Peering out the window, Bessie said, "There's a man and a woman at the door and I've never seen them before."

Hershel opened the door into the laughing faces of his brother Charlie and a woman he'd never seen before either. In barged Charlie, picking up Hershel and whirling around, saying, "Well, here you are, little brother. Long time, no see. Thought we'd never find you."

"Charlie, did you come all the way from Alaska?"

"Yes, I'm on furlough, and this is my new bride, Flo. Flo, meet my brother Hershel."

Flo was a sight to behold. Her close-fitting flowered dress was full of flounces and ruffles, her shoes had buckles decked out in rhinestones, her face was painted in a variety of shades—red on her lips being the most prominent, and her hair flared in an orange hue previously unknown to those observing it.

"Pleased, I'm sure," said Flo, closely studying her fingernails, also a brilliant red.

"I met Flo in San Francisco on my way home, and she decided she'd like to come east with me. We've got a room at the hotel, but I wanted to see everybody tonight. Where's Dad?"

"He's already gone to bed, Charlie. He's not very well."

Bessie stood, sort of dumbfounded, waiting to be introduced. Belle had made a hasty exit but stood just outside the kitchen door taking it all in.

"Now, Charlie, here's my wife, Bessie. She's Lucy's sister, and her husband Orie was killed in the Monongah mine explosion. Don't know if you ever met before."

"No, I only heard Lucy speak of you, but that was a long time ago."

"Let's go see if Dad's awake. We won't get him up, though. He lost a leg in a mine accident, but I know he'll want to see you."

As they left, Belle re-entered the kitchen, looked pointedly at Bessie, and asked Flo to have a seat. "Would you like some coffee, dear?" said Belle in her most innocent tone.

"Oh, no coffee for me. Would you have anything a little stronger?"

"No, we don't hold with that sort of thing in this house."

Bessie, embarrassed now by her mother's words, said, "You and Charlie can probably get beer or something at the roadhouse. It's just on the way out of town toward Shinnston. He'll know where it is."

"Okay, I can wait," said Flo. "This seems like a sort of quiet place. Is there any nightlife at this roadhouse? Any music? Any dancing? Sure ain't a thing like San Francisco."

"Is that where you're from, San Francisco?" asked Bessie.

"No, I was just passin' through there when I met Charlie. I was born in Kansas, which is also a quiet place. Had to get out of there or just die of boredom. My whole family don't know nothin' but farming, and that's not a life for me."

Hershel and Charlie had tiptoed back, saying that their dad was asleep and they didn't want to wake him. "How about some coffee, Charlie?"

"Oh, Charlie, Bessie was just telling me about a roadhouse we can go to," interrupted Flo.

"Well, I guess we'll do that, Hershel. See you tomorrow?"

Now Bessie interrupted, saying, "Yes, Charlie, please come at lunchtime tomorrow. It's Sunday, so we'll all be here." Taking Flo's hand, Bessie said, "Maybe we can get to know each other a little better tomorrow."

Flo and Charlie must have had a late night, because they didn't arrive until after 3:00, way beyond lunchtime. Bessie offered them a piece of her blackberry pie, which Flo declined, saying she had to watch her girlish figure, to which Charlie replied that he was spending quite a bit of time watching her girlish figure. Finishing off his pie, Charlie said, "Well, Dad, how do you like being retired?"

"You have no idea how people have to live, Charlie. I'm not retired; I'm out of work and damned unhappy about it," said Jeremiah. "Here I sit, day after day, with nothing to do but think about sitting here, day after day. Your brother has to keep us all, and some days we live from hand to mouth."

"Sorry, Dad. Maybe I can help out a little."

"Don't trouble yourself, son. We've got along without you all this time, and now you've done got yourself a fancy woman to keep. I wish you luck with that."

At that, Flo got up, straightened her skirt, and said, "Are you coming, Charlie?"

Bessie, trying to make up for Jeremiah's bluntness, said, "Oh, don't go yet. We haven't really had a visit."

Charlie gave a little wave and caught up with Flo, already halfway down the porch steps. "See you another time," he said.

"I'd like to see Charlie with a good woman, but she don't look right to me," said Jeremiah.

Belle replied, "Jeremiah, shut your mouth and drink your coffee," to pent-up laughter all around.

CHAPTER 19

1912

News of Mother Jones's arrival in southern West Virginia in the midst of a virtual war at Cabin Creek spread like either a welcome spring rain or a dreaded disease, depending on whose side you might be on—the striking miners or the coal operators. An organizer for the United Mine Workers, the eighty-two-year-old woman who some called rabble-rouser, some called miners' angel, had tried unsuccessfully to bring the union to the Fairmont Field of mines that included both Monongah and Riverview in 1902. Hershel remembered her vividly from an appearance she made at a ballpark on July Fourth. The dust and the locusts were bad that day and fourteen-year-old Hershel had never heard a woman make a speech, much less a speech filled with cuss words.

"I never got to see her, so tell us what she was like," said Bessie.

"Well, she was a small, little old woman with the face of an angel. Her words, though, were like they should have been coming out of someone else's mouth. She took the name of the Lord in vain without thinking a thing about it. She called the operators and their hired guards every kind of name, but she called out the union leader, too, saying he was a no-account nothing who stayed drunk all the time."

"What did she look like, other than an angel?"

"She wore a black dress and a black shawl, and she was very neat and tidy, even though it was a hot day, with the wind blowing dust every whichaway. Sometimes, the locusts called so loud it could have been hard to hear, but she had a very strong voice that she turned on full force."

"So, what did she say? What did she want people to do?"

"She said the Fairmont Coal Company was our worst enemy and our second worst were the scabs who worked through a strike."

"I had to work through a strike once to put food on the table. I guess she never heard of that," growled Jeremiah.

"She hates the owners, and she said if miners would all stick together, they could win better wages and safer mines, but that strike failed, and I guess this one will, too," said Hershel.

"I heard she got arrested in '02, but she made a big speech as they were taking her away," said Bessie.

"I wasn't there for that, but I wouldn't put it past her to just keep on talking while they carted her off," said Hershel. "In Fairmont, she arrived in style in a buggy at the end of a parade with a band and flags, so maybe she went to jail in style too, handcuffs and all."

"Somebody called her the most dangerous woman in America, because she wasn't afraid of the mine owners or their guards. Sounds a little bit like you, Belle," said Jeremiah. Laughter erupted until Belle cleared her throat.

"Mother Jones lost her whole family in an epidemic, so I guess she thinks maybe she's got nothing else to lose if she just speaks her mind and defies those who mistreat others. I've still got two boys to raise, so I couldn't take a chance on jail, but I do admire her for what she does," answered Belle.

Next day, Bessie brought home a newspaper that described the speech Mother Jones had made on the capitol steps in Charleston the day before.

"It was full of anger and lots of applause and shouts from the miners who came to listen," said Bessie. "She started out by saying that what was happening was 'an uprising of the oppressed against the master class,' whatever that means. She complained that the armed guards had 'Winchesters, a dangerous and deadly weapon,' plus three Gatling guns."

At that point, Hershel spoke up to say that he had heard of Gatling guns on one of Charlie's visits home from the army. "They just spray bullets everywhere and kill everything in their path," he said, "not like a hunting rifle that fires one shot at a time."

Bessie read that Mother Jones said the governor had to save the people from their "state of constant fear, unrest, and dread" by getting rid of the guards and giving back the "Constitutional rights of freedom of speech and peaceable assembly."

"Oh, listen here," said Bessie. "She says that these guards drag women and children from their homes and beat them like rats. Can that be true, Jeremiah? You've been through strikes before."

"Well, I never had to face these mine guards like she's talkin' about, but I do know they're mean sons-a-bitches. I know about bein' beat up, though, but it was at the hands of miners like me who wanted me to strike with them. I couldn't let my children suffer, so I worked, and a lot of good it did me. You remember all that, Hershel, don't you?"

"Yes, I remember, and I'm just glad I haven't had to choose one or the other. At least, not yet," said Hershel. "What else did she say?"

"She compares miners with the Israelites and says the labor movement is a 'command from God Almighty.' Then she turns right around and blames the miners for electing 'a whole gang of commercial pirates' to public office."

Reading further, Bessie laughed out loud and said, "Guess what she calls the company store? She calls it the 'pluck-me' store. I never knew I worked at a pluck-me store, but I guess I do."

As they finished packing lunch buckets for morning, Bessie confided to her mother that she wished she could be brave enough to do something important like Mother Jones. "Now, Bessie, you know good and well that, like me, you have bigger responsibilities right here at home, so stop thinking those aren't important."

For a few days now, Bessie had been feeling sick of a morning, and she knew well what that meant. It was a sweet secret she kept to herself. Soon, she would have to share the news with Hershel, and she wasn't quite sure how he'd take it. They'd never talked about children, and she hoped he would welcome more than Orie and Ivy. They'd again taken up sitting out on the porch after dark, and this night might just be the perfect time to speak of her fears and hopes.

The sound of cicadas filled the air, blending with the gentle clink of the chain as the swing moved slowly back and forth. Hershel controlled their movement since Bessie's legs were too short to reach the floor. She turned and leaned back, pulling her feet up and resting her head on his shoulder. "Hershel, I have something to tell you," she said.

"Sounds serious," he said, a slight grin on his face.

"Well, yes, I guess it is serious," she said, losing her nerve for a moment.

After a long pause, he said, "Well, out with it."

Sitting up, Bessie said, "Oh Hershel, I don't know whether you'll be mad or glad. I don't know if you want any more burdens than you already have. I don't know if it will be a burden or a gift."

"Bessie, just tell me—what is it?"

"Okay, we're having a baby. There, I said it," Bessie blurted out.

Hershel sat quite still, looking stunned for a minute. Then he burst into laughter and grabbed up Bessie and whirled her around on the porch and then down onto the front yard, laughing all the while.

"How can you speak of burdens when you talk about a baby?"

"But there will be another mouth to feed."

"Now, how much can a little baby eat?" He laughed.

"Hershel, be serious. Do you really welcome this news?"

"Bessie, if you think I wouldn't want a child, I haven't let you see who I really am. Come and sit down."

Bessie wondered what words were about to be spoken—thinking she knew him very well.

Hershel grew solemn as he said, "I've never told you much about my mother's death, but I think it's time. Jane and I were both twelve years old, and on her deathbed Mother asked Jane to care for the house and chores and asked me to see to the other children when I wasn't at the mine. Not long after that, Jane died, too, and my father refused to honor those wishes. Instead, he gave the younger children away, leaving just me at home with him. All at once, I lost my mother, my twin sister, who was my other half, and the little ones I loved, Virgil, Leonard, and Debbie. The pain and loneliness of that time have never left me. They don't live that far from here, but they've forgotten us and come to love others as their families. Then, of course, I lost Lucy, too."

Tears filling her eyes, Bessie said, "Yes, we share that loss, Hershel."

"I love your children as my own, and I want you to know that Orie and Ivy will always be my son and daughter, no matter how many others we have. Now, tell me how long you've known about this and when we can expect to add this new little 'burden.'"

"I've had the morning upsets now for about a month, so I think our baby will arrive in early spring," said Bessie, now smiling in relief.

"Spring is the perfect time for new lives to begin among the budding flowers and trees. I'll get started building a crib that I hope will be filled with more than one baby through the years. Bessie, I could not be happier at your news."

Autumn turned to winter, and Bessie's morning sickness disappeared as the baby grew. She could continue her work at the company store as long as her condition didn't show, but soon her clothing no longer fit, and by January, she had to give her notice. Mrs. Serilla, who had been promoted to manager, said she would try to keep her job open, but she made no promises. Bessie missed her work and especially the pay that came with it, but now she busied herself with making baby clothes and what she hoped would be plenty of diapers. With Ivy nearly nine and Orie six going on seven, she had nearly forgotten what it would be like with a new infant in the house.

Bessie tried to sleep, as Hershel seemed to struggle with something unknown but greatly feared. She thought it must surely be a nightmare, but she didn't know what she should do. She tried shaking his shoulder when suddenly, he opened his eyes and shouted, "Bessie, get up, get up! The roof is falling and you've got to help me hold it up. Hurry and help me brace this wall—hurry, hurry. If it falls, it will kill us both. Please, Bessie, help me!"

She scrambled up beside him, and they both now stood on the bed, bracing themselves against the headboard. "Hershel, wake up. Please, just wake up. We're not in the mine. We're here at home, safe and sound. Please, wake up and come to your senses." And just as suddenly as it began, it ended. Hershel sank down onto the bed, closed his eyes, and went back to sleep—no more thrashing or kicking, no more panic, no more calling for help, just peaceful sleep. *Thank God,* thought Bessie, but sleep didn't return as easily to her. She lay quite still, listening to him breathe, hoping and praying that no more dreams would come that night. When the sky began to lighten, she rose to get a head start on breakfast and wondered if he would remember their adventure holding up the mine roof.

Belle always got up early, and this day was no different, except for the puzzled look on her face. "What was all the commotion about in the night, Bessie?"

"Hershel had such a bad nightmare that he thought the mine was caving in. He demanded that I help him hold up the roof, so we stood there on the bed holding up the headboard. Finally, he just lay back down, and I don't think he ever actually woke up. I've never had many nightmares, but Ivy did for a while after Orie died."

"I've never had one, but I've always heard you shouldn't wake up somebody like that."

"It was really scary because I didn't know what to do except just do what he asked."

Hershel entered the kitchen and asked, "What was scary, Bessie? Is something wrong?"

"You don't remember your bad dream?" she asked.

"No, what bad dream?"

As she explained what had happened, a smile spread over his face. "There's nothing funny about holding up a headboard in the middle of the night, Hershel," she said.

"Oh, I'd love to have seen you there in your nightgown, holding up the mine roof. Wouldn't you, Belle? I'd rather laugh about it than cry about it."

"Hershel, are you all right?"

"Yes, I think I'm okay. I remember my mother telling me that I had nightmares when I first went into the mines, but I thought I was over it. Please don't worry yourself about it. We heard the roof working in the section we were wiring yesterday, and I guess I was thinking about that when I went to sleep."

"Do you have to go back to that place today?"

"No, we finished it up and we'll be moving on today. See, nothing to worry about, Bessie. Speaking of moving on, those buckwheat cakes smell wonderful."

CHAPTER 20

1915

With baby Walter now two years old and eating soft food and drinking from a cup, Bessie wondered if she might again find work at the company store. She had loved nursing her baby, but he was old enough now to stay home with Belle and play with his older brother and sister. Hershel's job as second electrician had ended once the mine was wired, so he was back to loading coal. Hershel and Bessie often sat talking over early-morning coffee since he came home too tired even to eat his dinner, much less have conversation. Still, he always took time to hug little Walter before lying down for the night. This day, they tried to speak of small matters, like the need to wrap the pump before it got cold enough to freeze, but Bessie had more serious concerns as well.

"Hershel, do you think I could leave the children with Mom and try to get my job back at the store?"

"Why would you want to, Bessie?"

"Guess I've just felt hemmed in lately. I really enjoyed being out and about every day, and I miss it. Besides, we could put that money away, just in case."

"What does Belle have to say?"

"What she always says: never turn away from money to be made."

"Does she mind the extra work she'll have when you're not here?"

"She says not, but mind, I haven't got the job yet."

"Well, for my two cents, you should do what you think best. There's the whistle." With that, he gave her a peck on the cheek and rushed out the door.

Much had changed at the company store in her two-year absence, and now they were looking for someone to mind the new post office that had been set up there. She didn't begrudge the extra work, and she loved the extra pay she would receive as "postmistress." That income came in the form of real dollars, not scrip, so between that and Hershel's pay, they would be able to add to her savings from Orie's death. One day, she thought, they might buy a house and some land, have a big garden, and avoid living in a coal camp.

"So what do you have to do in your new job, Bessie?" asked Hershel the morning after she went back to work.

"Well, first of all, I have to get to work in time to put the new mail in the boxes by eight o'clock. Then I'll sell stamps and fill in at the store. Later in the morning, I'll sort the outgoing mail for the afternoon train and take care of packages and shipments."

"Sounds like a busy day."

"Yes, but that's what I like. I get to talk to lots of people, and Mrs. Serilla is so nice to work for."

"That's good. I liked working for Jack, while it lasted."

"There was a lot of talk yesterday about this war and sunken ships and whether we'll get into it or not."

"What sunken ships?"

"Some passenger ship the Germans sank—the Lusi-ana or Lusi-something or other."

"Whose ship was it?"

"I think it belonged to England, but there were Americans on it and they were killed. The Germans have these underwater boats that sneak up on ships and sink them with underwater bombs of some kind."

"Well, I've seen a lot of explosions in my life, but never thought you could explode anything under water." One more peck on the cheek and he was gone.

Hershel came home that day with news of his own. Tired as he was, he wanted to tell the family about the plans for mine rescue teams, so after supper, they all remained around the table.

"Today, the foreman came around and asked for volunteers to be a part of a rescue team. We'd have training in all the things you need to save miners when disasters happen. I said I'd do it."

"What kind of disasters?" asked Belle.

"They didn't say exactly, but I guess it means things like Monongah."

"Oh, Hershel, do you mean you'd have to go into a burning mine and try to find people?" asked Bessie.

"A burning mine or a collapsed mine or a flooded mine—whatever it was that needed rescuers," Hershel answered.

"Would it be just at this mine in Riverview? It seems pretty safe." said Bessie.

"But it wouldn't be just here. You know when that siren blows, everybody comes running, just like they did at Monongah. If I had the training, I'd be expected to go wherever I was needed. But we do that anyway, with or without knowing any more than we already know."

"Yea, that's right. Every able-bodied man expects to help and be helped in this mining business. Been doin' it all my life," growled Jeremiah.

"I want to know how to do these things better, maybe to save a life rather than just carry out a dead body." Glancing at Bessie's stricken face, Hershel said, "I'm sorry, Bessie. I know this brings back all those memories you'd put away years ago."

"Maybe if you get the training, you'll be able to save your own life someday," she said. "I can't lose you, too, Hershel."

Two months later, Hershel and four other men began their training one day a week. Their first task was to learn to use the breathing equipment they would have to wear into a mine that was filled with gas. Helmets like those worn by deep-sea divers were heavy and awkward to use in tight places like coal mines, but that's all they had. In the training sessions, they wore the helmets while doing hard work like loading coal.

They practiced carrying each other for longer and longer distances to prepare for carrying the injured from a mine. Hershel was tall but thin, so this part of the training proved almost too much for him. One of his team members was a large man, but the others were of average size. Since they all felt they would sink or swim together, they decided that they should plan for their examination so that Hershel wouldn't have to carry the largest guy. If he failed, they all might fail.

Testing came after each segment of the training, and after four sessions, they all managed to pass the physical exam. By that time, they had been given lighter-weight breathing devices that were easier to care for and easier to wear. The helmets had allowed them to see only straight ahead, but with the new apparatus, they could turn their heads and see all around. Next, they would learn about the human body and how to give first aid for broken bones, bleeding, burns, and shock. This part of the training was such a revelation to Hershel; he tried to remember every detail to explain to Bessie.

"Did you know that putting butter on a burn is the right thing to do unless the butter has been salted? Then it makes it worse," said Hershel.

"Well, I've only made sweet butter. Who would put salt in their butter?" Bessie replied.

"They told us the butter you buy in the store might have salt added to it."

"Guess I better take a look at what we sell, just to make sure. If I scalded myself in this kitchen, the butter is the first thing I'd look for."

"The satchel they call a 'first aid kit' has some salve in it we're supposed to use for burns, so maybe we should have some of that here at home."

"I'll see if we sell anything like that at the store. So far as I know, nobody has ever asked for such a thing. So this week, you've studied about burns."

"And then we'll learn how to stop bleeding by putting a tight band around your arm if that's what's cut open or broke with the bone poking through. Over the years, I've seen plenty of broken arms and legs and even some cut clear off. People can bleed to death pretty quick if you can't get it stopped."

At that, Bessie's usually sunny face clouded over, and worry lined her forehead. "Oh, Hershel, why do we have to have such a hard life? Why can't we just live one day to the next without the thought of fires and explosions and poison gas? Every now and then, a picture of Orie sitting there about to drink his coffee comes into my mind and I just want to scream and run till I can't run anymore."

Taking her in his arms, Hershel tried to calm her fears, and he realized that unless there was something she needed to know, he wouldn't tell her any more about his first-aid training. The thought of keeping it all to himself made him sad. He'd shared his childhood with his sister Jane. He'd shared his early married life with Lucy. Now he needed to confide in Bessie, but she seemed too likely to cry, and he couldn't have that.

1916

Cars to load were becoming scarce, and with miners being paid by the car instead of by the hour, unrest was growing. Hershel had been paid for his training days an average of what he earned loading coal, but the threat of layoffs and mine closures loomed. This lack of cars, however, proved a godsend to the 250 men normally working at the Jamison Mine at Barrackville, a small town near Monongah, on the morning of October 19, 1916.

When the disaster siren blew that morning, a call went out for any help possible from those who had been trained in mine rescue. Hershel and his team members had finished their training but were already at work at Riverview and scattered through the mine, so it took some time for them to assemble and climb aboard the streetcar with their equipment. This would be their first rescue attempt, and each man felt both excitement and fear.

"Let's go over our training steps before we get there," urged Hershel.

"Yes, I don't know if I remember what to do first," said Dickie, the youngest member of the team.

"Well, let's just think back to the last time we competed against those fellas from Pennsylvania that had always got all the medals before. We knew what to do then, and we whooped 'em at their own game," said Hershel.

Another spoke up. "Okay, first, we check our equipment. We can do that while we wait for this damn car to get us to Barrackville."

"When we do get there, we take our assignment from the superintendent or the fire boss or whoever is in charge."

"Right, so by that time, I think our training will take over and we'll just do whatever is needed," said Hershel.

Even though they arrived several hours after the initial explosion, the rescue teams could not enter the mine. So many structures had been destroyed and so much smoke was still coming from the shafts, the only work they could do was clearing away the wreckage, necessary tasks but not what they had spent months training for. As time passed, hope waned that those trapped inside could be found alive. Since the mine was not in operation that day, no accurate count had yet been made of those inside. Early speculation said that six were known to be entombed and nine more were missing. They worked as electricians, pump operators, and machine operators who would be in the mine making repairs on such a day, even though no coal was being produced. Rumor had it that the cause had been exploding coal dust. Others said it was the fault of one of the men smoking.

"I've never worked this mine, have you, Hershel?" said Dickie. The two of them were working at the air-shaft opening, trying to realign the fan, which had been blown out several yards from its housing.

"No, I've only been at Monongah and Riverview. This one is known to be real gassy, so I hope I never have to be over here."

"My God, Hershel, I didn't know you were at Monongah. And you're still alive?"

"Stroke of luck, Dickie. That's all."

"How long did you stay after the explosion?"

"Just long enough to find another job. My brother-in-law was killed, and it didn't scare me as much as it got on my nerves. I would think I saw him every now and then, so I had to get out of there."

"I heard they tried to blame it on a careless miner."

"Well, they never came to a real conclusion about the cause, so we just all went back to work as if it never happened. Now let's see if we can get this fan back in place."

With the fan starting up and a passage cleared for rescuers, one squad entered the mine. Each man had a breathing apparatus, and one carried a canary in its cage. Smoke was still thick, so they knew a fire raged somewhere in the mine. Their job would be to find the fire before it reached the point of exploding again and try to put it out or at least contain it enough to search for the victims of the first explosion. As those in the lead rounded a corner, they heard a moan coming from off to their right, so one man entered a side corridor and found one of the pump operators lying between the tracks. It took two rescuers to pick him up and hurry him out to fresh air. Returning to the squad, they discovered that both the canary and two of their men were also down.

"Time to get the hell out of here," said one member.

"We've got to warn the others ahead of us," said another.

Their dilemma was clear. They'd run into a deadly pocket of black damp. Stay and collapse, or go if they could, leaving others behind.

"You go back out, and I'll take your oxygen and try to reach the others. Just run as fast as you can to get out of this gas. I'll be along." These were the last words of the Bureau of Mines rescuer who had come to Barrackville from Pittsburgh aboard the converted Pullman car that served now as a rescue car.

Just as the remaining members of the rescue squad reached the outside, a roar erupted from the shaft and the mine exploded again, knocking them flat but alive. All efforts to get back inside were suspended. The wreckage they'd moved was now replaced with more blown-out timbers, more frames, more equipment housing, and again, the main fan that ventilated the whole system. The force of the blast ignited the dry coal dust coating the already damaged tipple, bringing it down and setting nearby sheds ablaze. Thoughts of men caught in the inferno below their feet would haunt each person there for as long as they lived. Still, they remained—ready to try again to make sure no one was left to die alone in the dark.

The superintendent of the mine called for everyone to gather around to hear his plan for their next steps.

"Men, you all know we can't stop here. Once we are able to get enough air and enough water into the mine, we can get the fire put out and then find our brothers. That's how I feel about them, and I know you do, too."

He was interrupted by a cry of, "But they're dead—we'll all be dead, too, if we go back in there."

Others joined in. "He's right. Yeah, we'll die, too, and for what?

"For the profit of the company, that's for what!"

"To save his precious mine from burning, that's for what!"

The superintendent continued, "Now, men, right now, it's not about profits or losses for the company. It's about those still in there. Yes, they're probably dead, but they are our brothers and, alive or dead, we need to get them out for the sake of their families. We do that not just for them, but for ourselves, too. We all need to know that someone would come for us if the situation called for it. Now, how many of you are willing to stay as long as it takes?"

The crowd began to murmur "hopeless," and "fool's errand," and "not me," until one miner shouted, "I will."

Hershel yelled, "I will, too. It's only right."

At last, a general chorus of agreement went up, and soon, most were forming into ranks ready to start the work of putting out the surface fires and clearing away debris. A few ducked their heads and drifted away. An old man pushed his way through the crowd and said quietly to Hershel, "Thank you for speaking up. My son's in there, and his ma's about lost her mind."

"I'm sorry," said Hershel, "we'll do what we can." Then he and his team headed for the broken fan to see if it could once again be repaired.

CHAPTER 21

Bessie learned of the Barrackville explosion at the store that morning and assumed Hershel would go as a rescuer, but she'd had no word from him. Leaving the store at 2:00 in the afternoon, she rushed home to tell the family.

"We already heard about it, Bessie," said Belle. "Some fella's been going from house to house spreading the news so we'd know not to expect them home for supper. Or for anything else, for that matter."

"Oh, Mom, I'm so scared. They're in more danger than if they'd just finished out their workday. Somebody said one of the rescuers had been killed, even if he was wearing one of those breathing things."

Just then, the children got home from school with frightened looks on their faces. "Mama, what's happened to Daddy?" cried Ivy.

Hugging her daughter, Bessie said, "Now hush, Ivy, we don't know that anything's happened to him. He's just gone to help some miners who were in an explosion. We're not getting ourselves all upset till there's something to get upset about. Now, go find Walter and bundle him up. He needs a little fresh air, and your grandma needs a little rest."

Orie hung back, wishing to hold onto his mother, but at ten, thinking that boys were supposed to be strong. Bessie just grabbed him and held him close. "Orie," she whispered, "Your daddy will be home soon, and everything will be all right. Now give me a hug and go help your sister with Walter. He's been giving your granny a fit today."

She didn't know if that was true, but at the age of three, Walter was bound to be giving somebody a fit—into everything, opening all the doors, all the drawers, curious to a fault. Besides, these two needed a distraction, and their little brother could surely provide that. Russell and Wilbert, now fifteen and thirteen, had their chores to do and had gotten to them after a look from Belle—mostly finding coal along the tracks and tossing it into the bin Hershel had built just off the back porch. They also had taken up lately with Mr. Morris and Jeremiah, neither of whom could get around the house very well anymore. Both old men saved up jobs for the boys to do after school, and if there were no jobs, they might sit and tell stories about the old days. Neither boy ever wanted to work in a mine, but they loved to hear the old stories over and over.

"Tell us about being a trapper, Granddad," begged Wilbert, always the most likely to get the stories started. Jeremiah, at sixty-three, was the "granddad" of the house, even though he was unrelated to the two boys. He'd seen his sons, Charlie, Bill, Jim, and Hershel, through their growing up years, so he was accustomed to boys' ways. He still mourned Jane's death, which, in his mind, had separated him from his younger children. The thought of keeping them home with him was the furthest possibility he could imagine. How could a man and a half-grown boy raise little children—no, it was impossible.

As the day wore on and they still couldn't get into the mine, the men tried to find meaning in sorting through enormous piles of debris, trying to decide what was scrap and what might ever be used again. Some of the metal was still hot to the touch and some of the wooden timbers still smoked, so the job was dangerous as well as tedious. Still, it kept their hands busy and their thoughts occupied. Finally, after 5:00, they were called together again and told that another effort was about to be made to enter the mine and see what conditions were like. A Bureau of Mines team would go in first and send back word for others to follow.

Hershel and his team gathered their equipment and waited for instructions. A group of women came around with sandwiches and coffee, but few felt like eating, although the coffee was most welcome. Huddled near the shaft, now clear of smoke, they sat thinking their own private thoughts, hiding their own private fears. At last, a message was received that the team could now enter the mine. They were joined by a trained rescuer who worked at this mine, so that his mental images of the workings could help them survive their next few hours. Hershel's experience at Monongah had taught him, though, that very little of that underground world would look the same as it had before the double explosions.

The descent to the bottom of the shaft, usually a chilly ride, was tempered this time by warm drafts from below, a sign of the fire still burning somewhere in the mine. They wore their breathing equipment draped around their necks, ready in seconds if the canary dropped over. They'd been warned that there were pockets of deadly methane here and there. They hoped for living miners to bring out but prepared themselves for only the dead. If the few men inside had been working together, they would have had ways to wall themselves off from the fire and the gas. If they were separated, which was most likely, a man alone had little chance.

"God, look at that," said Jerry, the local miner, pointing to a mound of timbers splintered to the size of small nails and blackened by the fire. "I been here since she opened in 1909 and never saw anything like that."

"What's our best route?" asked Hershel.

"We need to move south, southwest, and put up as many stoppings as we can along the way," said Jerry, "so let's get at it."

They worked quickly but efficiently, listening all the while to the now-brittle roof cracking and talking and seeming to move as they moved. Other crews were working other areas, everyone with the same goals: find the trapped miners and put out the fire. They all kept at it throughout the evening and into the long night, finding first one man burned beyond recognition, then another dead from the gas, but with no sign of having faced the fire. They finally were relieved of their duties at two in the morning, tired, aching, and hungry. Outside in the cool autumn night, Hershel was both relieved and frightened to see Bessie's anguished face among the women sitting around a fire just beyond the ruined tipple.

"Bessie, how did you get here?" he cried.

"Oh, Hershel, thank God you're out of there! Your brother Bill came to see if you were involved in this rescue and offered to bring me here. I just couldn't stay at home walking the floor and not knowing anything."

"Bill's here?"

"Yes, he said he'd stay till we knew if you were all right, and then he said he'd take us home."

"My squad is scheduled to go back in at 8:00 in the morning, so I planned to bunk here for a few hours. Let Bill take you home, Bessie. Your mom needs you, and there's nothing you can do here." Giving her a hug and a little shove, he said, "Please, Bessie, go home. Let's go find Bill now."

Sleep, when it finally came, was filled with nightmare scenes of raging fires and burned bodies. Waking with a start at six a.m., Hershel sought only some water to wash his face and a good, hot cup of coffee. A crew had been brought in to provide food for the volunteers, and once he'd walked around loosening up a little, Hershel realized he was hungry, not having had anything but coffee for more than twenty-four hours. Turns out they had pancakes and sausage and even eggs sunny-side up, just like he liked them. It was starting out to be a better day than he'd expected.

The superintendent called the teams together at 7:30, just as other groups were coming up from the shaft, their six hours of work over. "Men," he began, "eleven bodies have been recovered, and we're not sure how many more we'll find. The job now is to put out this fire. We don't think it's set the seam on fire yet, but that's what we're worried about. If that happens, we'll have to seal off everything and hope it will go out for lack of air, but it could just burn for years, and every family here would be out of work."

"Have we got enough water to fight with down there?" demanded one angry-looking miner.

"We've been stringing pressure hoses down all night and trying to remove as much gas as possible all at the same time so the gas doesn't keep feeding the fire. As you all know, this mine releases lots of gas and with the fans going full blast, that dries out the mine, raising the risk of more coal dust in the air. We've got to work fast now before it explodes again, and the first job is to put out that fire, so let's go."

"Are you going down with us?"

"Yes, I am. Let's go."

As they descended once more into the shaft, their ears were assaulted by merging sounds, the loud whir of the fans operating once again, the ripping of canvas and pounding of nails as brattices were made and hung strategically to direct the flow of air, the distant but ominous roar of the fire deep inside the mine, and the sound of water rushing through the pressurized hoses. As they worked their way forward toward the fire, the separate sounds became a din soon drowned out by just its roar. All he'd ever been taught about hell, Hershel thought, could be no worse than this.

Pumping air onto a fire, of course, only made it burn hotter and faster, but it was necessary to blow the methane and other gases away from the fire to prevent another explosion. Hershel suddenly thought of his mother fanning embers with a piece of paper to restart a fire in the grate early in the morning. As he looked up to see her better, a loud cracking seemed to travel several feet along the roof where they were working. The sudden change in temperature of the mine as the water poured onto the fire had weakened all of the surfaces, making them unstable. Before they could set posts under it, the roof came down around them, pinning Hershel and Jerry under a large piece of slate.

Jerry began yelling for help, but no sound came from Hershel. He lay in a stupor, seeing his mother again and again, smiling and calling to him to wake up. Those visions faded, replaced with Lucy's pretty face, replaced then with dear Bessie, dancing around the backyard at Monongah, urging him to get up and dance with her. Someone tried to lift the rock but failed, and a knife of pain shot through his head, taking away the lovely faces and replacing them with nothing but blackness.

Jerry's shouts had brought help at last, and with the use of a mine jack, the slate had been lifted off them both. Jerry's leg was broken, but Hershel was unconscious, so his injuries were still unknown as they both were carried down the endless tunnels, up the shaft, and out into the crisp, fresh air of autumn.

CHAPTER 22

Bessie had gone to work that morning but found that she couldn't stay. Not knowing about Hershel made it impossible to concentrate on anything but worry. Why did he have to do this volunteer rescue work? What was the purpose, if everyone in this mine was dead anyway? she wondered. Her only experiences with mine accidents had resulted in real sorrow—her father's death early on, followed by the Monongah disaster that took her husband. Now here was Hershel, tempting fate.

Begging Mrs. Serilla for understanding, she rushed out the door and ran for the streetcar that was just starting up in the direction of Fairmont. She'd have to change trolleys once on the way to Barrackville, but she couldn't stay put any longer. *Thank God for Mom there at home with Walter.* The other children had resisted going to school that morning, but with their mother and grandmother both insisting, they had no choice but to give the screen door a slam and stomp off the porch. Bessie knew it was fear rather than anger that came out in this behavior, and she felt like doing the same herself.

The streetcar stopped at last in Fairmont and she looked around in a panic, trying to figure out how to find the right one to Barrackville. She'd asked the driver which one to take, and he said they didn't have numbers, but to look for place names. She spotted one with a list of stops on the front that started with Ida May, then Barrackville. Already crowded with what could only be sightseers, the car was barely standing-room only, but this part of the trip would be only a few miles, so she paid her nickel and found a pole to hang onto. The car jerked to a start and then rolled smoothly and silently along, electricity crackling overhead as the long pole atop the car made contact with the wire above. No one got off at Ida May, though several more squeezed aboard. It seemed everyone was headed to the disaster. No laughter and little conversation accompanied the travelers on this nearly hypnotic ride. *Oh, please God, let him be all right,* prayed Bessie.

She arrived at 2:00 in the afternoon, just as shifts of volunteers were changing. Those with blackened faces were moving slowly away from the shaft, whereas fresh-faced men were moving swiftly toward it. Hearing a call of "Bessie," she turned, expecting to see Hershel, but it was his teammate, Dickie.

Looking around, she asked, "Where's Hershel?"

"I'm sorry, Mrs. Martin, for using your name, but that's what he calls you."

"So where is he?" she insisted.

"I'm so sorry to have to tell you that there was a roof fall and they carried him out a couple of hours ago. That's all I know."

"Was he alive?"

"I'm sorry, ma'am, I don't know."

At that, Bessie scoured the scene for someone, anyone, who could give her information. Running now toward a group of official-looking men dressed in suits and bowlers, bent over a map, she screamed, "Where's my husband?"

One of them took off his hat and came toward her with his hand outstretched. "Who are you looking for?" he said.

"Hershel Martin, one of the rescuers who was hurt this morning. Please tell me where you took him. Please tell me he's not dead."

"Yes, we had two men covered up in a roof fall. One had a broken leg and the other was sent to the hospital in Fairmont, unconscious. Let me see if I can find their names. Yes, here they are—the unconscious man was Martin, but he was alive. That's all I can tell you."

"I just came on the streetcar and have no way back. How can I get to that hospital? Can you help me?"

"Is there no one you can call on to come for you?

"No, there's no one."

Just then, another of the important-looking men came forward, but this one had no sympathy. "Just you run along, now. This isn't New York City, and we're not running a taxicab service here."

At that, a spark of her mother ignited in Bessie. "My husband works at Riverview Mine, but he came here out of the goodness of his heart to help in your rescue operation, and you tell me you don't run a taxi service. He was hurt in your damned mine, and I'm stuck here with no way to get to him. I don't know if he's alive or dead and you tell me you don't run a taxi service? What kind of people are you?"

Her voice rose as she spoke, quickly drawing a crowd that was anxious for any sort of sensation. Another man left the map table and approached with determination. Here was an angry woman who might turn the onlookers into an angry mob. His solution was to take her arm, lead her away from the crowd, and shush her like he would a child.

"You let go of me!" shrieked Bessie.

"Now, just calm down. Lower your voice and we'll find a way to get you to Fairmont, just as you wish," he whispered. "Can you do that?"

"What will you charge to take me? I have one dollar to my name, and I'll need it to get home—if I ever do," she said.

"Now, now, we'll take you for free and hope you find your husband in good hands and in good spirits when you get there." His clammy hand on her arm reminded her of Mr. Humphrey, so she was relieved when he turned her over to an assistant who would drive her to Fairmont.

The automobile ride took only half an hour, and she thanked the young man who let her out at the hospital steps.

"You're welcome, ma'am. I hope you find your husband well."

"I hope I find my husband alive," she said, slamming the car door.

The lobby was largely empty, huge, and frightening in itself, and she wondered how on earth to find Hershel. A young woman in a uniform appeared, seemingly out of nowhere, and said, in a no-nonsense voice, "May I help you, madam?"

Remembering the kindness she'd received at the hospital in Clarksburg with Jeremiah, Bessie said, "Oh, yes, I do hope you can help me. My husband was brought here from the Barrackville Mine a few hours ago, and I don't know what's happened to him since."

"And what is his name?" said the nurse.

"Martin—Hershel Martin."

"Let me look at our patient roster. Just a minute."

Bessie stood on first one foot and then the other as she waited.

"Yes, here he is. He's in Ward C on the second floor. I'm afraid visiting hours are over for the day, however. Can you come back tomorrow afternoon?"

At this, Bessie's face crumpled. "Don't you understand? He was hurt in the mine, and I haven't even seen him since. I've been afraid he was dead, and now you tell me he is in a ward in this hospital and I can't even go to him?" For the second time that day, she said, "What kind of people are you?"

"We have our rules for our patients' well-being, and we can't break them just because you would have us do so."

"I must see my husband, and someone here is going to let me," Bessie proclaimed. Once again, her voice rose, calling attention to herself and the young woman so sure of herself and her rules.

A door opened and an older woman came bustling out, scowling and asking, "What's going on here?"

The young woman answered. "This woman has arrived demanding to see a patient, and I've explained that visiting hours are over for the day."

Unwilling to let that define her situation, Bessie stood tall and said, "My husband was injured in the Barrackville Mine today, and I need to see for myself that he's still alive. They took him out of the mine unconscious, and, as I see it, this is an emergency and nothing to do with visiting hours."

"Miss Rogers, I'll take care of this," said the older woman. "You can go back to your duties."

As Miss Rogers disappeared once more, the other woman introduced herself as Mrs. Johnson and said, "I'm sorry for that. I'll take you to him immediately."

"Oh, you're so kind," said Bessie. "She said he's in Ward C."

"Yes, that's where we take miners, so let's hurry on and find him."

The ward was nearly empty, reflecting the fact that none of those recovered from Barrackville had survived. Hershel lay completely still, his head wrapped in a white bandage, his face and hands still streaked black with coal dust they hadn't bothered to remove. The only other patient had his leg lifted with a pulley and encased in a white cast from his hip down to his toes. He seemed to be unconscious as well. However, when he heard Bessie say, "Oh, Hershel, there you are," the other patient opened his eyes and said, "Is that you, Bessie?"

Shocked at both the sight of Hershel and the sound of her name, Bessie said, "Yes, who are you?"

"I'm Jerry. I was with Hershel when the slate came down. He hasn't made any sense ever since, but he's been calling out the last hour or so."

"What's he said?"

"More or less just moaning, but a while ago, he said 'Bessie,' clear as a bell."

Touching his face, Bessie said, "Open your eyes, Hershel. I'm here."

Mrs. Johnson suggested that she could wash the coal dust from his face if she wanted to. "Here, let me get you a washcloth and some warm water. I don't know why that hasn't been done before now. I guess they were just anxious to get him bandaged and maybe worried about burns on his face."

"Oh, yes, let me do that. He's always so careful to wash at the mine before he comes home. Says he doesn't want to scare the kids—always making little jokes like that."

"Here you are, dear. I think you'll know whether it hurts him or not."

As Bessie gently cleaned first his hands and then his face, she thought about how much he would hate to be lying here, helpless. She wondered if and when he would ever wake up and what she would do if he never did. Daylight faded and still, he didn't open his eyes. Nurses came in and out, checking on Hershel and Jerry, and finally, a doctor arrived on evening rounds.

"Mrs. Martin?" he said.

"Yes, doctor, what can you tell me?"

"What we know for sure is that your husband has had a serious head injury, possibly a concussion, and that his future depends on how soon he wakes up and whether he knows you when he does."

"Well, this other fellow said he called out my name."

"Yes, that's a good sign, and sleeping for a while longer may be good for him. Still, we want to determine how much damage has been done, and we can only do that when he wakes up."

"Can I stay with him? I won't be any trouble. I'll just sit here in this chair and hope to see him open his eyes."

"It's against every hospital rule for anyone to stay overnight in a ward. Still, there are just two patients, and they were in this together. We'll just pretend you're not here."

"Thank you, doctor. You have a kind heart, just like my Hershel."

The doctor continued his rounds and was replaced by Mrs. Johnson, who said, "I bet you're hungry, aren't you? Since he couldn't eat his supper, we'll have it brought to you."

"I couldn't eat a bite, but a cup of tea would be very nice."

"We'll see to both. Maybe you'll be hungrier than you think."

Along with the meal and tea, Mrs. Johnson brought a blanket and pillow. Sitting down for a little chat, she said, "I'm off duty now, but I can't bear to leave you here alone. I lost my husband in the mine a long time ago, but it all comes back on a day like this."

"Oh, I'm so sorry to hear that. My first husband died at Monongah, and I've been trying to make a new life with Hershel. I keep wondering why we have to live like this." I've sworn a solemn oath that none of my children will ever set foot in a mine. Still, what else will they do?"

"They'll have to go to school, is what else they'll do," said Mrs. Johnson. "It's their only hope. You just make them go, whether they like it or not."

"Oh, I do."

Just then, Hershel moaned and began thrashing from side to side. Bessie and Mrs. Johnson tried to calm him, but just as suddenly, he lay quiet again.

"I don't know what that means, but at least it's a change," said Mrs. Johnson. "I'll stay while you try to eat some supper, and then perhaps you can catch a cat nap or two."

Sunlight came flooding in the east window over Jerry's bed and lit up Hershel's bed on the opposite wall. Bessie awoke with a start and, glancing at Hershel, saw that he was moving his head and fluttering his eyelids in the light. Slowly, he opened his eyes and saw Bessie standing at the side of his bed, looking distressed.

"What's wrong, Bessie? Where am I?" he said.

"Oh, Hershel, you woke up. You know me!" she cried.

"Why wouldn't I know you?"

"You don't remember the roof coming down on your head in the mine?"

"I remember the roof talking and a loud crack in the mine, but that's all."

"Seems you've lost a day of your life, but not the whole thing," said Jerry from across the room. "I was there with you and got my leg broke, but you got hit in the head."

"How'd they get us out? I remember being pretty close to the fire."

"They had to jack up the roof and pull us out. Then they brought us here to Fairmont in that Pullman car, so we rode in style, brother."

"Is the fire out?"

"No news since we got here. Do you know, Bessie?" asked Jerry.

"I don't know either. I just know neither of you will be going back to see about it anytime soon," said Bessie.

CHAPTER 23

After three days in the hospital, Hershel was sent home with orders to rest not only his weary head but also his shoulder, which had been dislocated in the accident. They had forced it back into place while he was still unconscious, sparing him that pain at least. He'd been trying to work out the stiffness, shrugging and rolling the shoulder for the last two days. A coal miner with a bum shoulder wouldn't be able to do much, not to mention one with a concussion. Just as they were leaving the hospital, Bessie noticed a man walking toward them that she recognized but couldn't quite place.

"Mrs. Martin?" he said.

"Yes, I'm Bessie Martin, and this is my husband, Hershel."

"You may not remember me. You were quite upset when we met at the mine a few days ago." Turning to Hershel, he said, "And how are you doing by now?"

"Fair to middlin'," Hershel said with a smile. "What can we do for you?"

"Well, I've just come to pass on a little token of our appreciation for your rescue services at our mine. I'm sorry you were hurt in the process, but things have quieted down now, and we're able to see more clearly. We owe you a debt, and I'm here to pay it," he said, handing Hershel a sealed envelope. "I'll be on my way now."

With that, he turned and walked toward a waiting car.

"Wait, what is this?" said Hershel, holding up the envelope. The man just waved, and the car drove away. Bessie and Hershel looked at each other and she said, "I remember him now. He's the only one who seemed to understand that I was in trouble and needed help. The other men with him had no feelings at all. They just wanted to shoo me out of the way and get on with their own business. Someone decided to bring me to the hospital and it may have been that one. What did he give you?"

Hershel put the envelope in his pocket and said, "Let's wait till we get home. We've got a streetcar to catch, and I can't wait to see the children." Hershel had been lying in the hospital worrying about whether they'd be put out of the house if he couldn't get right back to work. He felt weak and exhausted after lying in bed for three days, but he fully intended to go to the mine the next morning. Bessie would fuss, he knew, but that couldn't be helped. Her job at the store and what Belle took in from her sewing wouldn't see them through, so the sooner things got back to normal, the better.

Their arrival in Riverview was met with cheers from several miners gathered at the trolley stop. "Glad to see you're all in one piece," said one. "Welcome home," said another. Word had spread in the small community that one of their own had been sent to the hospital, and more often than not, injured miners didn't come home. Hospitals, it seemed, were where you went to die. Rarely did a miner come home and return to work. Loss of life and limb was much more common than recovery, so Hershel's return was a cause for celebration.

The children were playing in the yard on this chilly but bright fall afternoon, and they came running when they saw Bessie and Hershel walking slowly home. "Now, don't come crashing into your daddy," said Bessie. "He's not well yet." Tentative hugs all around were all she allowed, but Hershel just beamed and hugged them back with his good arm.

"We made you a cake," said Ivy, "chocolate with white icing, just the kind you like."

"And I've got a good fire going in the grate, so you'll be nice and warm," said Orie. Tearing up, he said, "Oh, Daddy, I'm so glad you're home."

Reaching out to his children, Hershel said, "What would I do without the two of you? Thank you for helping your mother while I was gone. Now, where's that rascal, Walter?" Hershel asked as he spied the little boy peeking out the screen door.

Walter ran squealing down the steps, indeed crashing into his father. Bessie quickly took him in hand, letting Hershel greet Belle and Jeremiah, who'd come out onto the porch. Old Mr. Morris had taken to his bed that day, saying he was feelin' poorly, but he brightened up seeing Hershel coming in to check on him. "What's happened to you?" said Hershel. "I'm supposed to be the sick one in the family."

"Well, son, I just don't feel like sittin' up today with this cough. I just can't get a good breath. Too many years breathing coal dust, I expect. A little rest and I'll be fit as a fiddle tomorrow." Mr. Morris grinned.

"A bite of chocolate cake might do the trick," said Hershel.

"No, don't think I could keep it down. Maybe tomorrow."

Later that evening, Hershel crept into the room Mr. Morris had shared with Jeremiah to see if he was all right. "Do you need anything—a glass of water, cup of coffee maybe?"

"No, nothing for me. How are you feeling?"

"Well, I might not be fit as any fiddle, but can't complain." Pausing, Hershel said, "I've been wondering about something for a while now, so I may as well just ask you."

"What is it? You're looking mighty serious."

"I've just wondered if you ever had any hard feelings about Orie's kids calling me Daddy and thinking I was their daddy."

"No indeed. If it wasn't for you, they'd have no daddy at all. I wish Orie hadn't had to leave them so soon, but I've always been grateful that you stepped in and treated them like they were your own. Now I'll say good night," he said with a sad smile.

As Hershel came out of Mr. Morris's room, he met Bessie going in with a poultice for his chest. "Don't know if this will do any good or not, but can't hurt to try."

"Guess not," he said, absently putting his hand in his pocket and coming out with the envelope they'd both forgotten about.

"Hope that's not a bill for my taxi service," she teased.

"Your what?"

"One of those men I told you about said they weren't running a taxi service so they couldn't take me to the hospital."

"What's a taxi service?"

"Something they have in big cities to take people places if they don't have a car or a streetcar."

"Okay, let's see if it's a bill." Slitting the envelope with his pocketknife, Hershel discovered something he'd never seen before—a one-hundred dollar bill.

"Look at that, Bessie. Is it real?"

"I've seen the operators flashing those around at the store, but I never thought of having one myself."

"I can't believe that guy handed one out just like that. What should we do with it?"

"From what he said, it was a reward for your rescue work at Barrackville. I expect there was a little guilt that you were hurt and he only knew what rich people know—throw some money at it, and it will go away. That's what they did with me—didn't give me money, but gave me a ride."

"Well, I think there was more kindness to it than that, but you may be right. Should we add it to your savings?"

"Yes, I'll put it in the bank in the morning. And, by the way, it's not *my* savings, it's *our* savings."

Hershel went back to work the next morning and came home worn out that evening, but as the days went by, he recovered—but Mr. Morris did not. Growing weaker, the old man couldn't get out of bed, and when the doctor came, the family was told to prepare themselves for the worst. At seventy-seven, his life as a miner had taken its toll. He didn't have TB, but the coal dust he'd breathed in over the years seemed to have filled up his chest, causing him to wheeze and cough and fight for every breath.

The children, even little Walter, spoke in whispers and tiptoed through the house trying not to disturb him.

Bessie had gathered them all, big and little kids, and told them that Mr. Morris, their second granddad, wouldn't be with them for long.

"But why, Mama, where does he have to go?" asked Walter.

"Well, he's lived a long life, and now it's time for him to go to his reward in heaven," she said.

"Will he see the pearly gates?" asked Orie.

"I don't know what he'll see, but he won't have to cough anymore, so he'll feel much better."

The constant struggle behind his closed door became more and more difficult, and the doctor had no remedy except rest. All of those in the house found themselves trying to breathe for him and failing, of course. At last, the battle ended, and Mr. Morris could rest once more. They took him back to Monongah and buried him next to his son, Orie.

1918

The war they were calling the Great War raged in Europe and demanded ever more coal, so Hershel was getting overtime hours and overtime pay. Still, Bessie knew they could never count on that money lasting. One day, the war would end, and the company would cut back on wages and hours to save their precious profit. Hershel and the other coal miners had a wartime exemption from the draft, which took so many other young men. There was a catch, and a big one, to that situation, however. Anyone who failed to work "hard enough" would have the exemption taken away and be sent off to fight. The question of what "working hard enough" meant was never really answered, and it could stand as an excuse if a foreman didn't like somebody or if anyone breathed the word *union* at any time.

Bessie was hiding the fact that they were expecting another child so that she could keep her job as long as possible. Her work at the post office, however, had become so unpleasant that she would have quit long ago if they didn't need the money. The mine owner was now insisting that she inspect every piece of mail that passed through the post office for the slightest tinge of "union propaganda." She wasn't quite sure what *propaganda* meant, but she had to be constantly on the lookout for any newspaper, circular, or letter supporting a miner's union. Then she was required to turn in the names of those who had received such mail.

Talking with her mother one evening, Bessie said, "Mom, what would you do if you were in my predicament? They're trying to turn me into a spy."

"Looks to me like you've got two choices: be a spy or quit the job. Could you keep the store job and give up the post office job?"

"I'm not sure. I can ask Mrs. Serilla. She has been so understanding about me wanting to work as long as possible while I wear loose clothes and a duster so the baby won't show. Don't know what she'll think about the post office job."

"How many names have you had to turn in so far?"

"I haven't turned in any. I just said I hadn't noticed any of this propaganda yet, but that I would watch very carefully. I've burned a bunch of union newspapers in the barrel out in back of the store rather than putting them in the boxes."

"I didn't think you had it in you to be so sneaky, Bessie, but that's what I would have done."

"I can't get anybody fired over this. They'd lose their homes and maybe be sent off to France, and that would be on my head, but I don't know how long I can keep it up."

Next day, Bessie discovered that union materials had been sent to every person with a mailbox at Riverview—miners, bosses, those who worked in the mine office and the company store, and the operators themselves. Someone had gotten all the names and addresses and sent out invitations to a union meeting to be held in Clarksburg in one week. She couldn't very well tamper with that much mail, because a sign in the post office said to "tamper" with any mail was a "federal offense punishable by a prison term." What could she do now?

The simplest of answers came to her in the middle of the afternoon. Just put all the mail in all the boxes, and let the operators see that people got mail like this whether they wanted it or not. Now she wouldn't have to single anybody out. Dutifully, she wrote down every name, hers included, and had it ready if requested. Now maybe they could send willing spies to the union meeting and leave her alone. The outrage that followed proved her point. You didn't have to be a union sympathizer, even though you might be, to get union mail.

Since January, the family had lived with the "voluntary" food restrictions set by the government as a response to the serious needs caused by the war. Mrs. Serilla had put up a poster in the store that said, "Food will win the war. Waste nothing." They were called on to observe "meatless" Tuesdays and "sweetless" Saturdays, as well as "wheatless" Mondays and Wednesdays. Belle's beautiful white yeast rolls now had to contain other grains besides wheat, which made them darker in color. They ate them, but they didn't like them. The next indignity called for "gasless" Sundays, "heatless" Mondays, and "lightless" nights. Since they had no gas, that rule was no sacrifice. January and February in West Virginia without heat, though, was unthinkable.

One Sunday morning, Hershel glanced out the window and saw a bundled-up figure coming up the snow-covered road, leading some sort of large animal on a leash. Curious, he continued to watch as the person turned into their yard and approached the front porch. Opening the door, he realized it was Bobby, and the object on the leash was none other than a pig.

"Bobby, what are you doing with that pig? And why are you bringing it here?"

"Just let me in out of this cold and I'll tell you," he said, tying the animal to the porch railing.

The commotion he made stamping the snow from his feet and rubbing his hands brought all of the kids into the room, wondering what was happening on a normally quiet day.

Bessie appeared and said, "Here, Bobby, give me your coat, and come and stand by the fire."

"So, Bobby, what's the story with the pig?" asked Hershel.

"Where's a pig? I want to see a pig!" shouted Walter.

"Hush, son; let him talk."

"Well, it's like this," said Bobby. "Last night, I got real lucky in a poker game. Old man Sweeney didn't have enough money to cover his raise, so he put an IOU in the pot for a hog worth about forty dollars. His hand wasn't quite as good as he thought it would be. As you can imagine, they won't put up with a hog at the boarding house."

"So what do you plan to do with this hog?"

"I sure don't know what to do with it, but I thought maybe someone in this family might have some ideas. We could go halves."

"That would be a big help with all this food rationing, but I wouldn't know where to start," said Belle. "We never had any livestock ourselves."

Jeremiah spoke up. "I remember helping my father butcher hogs when I was a boy. I couldn't do it myself now, but I could tell you where to start."

"I'll believe that when I see it," said Belle.

"Now, listen here, woman—" Jeremiah spluttered.

"Dad, do you really know how to do this?" interrupted Hershel.

"Yes, by God, I do, and I'll be glad to show this dear lady just how little she knows."

Following Jeremiah's instructions, they killed the hog and then bled it out and began the butchering process after first scalding it to remove the bristles in a large tub of hot water over an open fire. Setting up a long table of sawhorses and pieces of lumber, Hershel and Bobby spent the cold afternoon separating the hams and loins from the side meat, the organs, and scraps. Bessie and Belle began rendering lard from the fat scraps on the kitchen stove, skimming out the cracklins as they went along, all under the watchful eye of Jeremiah. Grinding up the lean scraps for sausage, they added some hot peppers from last summer that they'd hung in the cellar to dry. Ten- and twelve-year-old Orie and Ivy ran back and forth fetching peppers and onions from the cellar, while Russell and Wilbert were now old enough to help out by keeping the fires going and helping lift heavy pots and tubs. What Hershel and Bobby lacked in experience, they made up in enthusiasm, realizing what a gift this poker win really was. Nobody but Jeremiah wanted liver and onions for supper that night, but that's what they had anyway.

Belle said, "Well, you old curmudgeon, I have to give credit where credit is due."

Jeremiah responded, "It's about damned time."

By the time they'd paid to have the meat smoked and divided it up with Bobby, they ended up with a ham, some bacon, and lots of sausage and lard. Still, in this time of shortages, nothing could have been more welcome.

Bessie kept the new baby girl, Emma Jane, wrapped in quilts till June, when the weather finally took a turn for the better. "That baby won't know how to act now that she can wave her arms and kick her legs," noted Belle the first afternoon they spent outdoors.

"Yes, at three months, she's ready to run off, isn't she?" said Bessie.

"Won't it be wonderful when the garden starts to come in? What I wouldn't give for a fresh tomato."

"Willard said the root cellar's about empty, but there's still a few jars of pole beans and some blackberries. If I just had some sugar, I'd make us a pie for supper. That's one thing the government won't have to worry about. There's not enough sugar to make anything sweet."

Emma began to wail, so Bessie took down a clean diaper that had been flapping in the breeze on the clothesline and said, "You stay in the sunshine a while longer, Mom. I'll get supper started. How about some of Jeremiah's sausage?"

CHAPTER 24

The heat of summer was finally fading, but rumors of a terrible sickness began to circulate through the coal camps. It seemed to have struck especially hard among the thousands of soldiers in military units coming and going to war. They called it the Spanish flu, and it seemed to strike and kill suddenly. The combination of food restrictions and the birth of Emma Jane had seriously depleted Bessie's energy, and she found herself sleeping poorly and waking as tired as she had been when she lay down at night.

One morning, a telegram arrived for Jeremiah. "Here Bessie," he said, "read this for me. It can't be anything but bad news."

Opening the envelope, she read words glued onto a piece of Western Union paper that said, "Coming home. Stop. See you on the 15th. Stop. Charlie. Stop. Oh, Jeremiah, that's good news. Charlie will soon be home from the war," she said.

"What are all those stops for?"

"That's just the way they do it, I guess."

Shaking his head and tsk, tsk'ing, Jeremiah took the paper and tucked it into his Bible for safekeeping. "Stop, stop, stop," he muttered as he headed for the kitchen and his second cup of coffee.

Hershel received the news of his brother's return with mixed feelings. Their long history together had had its share of good times outweighed by bad times, but he was greatly relieved that Charlie had not been killed in the war. He wondered what Charlie would have to say about the draft exemption that had kept him underground instead of in the trenches. He wondered as well about how the company would deal with returning miners who had volunteered to go to France. Would they get their old jobs back, and what would that mean for those who'd stayed? All these thoughts swirled through his head as he stood on the platform waiting for Charlie's train to arrive in Fairmont.

Bessie had wanted an outing, so she left the children with Belle and rode along on the streetcar. She didn't feel like standing to wait, so she sat in the station, overhearing conversations whether she tried to or not.

"I heard this flu is the most dangerous for people who ride streetcars," said one high-pitched female voice.

"Well, I heard that trains were the worst, what with all these soldiers bringing back the disease from France, or was it Spain? I don't know where, but over there somewhere," said another.

A man chimed in, arguing that there wasn't any danger since Americans were so much healthier than "those foreigners."

About that time, Charlie burst through the door, with Hershel right behind. "Bessie, I'm so glad to see you. Are you well? You're looking a little peaked," he said.

"Not peaked, just hungry, Charlie. Let's get home to supper," she replied, giving her brother-in-law a hug.

Charlie had arrived fresh from a troop transport across the Atlantic that was crowded with soldiers eager to get home to families starved both for news of their loved ones and for the food they'd sacrificed in the name of patriotism. Little did anyone know that the ship was crowded in another way—crowded with the deadly but unseen infection called influenza.

Charlie seemed to wilt on the streetcar ride home. "You're looking a little peaked yourself, Charlie," said Bessie.

"Well, to tell you the truth, I couldn't sleep very much on that ship. Seems like there was a storm every evening. We stopped over in

New York for one night and then got right on the train, so I'm pretty wore out."

"Dad's been real worried about you all this time you been in the war," said Hershel.

"I hope he won't ask me too many questions, 'cause I don't have too many good answers. I been in the army a long time, but I never saw anything like it—what with the bloody trenches and the bodies tangled up in the barbed wire. The worst part was the poison gas the Germans lobbed at us. If you got caught in the gas, you died. Whole platoons would die, maybe the next day after the gas attack, and they might not even know they'd been hit. All that's part of why I can't sleep, I guess."

"Is that the same kind of gas that kills coal miners?" asked Hershel.

"No, they call it mustard gas, and you can't see it, but you might be able to smell it. It burns whatever part of the body it touches—eyes, skin, throat, lungs—and it stays in the ground for days, so if you happen to blunder into it, you might go blind and not know why."

"What about this flu?" asked Bessie.

"There were a lot of guys down with something on the ship, but it was hard to tell the flu from the seasickness."

Charlie arrived in Riverview along with the long shadows of evening but in time to greet his father and meet the children, having spent long years in the army serving in Alaska.

"Tell me, son, will you have to go back to the war?" asked Jeremiah.

"Well, Dad, recruits are still heading back that way, but word is it seems to be winding down. I sure hope never to see such death and destruction again. I'm on furlough for a month and on standby orders, so it's all up in the air for now."

"We're glad to have you home. Now, how about supper?"

"I'm not hungry at all, but I think I might lie down a little while. You all go right ahead and eat."

"I'll show you where to put your things, Charlie. I've put you in with your dad. I hope that's okay," said Bessie.

"Anywhere that's not moving is fine with me, thanks."

Belle had dinner warming in the oven, so everyone but Charlie sat down to their meal.

"Wonder what's wrong with him. He don't look right," said Jeremiah. "He's always been ready to eat."

"I guess he hasn't had much sleep, being on that ship and then on a train," said Hershel.

"He just don't seem like our Charlie," insisted Jeremiah.

By morning, Charlie had first fever, and then chills—normal enough symptoms of the grippe so many suffered in most winters. Bessie tried to encourage him to drink a little broth, but he turned it down, saying he was afraid to try to swallow anything—even water. When he seemed too exhausted to hold up his head, they all hoped it was just the result of months at war. Late in the evening of the second day, he began coughing. He tried to spit up the red-tinged foam that clogged his throat, but more kept coming. Hershel was taken back to Lucy's last days when she couldn't breathe, but surely Charlie didn't have TB. He'd shown no signs of illness in Fairmont, just a couple days earlier. Thinking it might be safer, Bessie bundled up the five children and Hershel took them out to sleep on pallets on the porch.

"Emma's too little to go out there. She can sleep in my room," said Belle.

"Yes, that's better, Mom," said Bessie. "I'll keep an eye on Charlie, but I don't know what I can do for him, do you?"

"Maybe just keep him from throwing off the covers. He's been thrashing around a lot. Spittin' up blood like that looks like a bad sign to me."

"I'll try again to see if he could drink a little water. He's burning up with fever."

By morning, Charlie was gasping for every breath. The doctor arrived early, but he took Bessie aside and said there was nothing he could do. He had heard about the symptoms of this flu and said it looked like Charlie had a classic case. When they got this bad, this quick, death would come just as quick. She should begin making Charlie's final arrangements as soon as possible and, by the way, he said, they should all stay as far away from him as they could because it was what he called *infectious*. Flu victims, the doctor said, had to be buried within twenty-four hours—no exceptions. All that night, she'd bathed Charlie's head with cool water and disposed of the bloody cloths he'd spit into. How could this nightmare be happening to them? she wondered. A strapping fellow gets off a train one afternoon and is going to die in just a few days. She already mourned his passing but was terrified that everyone in the house might be dead by the next day.

Bessie carried the news to the family that had come back into the house for breakfast after two nights on the porch. She insisted that while Charlie was still alive, she would be the only one allowed at his bedside. Hershel should go to work, and the children should go to school, she said, because there was nothing they could do to help and because she wanted them all out of the house and away from the disease. Belle shooed the children out the door with biscuits and glasses of milk.

"Leave the glasses on the porch, and take the biscuits with you," she ordered. "Now, be on your way."

Too frightened to argue, off they went, wondering who would be sick when they got home. Hershel refused to leave Bessie to handle this crisis, so he paced the floor, listening for Charlie's cough and hovering at the door when the sound of his breathing became labored, then shallow, and finally didn't come at all.

"He's gone, Dad," Hershel said to Jeremiah, "just like that."

"Oh, my poor boy, my poor boy. He lived through the army all these years and then the war. What did he do to deserve this?" mourned Jeremiah.

Belle, overhearing, said, "Jeremiah, he didn't do anything to deserve such a death, but his suffering is over. Maybe you can take comfort in that. Be thankful he didn't die on some misbegotten battlefield unknown to anyone but God himself."

Belle took the children aside as they straggled home from school, fearful as their leaving had been that morning. "I have something to tell you," she said.

Fearing the worst, Ivy whispered, "It's not Mama, is it?"

"No, child, it's your Uncle Charlie. Remember when Grandpa Morris died and the angels gathered around to carry him to heaven?"

"Yes," they said.

"Well, that's what's happened to Uncle Charlie. He's safe in the arms of the Lord now, so don't be afraid for him."

Charlie's became the first influenza death at Riverview, but it would be far from the last as the disease spread across the country from the eastern port cities even into the hills and hollows of West Virginia. The doctor came and tacked up a "quarantine" sign on their door warning others away and forbidding them to send the children back to school till further notice. The order didn't prevent Hershel from returning to work, however, since coal was still in short supply for the war effort. The twenty-four-hour burial period required the doctor's and the undertaker's cooperation, so Hershel made trips to both and signed agreements he couldn't read.

Hershel walked the few miles from Riverview to Shinnston to purchase a wooden coffin from Harmer and Son, who provided not only funeral services but built wagons and furniture as well. Since the house was under quarantine, Hershel hired a wagon and arranged to place the body in the coffin and meet the undertaker at the old family cemetery in the small town of Bethlehem where his mother was buried. He and his brother Bill had spent the best part of the previous night digging the grave in the plot reserved so many years ago for Jeremiah next to his beloved wife, Lucinda.

"I've got to go with you, Hershel. Somebody'll have to speak to the Lord for this boy, and I want it to be me," said Jeremiah.

"Dad, you know you're not supposed to go out of this house because of the flu."

"Nobody can keep a man from buryin' his son, can they? And besides, I ain't sick."

"All I know is that you'll be breaking the law if you go. I'm sorry, Dad, but can't you say the words here and leave the buryin' to me and Bill? It'd be a sad day if you had to go to jail."

"Well, I'll be a goddamned son of a bitch. It ain't right."

"Now that you've got that said, what are your words for Charlie?" asked Belle.

Jeremiah asked the Lord to welcome his son into his house of many mansions and to keep him safe unto eternity, and Bill read the 23rd Psalm from the front porch loud enough for everyone to hear. Wilbert, trying his best not to breathe, helped Hershel put Charlie's body into the coffin. Bill drove in his car, and Hershel followed along in the wagon. Neighbors along the way, having heard of the influenza, went indoors and watched the procession behind the safety of glass panes.

Mr. Harmer, as was his custom, said a few words as Bill and Hershel lowered the coffin into the grave. He'd never met Charlie, but he had presided over soldiers' burials and applied that experience to this one, thanking Charlie for his suffering and service in France and lamenting his having to come home and die of this unknown plague. After Hershel and Bill had filled the grave and placed some red oak leaves on their mother's grave, Bill offered to take Hershel home in his car, but Hershel said he wanted to walk to clear his head. What he wanted was to make sure he didn't leave any traces of this disease in Bill's automobile.

Hershel returned the horse and wagon to Mr. Harmer, and as he made his way home in the late-afternoon shadows, Hershel wondered at the random chance of life itself. So many good people had been lost to him over his thirty years: his mother, his sister, Jane, his lovely Lucy, Bessie's Orie, and now Charlie. As he approached the bridge over the West Fork River, a gentle rain began to dimple the still water near the bank. It must be a thin cloud, he thought, because the sky above held onto the blue it had displayed all day. Raindrops coming out of the clear sky seemed like a mystery—nothing frightening, but yet a puzzle. Holding up his face to the mist, he felt a rare sense of peace. He'd go back to a quarantined house this evening and he'd go back underground tomorrow, but for this moment, he would just stand on the bridge, look at the water as its surface filled with little circles, and breathe.

CHAPTER 25

It began for Bessie with a little tickle in the back of her throat, like she was coming down with a cold. Funny, though, she had no sneezing or sniffling, like a cold. Fearing she'd give her cold to the baby, she turned Emma Jane over to her mother. Hoping earlier that she'd be given the chance to return to work, she'd stocked up on canned milk and the kind of bottles they were using to feed babies with these days. The so-called "condensed" milk had to be mixed with water and warmed, but it would have to do while she couldn't nurse the baby. Belle had resisted at first, calling baby bottles a bunch of nonsense, but things looked different in the wake of Charlie's death.

Bessie's cold worsened, but she didn't seem to have the terrible cough that was the first real sign of Charlie's illness. Still, she had trouble keeping down anything she tried to eat and grew weaker by the day. In terror, she looked for signs of red on her pillow each morning. So far, no one else in the family had gotten sick. The doctor prescribed warm milk with cinnamon, but she couldn't manage it. The third day, she slipped into a dream, not knowing whether she was asleep or awake. She was alternately hot and cold, and Hershel either put cold cloths on her forehead or covered her with blankets warmed by the stove.

"Belle," he said, "do you think she'll go like Charlie?"

"Well, son, so far she hasn't spit up any blood, and she seems able to breathe. That's what killed him, I think. He couldn't get a breath."

"I've already lost one of your daughters, Belle, and I can't imagine living without Bessie. I wouldn't want to live without Bessie."

"Now, Hershel, listen to me. You have to be strong for everyone: your father, who's just lost a son; Bessie and Orie's children, who think of you as their daddy; your own little Walter and your beautiful baby girl. You can't afford to lose hope."

"Not to mention you and your boys," Hershel said, smiling at his mother-in-law. "I couldn't keep this place going without you and without them, you know."

"Yes, they're good boys." She smiled.

"Are you able to hold up under all this, Belle?"

"We do what we have to do."

"Yes, but maybe we could find someone to help you—to help you till Bessie is back on her feet." His thoughts of Bessie lying so ill filled his eyes with tears, so he turned his back and walked away as Belle said, "If you know anybody willing to come into a quarantine house, I'd take the help."

Asking around the camp for someone he could hire, Hershel heard about a Negro family desperate for work since the coal company refused them jobs. He found them in a lean-to down by the river and approached gingerly, since he'd never spoken to such people before.

"What do you want?" called a woman's voice.

"Well, ma'am, my wife's real sick and her mother's old, and we need some help."

Coming out of the shelter, she said, "Has she got that flu, you think?"

"My brother died of it, so I know what it looks like, but she's not having it like he did, at least so far."

"What would you need me to do, and how much would you pay?"

"Well, there's a lot of clothes to wash, what with a baby and the kids, but my mother-in-law would take care of the cooking. I never paid anybody before, so I don't know how much to pay you. What would you ask?"

"Well, sir, I guess I'd ask half a dollar a day. Could you pay that much?"

"That's an awful lot, but I'll pay what I have to. Can you come in the morning? We're the first house on the left down toward the mine."

"Is that the one with the yellow sign on the door?"

"Yes, I'm afraid it is."

"If she's not sick like your brother, I'll come. I done nursed people before. Will I have to haul water for the washing?

"No, we've got a well by the back porch, and you can heat water on the coal stove."

"All right. I'll be there bright and early."

"Thank you. What's your name, by the way?"

"I'm Molly. And you?"

"I'm Hershel, and my wife is Bessie and her mother is Belle."

Bessie had worsened overnight. She'd begun to cough and found it hard to breathe. She lay first in a pool of sweat; then she shivered uncontrollably. When she awoke, she begged Hershel to leave her there and go to work. "We need the money," she said.

"We'll be fine," he said.

She thought she must be dreaming again when she saw a small woman with glistening black skin coming into the room with Hershel. "Bessie, this is Molly, and she's come to help your mother while you're sick."

So it wasn't a dream, she concluded, as she sank back onto the pillow, now tinted with tiny flecks of blood. The doctor came once more and said that if she lived through the night, she might recover, but he had no guarantees. He'd seen this sort of pattern among the flu patients. If they didn't turn blue and die immediately, like Charlie, and if they could hold on for a week or more, then they might live, but they would be quite weak and subject to other ailments.

When Bessie awoke the next morning, she found that she could breathe easier, but she slept most of the day. The fever seemed to have broken, and by the next day, the milk and cinnamon Belle brought in tasted good. She asked to sit up in bed but soon found herself too weak to stay up long. As the days passed, though, she regained enough strength to walk into the kitchen and sit at the table. There she found Belle and Molly sharing cups of coffee and conversation about the day's washing.

"Now that you're up, Miz Bessie, we'll get your sheets washed and back on before you know it," said Molly.

"What would you like, Bessie? How about a nice cup of tea?" said Belle.

"Oh, yes, I'm ready for tea today."

Molly put the wash water on to boil and took Bessie's bedclothes outside to try to remove the specks of blood under the cold water from the well. Even lye soap wouldn't take out the stains if she put them in the hot water first. Satisfied that they were ready, she mixed some cold water with the hot and plunged her hands into the washtub along with the sheets.

Bessie, still sitting at the table, gasped and rose to witness a sight she'd never thought to see—black hands and white sheets in the wash water.

"Why, what's wrong, Miz Bessie?" said Molly, quickly wiping her hands. "You look like you seen a ghost."

Her face red with embarrassment, Bessie sat back down and admitted, "Oh, Molly, I thought it would come off. I thought the sheets would come out black."

At that, Molly began to laugh. "My land, child, that's the funniest thing I ever heard. This color don't come off. It stays with me for life."

As the family mourned the loss of Charlie, Bessie continued her slow recovery. Food to buy was still in short supply, but Hershel had taught Russell and Wilbert, along with Ivy and Orie, how to grow a garden, and they'd had a fairly good harvest. In July and August, Bessie and Belle had put the potatoes and cabbages in the root cellar and canned the blackberries. They'd started canning the tomatoes, but more were coming in and Belle needed help.

Hershel could afford Molly only one day each week now with the prices of everything rising, but Belle and Molly found a way to barter food for work. Every fourth jar of whatever they canned went home with Molly—and that included pumpkins turning to gold in the backyard. When the children came in with beans dried on the stalk, Belle and Molly broke open the pods and laid the beans out on paper to harden before hiding them away from marauding mice. If Hershel was successful in bringing home a deer later in the fall, that meat would be canned, too, and shared with Molly.

After several days of rain, Hershel was out salvaging the last of the vegetables in the garden when he heard someone pounding on wood. He thought nothing of it till he began hearing faint cries for help. Looking in the direction of the sound, he couldn't believe his eyes. The outhouse in the yard next door seemed to have begun a slow process of sinking into the earth with someone inside. It must be their new neighbor, Sarah, he thought.

Hershel ran for his crowbar, hoping it would be long enough for leverage to pry up the privy far enough to get the door open. Suddenly, one side of the hole gave way and the person inside began shrieking and crying, "Get me out; get me out!"

Hershel said, "I'm here. Don't worry—we'll get you out." He hollered for Russell to go for help and for Wilbert to find a long pry bar. Neighbors began gathering, some laughing, others worrying. When the privy tilted to one side, several men rushed forward to help press down on the pry bar to lift the structure up out of the hole. The door was flung open, and Sarah escaped. The crowd roared its approval, and about that time her husband, Ben, came out of the house, pulling up his suspenders, looking like he'd been asleep. "What the Sam Hill is going on here?" he shouted.

"Well, we just got your wife out of a hole in the ground," someone said, to a new burst of laughter.

1919

The war in Europe came to an end with only an armistice, not a peace treaty. For coal miners, that presented a problem, since they had agreed to a wage set for the duration of the war, which the operators insisted still applied. Unionization had come to northern West Virginia in 1916, but wartime conditions had been so favorable that no action had seemed necessary. Now, however, prices went up and up, while wages stayed the same, even though coal profits had risen greatly due to wartime need. With that need coming to an end, hours were cut, and miners soon found themselves unable to keep up. Caught in the middle, their answer was to go on strike. The same law that had been used to urge the public to go without food and fuel during the war was now about to be used to prevent the strikes that had started in the steel industry.

"What's about to happen, Hershel?" asked Bessie.

"Well, as much as I hate to do it, I think we'll be walking out in a few days," he replied. "I joined the union for our protection, and now I'll have to go along with whatever John L. Lewis decides. He's the boss."

"Will everybody strike?"

"I think they will. That's all the talk at the mine."

"Will they put us out of the house?"

"If it lasts very long, they might. If they bring in strike breakers, they'll need someplace to live, and these company houses would serve the purpose."

"Oh, Lord, I can't imagine having to move right here when the cold weather's starting. Where would we go, anyway?"

"I don't know, Bessie. Let's not borrow trouble, okay?"

Hershel arrived home late that night. It was Halloween, and the secret union meeting could be hidden behind the holiday revelry in the coal camp. A courier from union leaders in Pittsburgh brought the news that Lewis planned to call out his four hundred thousand members the next day, November 1, 1919. Hershel had not yet spoken at the meeting, but he had listened carefully to the arguments made for joining the strike. Certainly, it seemed only right that some of the operators' wartime profits should be shared with those who had worked so hard digging the coal. Certainly, it made no sense that with wages staying the same, prices should be going up for goods in the company stores—the only places the miners were allowed to buy them.

"But what about our homes?" shouted one miner. "Will we be thrown out in the muddy street?"

Several others joined in with, "Yes, where will we live?" and, "We have a new baby;" and, "My wife just go over the flu and she can't be left out in the cold."

Hershel's angry memories of being taunted by other boys because his father refused to go on strike rose to the surface, and he stood to speak. His plea for unity against the power of the operators fell on deaf ears, however, as his voice was drowned out by shouts of, "Strike, strike, strike!" Those who didn't agree, he was sure, would be hounded out of town. All he could hope was that their demands would be met quickly and the strike would end before any eviction notices were handed out. Surely, Lewis wouldn't let them down, with so many innocent lives at stake.

The cold rain of November turned to the ice and snow of December, and still the strike went on. Men accustomed to rising early and working hard found themselves with time on their hands and anger in their hearts. Women accustomed to spending their days cooking or canning, quilting or sewing, making lye soap, or singing the ABCs with their children now had men underfoot all day. With no money coming in for more than a month, tempers flared. Hearing foreign-sounding words like *Bolshevik* applied to themselves, being accused in the newspapers of being revolutionaries led by Russians named Lenin and Trotsky, whoever they might be, added dry tinder to their frustration. Hershel tried to swallow his feelings, as he had done since childhood, but other men drank more, shouted more, and became abusive to whoever happened to be close by.

New neighbors had replaced old friends in the house next door just before the strike began. Bessie and Belle had welcomed Sarah, who had come over for coffee one morning. They'd never been invited back across the adjoining yards, however. Belle said they were just unfriendly, but Bessie tried to blame the lack of hospitality on the strike. In the last few days, though, some ominous crashing sounds had come from that direction, and Bessie had caught a glimpse of Sarah's bruised face as she hurried to hang some clothes to dry. *Surely she's had an accident,* Bessie thought; *I should go check on her.*

The miners were called to a meeting scheduled for that afternoon, which gave Bessie a chance to run over to her neighbor's just long enough to make sure she wasn't seriously hurt. Stepping up onto the porch, she noticed a curtain move, but there was no answer to her knock on the door.

"Sarah," she called, "are you all right?" Still, there was no answer.

As she turned to leave, she came face-to-face with Sarah's husband, Ben. "What do you want?" he growled. "There's nothing for you here, so get out."

"I've only come to see Sarah," she said, backing away.

"Well, Sarah doesn't want to see you, so just get out, now!" he roared.

The door opened and Sarah said, "Please, Ben, leave her in peace."

Ben swiveled around at the sound of his wife's voice and Bessie took her opportunity to escape from the porch, but not before seeing the true extent of Sarah's injuries. The woman stood stooped, as if she suffered a severe pain in her side. Her face was not only bruised but also scratched or scraped from forehead to chin, and on her neck were marks left by the fingers of both his hands. As Bessie ran for home, Ben's voice could be heard saying, "And don't you ever come back. Now, get in the house, Sarah."

CHAPTER 26

The strike ended on December 10 with a disappointing outcome for the bituminous miners of the northern coal fields. The 60 percent wage increase they'd asked for, along with the six-hour day and the five-day week, dwindled to just a 14 percent increase alone, with the promise of a commission to study further changes. Safety and working conditions were ignored in the settlement, so miners would still be required to push loaded coal cars through sidings and onto the main headings where electricity moved the coal on out of the mines. With coal supplies running low, schools and factories had begun to close, union leaders were threatened with jail, and public opinion turned against the miners, who were still being labeled socialists.

"What's a socialist?" Hershel asked Bobby on their first day back at work.

"Hell if I know," said Bobby. "Seems like they're saying we want the government to take over the mines."

"Well, then, what's a Bolshevik?"

"Somebody told me that's a person who overthrew the government in Russia."

"What's that got to do with us? First they're saying we want the government to own the mines and then they're saying we want to overthrow the government. None of that makes any sense to me."

"Me neither."

"It just makes me mad as hell that these sons-a-bitches that own the mines made all this money off of the war and we're stuck with 14 percent. What does that come out to—a quarter a day more?"

"Maybe not even that much. Next thing you know, they'll raise our rent on the company houses."

"I've got to find a way to have a house of our own. Some places were on strike longer than we were, and they got evicted and had to live in tents. I won't have Bessie living in a tent," vowed Hershel.

"Yea, looks like the union didn't do us any good. Have you been hearing about this new group of men calling themselves knights?"

"Is that the Knights of Labor?"

"No, they're some other kind of knights."

At that moment, the whistle blew ending the shift, so Bobby said, "I'm going to a meeting tonight. I'll tell you all about them in the morning."

Bessie had avoided telling Hershel very much about their problem neighbors. Not knowing what he might do, she certainly wouldn't tell him she'd been ordered off the property by such a frightening, angry man. She'd watched for signs of life from the house, however, and observed that Ben worked at night while Hershel worked the day shift, so their paths may not have crossed. Trying not to worry about Sarah, she decided to concentrate on Christmas preparations, a much happier thought. As soon as she'd recovered from the flu, she'd gotten her old job back and so was able to put things on layaway for the children. All that remained were gifts for her mother, Jeremiah, and Hershel. After supper, Hershel suggested a few minutes on the porch, so they wrapped up and took their accustomed places on the swing. The wintertime sky was brilliant with stars, and there lay Orion the Hunter just above the horizon in all his glory. Huddling together in the cold, Hershel and Bessie began to speak at once. Laughing, she said, "You start."

"I'm wondering how much money we have in that bank account of yours," he said.

"Why, Hershel, you've never once talked about money."

"Maybe now's the time, Bessie. I'm worried that if there's another big strike and it lasts long enough, we'll be put out of this house. Nobody I've talked to is satisfied with the way this one turned out, so it probably won't be long before we strike again."

"So what do you want to do?"

"I want us to have a house of our own, with our own garden and our own fruit trees and a cellar to keep our food in that no one can take away from us. That's what I want."

"Oh, I'd love that, too! Orie's money from the Relief Committee, plus the extra $300 from the company, has been making interest for these thirteen years, and I've put away as much as I could from my pay and yours, too. Let me go to the bank in the morning and see how much we have."

Bessie dreamed of having a home of their own as she rode the streetcar to Monongah. She had no idea how much a house with at least an acre of ground would cost, and she had no idea how much money they might have in the bank by now. What she thought of as "Orie's money" had been placed in a savings account in Monongah, and the deposits from her earnings were in the Shinnston Bank, so she had two trips to make today and just enough time to get to work at noon. She'd neglected to change the name on her first account when she married, so the lady behind the teller's cage, reading her account number and name, said, "What can I do for you, Mrs. Morris?"

"Oh, that sounds so strange," said Bessie, "I haven't been Mrs. Morris for a long time. I'm Bessie Martin now."

"Well then, Mrs. Martin, what can I do for you?"

"I've come to see how much interest my money has earned in the thirteen years since my husband died. I'd like to buy a house of my own."

"Well, that's certainly ambitious of you," said the teller with a sly smirk on her face. "Just let me look up your account. Take a seat while I find the right book."

Worrying that something might be wrong, Bessie sat fidgeting in the ornate bank lobby. No women seemed to come through the door, just men in fancy suits. Suddenly, there was Hershel's brother Bill, looking just as dapper as the others, she noted. He looked through her at first, but then broke into a smile and opened his arms for a hug.

"Bessie, how nice to see you this early morning. Is someone helping you?"

"Yes, Bill, that young lady behind the window there is looking up my account. You remember, I followed your advice and put Orie's money in a savings account when I finally got it all in one lump sum."

"And what a trick that was—sending your mother to threaten them."

"Well, she does have a way of getting down to brass tacks." Bessie smiled. Looking around, Bessie said, "I wonder what's taking so long. I've got to get back to work."

"Let me see if I can help," said Bill.

Mysteriously, Bill walked right through the gate and behind the tellers' windows. He stopped to speak to the woman who told Bessie she'd have to wait and in a few moments came out carrying a ledger sheet with "Bessie Morris" written at the top.

"Here you are, Bessie. It looks like your $848 has earned compound interest in the amount of $397.31, which makes a grand total of $1,245.31."

"That's more than I expected, but how did you do that, Bill? Do you work here now?"

"Well, no, Bessie, but I've been promoted at work, and along with it came a seat on the board of directors at this bank."

"I guess I'm almost speechless, Bill. I can't help but think of you and Hershel out there digging Charlie's grave by yourselves in the bitter cold not that long ago, and here you are, a banker."

"Sometimes things just work out, don't they, Bessie? What are you and Hershel planning?"

"He's afraid of another strike and he's worried we'll be evicted, so we want to get a house of our own."

"Looks like you've got a good start here. Let me know if I can help. How's Dad?"

"Jeremiah's his usual self—misses old Mr. Morris and shushes the kids a lot, but I think he's happy enough most of the time. I've got to catch that next streetcar. Thanks, and congratulations on your new job."

At the Bank of Shinnston, Bessie discovered that her savings there amounted to a little over $300, which meant that she and Hershel had more than $1,000 to spend on a house and lot. The next step would be to figure out what that would buy. Her good news was met, however, with bad news when Hershel got home from work.

"I asked around today about moving out of the company house and learned that it couldn't be done," he said.

"What can that mean, Hershel, 'couldn't be done?'" she asked.

"It seems that when you're hired on at this mine, you sign a contract that you'll agree to live in a company house. When I came to work here, they handed me a wad of paper that was filled up with tiny print and they said, 'Sign here on this line,' so I did. I didn't say that I couldn't read and that I'd have to bring it home to my wife to read for me. I just signed the damned thing."

Bessie stood silently stirring the pot on the stove, disappointment written on her face. "Can't you say anything, Bessie?" he said.

"Well, Hershel, all I can think of is that they've got us under their thumb no matter which way we turn."

Raising his voice, Hershel said, "It makes me want to quit. Hell, I was looking for a job when I got this one, and I can get another one if I want to. Nobody in this goddamn coal mining work stays put for very long. Everybody moves."

Panicked, Bessie said, "Now Hershel, think about what you're saying. You've got a good job here. They paid you enough during the war for us to put money in the bank, and now we can just leave it there making more. When the time is right, we'll have enough to buy a home."

"Bessie, I won't have you living in a tent, and that's what could happen, you know."

"I know, but, as you always say, let's don't borrow trouble. Maybe things will settle down and we can live in peace a little while. I didn't get to tell you my news today."

"Well, what is it?"

"You'll never guess who I saw in the bank at Monongah—your brother Bill, all dressed up and working at the bank or something like that."

"Bill—at the bank? What happened to his job at the mine?"

"He said he had a promotion at the mine and a place on the bank board, whatever that means. He waltzed right in and took over figuring out how much was in our account—over $1,200, by the way."

"Twelve hundred? I thought it was about eight hundred."

"The extra came from the interest we earned. That's the way it works."

"I guess that's how the rich get richer." Hershel laughed. "If you're not upset, I guess I can try to be all right, too, Bessie. It still makes me mad as hell, though, that we have to stay in this coal camp even it we could afford to get out."

Hershel wondered why Bobby had been so closed-mouthed about the meeting he'd attended. When he asked about it that morning, he just said he'd tell him about it later. It wasn't something he could talk about with anyone else around. Before the shift started the next day, Hershel took his friend aside and said, "Okay, what was it all about?"

Looking around to see who might be listening, Bobby said, "Well, it was real strange. They seemed like all right fellas at first, said they were 100 percent American and all that, but then they started talking about the kind of people they hated. They said people thought of them as just hating Negroes, but that they also hated wife-beaters and bootleggers. You're not a drinker, Hershel, but I make regular trips to the bootlegger, so this bunch is not for me."

"Tell me more about this wife-beater thing. Bessie seems to think our next door neighbor might be one."

"Well, they said a man will get drunk, and when the wife complains, he just beats her up so he won't have to hear it."

"They may be right about that. My brother Charlie drank a lot, but he didn't hit any women that I know of. I'll see what else Bessie knows about it."

Hershel didn't have long to wait for his answer. As he and Bessie sat on the porch again that Friday evening, they heard a clatter from the darkened house next door followed by a muffled cry. Suddenly, the front door crashed against the wall and the screen door was ripped from its hinges as the man of the house lumbered out and down the steps shouting, "That's enough out of you, you ugly bitch!" As he disappeared into the darkness, Bessie jumped up and ran across the yard with Hershel following behind. The sound of weeping led them to the kitchen where a table full of food had been lifted up and slammed upside down to the floor.

Sarah's nose dripped blood onto the floor, and her face was beginning to swell. Looking dazed, she tried to salvage what she could from the wreckage of her supper. Bessie said, "Here, Sarah, you just sit down here, and we'll try to help clear up this mess."

"No, you mustn't let him find you here. He'll kill me, and you, too, if you're a witness to his temper. Please, just go."

Hershel stood, shocked at the destruction of both the woman and her kitchen. Coming to himself, he took Sarah by the arm and led her to the living room, where he convinced her to lie back on the davenport while he went in search of a cold cloth for her face. Bessie set the table upright, scooped the broken dishes and globs of food from the floor, and looked around for a scrub bucket and mop. She couldn't let poor Sarah with her blackened eyes and God knows what other injuries clean up what her husband had wrought. Hershel's rescue training came in handy as he discovered that Sarah indeed had a broken arm, which he bound up in a sling. Ben might come looking for those who had helped his wife, but that couldn't be helped. Sarah finally convinced them to go home and try to forget all about it.

"When he comes home, he'll be ever so sorry and he'll promise it will never happen again," she said. "But I know better."

CHAPTER 27

Hershel lay awake thinking that he'd like to do to Ben what Ben had done to Sarah. Although he usually kept a tight control over his own temper, the violence next door reminded Hershel of the punishment he'd taken as a child at the hands of bigger boys. He'd been fairly helpless then, but now maybe he could join this group that opposed such cruelty. Maybe they really could help women like Sarah.

Catching up to Bobby on the way to work on Monday, Hershel said, "Who do I have to see to join up with this group—these knights—you talked about last week?"

"Well, their whole name is the Knights of the Ku Klux Klan, and I'll round up one of 'em for you."

"What in the world does their name mean—Ku Klux Klan?"

"I don't know what it means, but it's been around since the Civil War, just not in our part of the country."

"You said they hate wife beaters, so what do they do about them?"

"I don't know any more than you do. I'm just telling you what they told me. As I said, I don't want any part of them. What's got into you, anyway?"

"You find me one of those guys and I'll tell you why I want to meet him."

That night, as the family sat around the dinner table, there came a knock at the door. Bessie started to rise, but Hershel quickly said,

"Let me see who's here at this time of night." Opening the door, he saw Bobby standing beside a tall, thin, older man he'd never seen before. Slipping outside, Hershel closed the door and said, "Are you from this Klan group?"

"Yes. I understand you're interested in our organization. Can we talk? I have a car just down the road."

"Fine, just a minute." Hershel opened the door and said, "Nothing to worry about. I'll be right back."

"But—" Bessie said to the now-closed door.

Bobby took his leave, and Hershel followed the other man to a black sedan parked along the unlighted road. Inside were two other men, but no introductions were made. Robert, the one who'd come to the door, said, "What's your interest, and what do you want to know?"

"Bobby tells me you don't like people who beat their wives. Is that true?"

"Why, yes, that's true. We also oppose drinkers and bootleggers and fornicators. We're a Christian group, and so we try to promote righteous living."

"So what do you do with wife beaters?"

"Well, sir, we take the opportunity of showing them the error of their ways."

"What do you mean?"

"I mean, if a good, serious conversation doesn't work, we give them a dose of their own medicine."

"Do you treat them as they treat their wives?"

"In a way, yes, we do."

"And if that doesn't work, then what?"

"Well, after that, we come to them as a group and scare the bejesus out of them. So do you want to join us or not?"

Opening the car door, Hershel said, "Let me think about it. How much does it cost to join?"

"It's just ten dollars a year—money well spent, of course, if we can rid the community of these people, don't you think?"

Hershel was, once again, sleepless over what to do. He had avoided Bessie's curiosity about the evening visitors, telling her it was just Bobby with one of his damn fool ideas. Those he'd met tonight were shadowy and hard to pin down. He'd never thought much about the ideas they talked about—he had never been a drinker, but he didn't object to others drinking—unless they lost control, like Ben. The sight of Sarah, so hurt and so helpless, preyed on his mind, though. If he could prevent such harm, why shouldn't he? Maybe this Christian group with the funny name really could help people like Sarah. He sure didn't want to spend ten dollars on a lost cause, though. His thoughts went round and round. His decision went back and forth until by morning, he'd made up his mind to join and see what happened.

He attended a meeting in Clarksburg on an impulse propelled by the sight of Sarah trying to hang up the washing in the yard, her face still blue from the beating. All she could manage with her broken arm was to fling the clothes over the line. She'd covered her hair, which had been pulled out in handfuls, with a scarf, but he'd seen the torn and bloody scalp the night of the attack. His anger at Ben had found no outlet, so it just festered. Approaching the church that sponsored the meeting, he fingered the ten-dollar bill he'd brought along, wondering if he should take a chance or not.

When he entered the meeting room, he was surprised that there were only about fifteen people seated there. He'd never seen any of them before. A man who introduced himself as James suggested that they could start, even though some members would likely be late. "They had a little job to do," he said, to laughter scattered around the room. Those who didn't laugh looked puzzled, Hershel among them.

James began by describing the purposes of the group, both to remind the members and to enlighten the newcomers, he said. "We all need to be encouraged every now and then to keep up the good Christian works that we perform in our quest to be useful and patriotic citizens," he added. Never mentioning the word *hate,* James outlined those who were considered objectionable, such as moonshiners, bootleggers, and abusive husbands and fathers who drove helpless women and children from their homes. He made a little joke out of the presence of "moonshiners here in the hills of West Virginia," but he scowled and slapped his Bible on the lectern when he spoke of wife beaters. "Now, I know some of you have come here tonight because of those very sins, and I want you to know that we are here to do something about them."

Moving his appeal to the wives of those present, James said, "I'm wondering if any of your fine spouses belong to that venerable organization, The Women's Christian Temperance Union." Several hands went up. He continued, "I'm wondering if you know that our Klan is associated with that wonderful group of ladies, who work hard to eliminate the evils of drink." Heads nodded. "I have another question for you," he said. "How many of you signed the WCTU pledge as children, never to let alcohol corrupt your life?" Now Hershel had the opportunity to raise his hand in solidarity with the goals of this group.

When James brought up the failure of the miners' union to achieve anything but a 14 percent wage increase from the last strike, the crowd came alive. Several more had filled the chairs and they began to chant, "The Klan can help; the Klan can help; the Klan can help." Caught up in the moment, Hershel found himself chanting, too. It was a simple enough slogan, and he'd lost any faith he'd had in the union ever doing anything to improve the lives of miners. James ended the meeting by welcoming new members who could now "pay your ten dollars and join us in this great cause."

Riding home on the streetcar, a large box occupying the seat beside him, Hershel felt a moment's doubt, thinking he probably shouldn't tell Bessie what he'd done with their hard-earned ten dollars. He hadn't seen what was in the box, but had been told it was special clothing he could wear only on special occasions. The sense of belonging he'd gotten at the meeting felt better than anything he'd known before. Anything he'd known, at lease, since the death of his twin sister, Jane. They'd been so close, almost like one person, but all of a sudden, one day, she was gone. Maybe now he'd found something meaningful.

A few weeks later, Hershel found the first occasion to wear the special clothing—a parade in Fairmont. A miner he didn't know had sought him out at work to say that the group would meet that Saturday at 8:00 a.m. at the Christian Church to prepare for the parade and that he should bring his clothing in the box he'd been given. Several men on the streetcar had similar boxes, and he felt proud to be carrying one, too. He was glad Bessie had to work that morning so there'd been no need to explain his trip to Fairmont. He'd simply said to Belle that he'd be gone for a few hours.

The meeting room in this church was packed with men in white robes. Hershel put his box on a folding chair and carefully unwrapped its contents. Fortunately, he'd chosen the box marked tall, so the robe fit him perfectly. He wondered how in the world they could see out of the small eyeholes, but he let that thought drift away as the leader began speaking. "We're here on this day to march in support of our brothers who are leading the fight against the sins of the world. I've used that phrase, 'the sins of the world,' on purpose because it's part of the heathen service of the Catholic Church, which we oppose in all its forms. As you know, this community of Fairmont is filled with un-American immigrants from Italy and Poland who practice this religion. Our banner today proudly proclaims the Klan as 100 percent American, 100 percent Christian, and 100 percent Protestant. That's who we are and proud of it. Am I right?"

"Yes!" roared the crowd.

Hershel felt a chill. He'd never heard this kind of talk before. What else would he learn today? he wondered. Surely, they weren't all like this. Not wishing to lose his place in the parade, he listened for his name to be called and tried not to think about what it meant to be 100 percent anything. He remembered his Italian friends from Monongah, one of whom had died in the tragedy, so how could he hate them for their religious beliefs?

Once the parade got underway, the whistling and cheering from the crowds along the sidewalks encouraged him to think that this was the right course after all. They were cheering for the marching bands and other groups, but they were cheering for the Klan, too. After the parade ended, he was among a group that took boxes of food and clothing to people who looked no poorer than his family, but still it felt good to be doing something for others.

At supper, Bessie told funny stories about her day at work, so no questions were asked about his Saturday. Later, on the porch, they once again heard a crash and a sob from next door. After that, there were no sounds at all. Hershel determined to do something more than pick up the pieces this time. The next day, he reported Ben to the Klan for mistreating his wife, noting that it seemed to be a regular weekend occasion probably related to his drinking.

The next Friday night, Hershel prepared to join in the Klan's "visit" to Ben. Holding up his robe carefully for inspection in their bedroom out of sight of the children, Hershel was interrupted by Bessie.

"Hershel, have you seen my sewing basket? I thought it was in here," she said.

Seeing the robe, she gasped. "Hershel, what have you done?"

"Now, Bessie, just calm yourself. These men are going to warn Ben against hurting Sarah—don't you want that?"

"Hershel, I can't understand why you'd want to be a part of the Klan. All they do is hate people who are different from them. Of course, I don't want Sarah getting beat up every weekend, but I don't know why you think this will fix it. When did you get mixed up with this crowd?"

"Right after I helped you help Sarah. You remember that night, don't you?"

"Yes, I remember, but now I understand why that Klan woman came here to get me to join up with her group."

"Someone came for you?"

"Yes, and I just ran her off. She talked about fighting against Catholics and Jews, saying they wanted to take over the country. She said immigrants like Italians and Hungarians didn't belong here because all they did was take jobs away from real Americans. Then she said that black people were the worst and how come I didn't know that. That's when Mom and I showed her the door. I won't tell you the language Mom used."

"I'm sorry, Bessie. I didn't know they'd come here after you."

"Now, take off that hateful outfit and I'll cut it up for a quilt."

"No, Bessie, I have to do this—it's a matter of honor. I'm going now to meet the others at the mine office."

"You mean to tell me the mine owners are mixed up in this, too?"

"I don't know who's mixed up in it, but that's where we're meeting.

"Hershel, if you do this, I don't know if I can live with you anymore. You're not the man I married. Please, don't go," she cried.

"I've promised to go and I'm going, no matter what you say." At that, he stormed out of the house.

The Klan marched silently, the way lit only by torchlight, from the mine to Ben's house. Armed with shotguns, a bucket of hot pine tar, and a pillowcase filled with chicken feathers, the eerie procession gathered a crowd of onlookers along the way. Hershel was handed the bucket of tar and feared what they'd expect him to do. The procession arrived at Ben's house, and one hooded man stood in the yard bellowing for the coward to come out and take his medicine. Ben, drunk again on a Friday night, staggered onto the porch and fell down the steps. The gathering crowd broke into laughter, but the marchers were deadly serious. Two Klansmen ripped off Ben's shirt. Another yanked the tar bucket away from Hershel and yelled, "Here, let me show you how it's done!" He began smearing the hot liquid on Ben's bare shoulders, while another threw handfuls of feathers at the tar and finally just dumped the rest on Ben's head.

Ben moaned in agony. Hershel, not realizing the pain they had planned to inflict, stood dumbfounded as Ben writhed on the ground. Sarah, worried she'd be attacked, too, stood behind the screen door staring at her husband. At a whistled signal, the group re-formed their lines and marched off into the night, torches slowly extinguishing one by one. Hershel stumbled along with the rest, wishing he could just go home and be done with this night, but he had been warned that they must all meet back at the mine. Passing his house, he saw his own family standing on their porch, the children wide-eyed, not knowing that he was there behind his white robe and hood. Bessie knew, though, and he saw her head off across the yard, no doubt to see what she could do to help Sarah.

Bessie turned, after seeing the children following her. "You kids get back in the house right now!" she yelled.

"What in the hell was that?" said Belle. "And who were those with the Halloween faces?"

"It's that Klan mob hiding who they are. They just tarred and feathered our neighbor, and if you'll keep these kids inside, I'll go see about Sarah."

"My land," said Belle. "I never saw such a sight."

Bessie found Sarah trying to pick the feathers from Ben's shoulders as he sprawled on his stomach on the living room floor. "Why did they do this, Bessie?" asked Sarah.

"They have some misguided notion that they're protecting you, Sarah."

"Oh, my God. What will he do when he wakes up? They don't know what they've done. He won't rest till he's paid every one of them back for this."

The tar hadn't spread down his back, but where it had landed lay red, blistered patches and feathers, masses of feathers. Ben seemed to be barely breathing, whether from the whiskey he'd consumed or the burns to his skin. If he could sleep through the night, he might be better able to cope with the pain in the morning, Bessie thought.

Reaching the mine office, all of the members began taking off their garb and placing the robes and hoods carefully back in their white caskets. Robert, the leader, called for order and then congratulated them on a good night's work. Hershel's face must have reflected his stricken feelings, because when Robert sought him out, he said, "Now, Hershel, don't think of this as a bad deed you've done. Did that man think of the pain he inflicted on his wife? No, I can tell you, he never gave it a moment's notice. He got what he deserved, and we'll do it again if we have to. You just keep an eye out in that direction."

Bessie and Sarah sat on the floor most of the night, removing as many feathers as they could while Ben lay unconscious. He would not welcome her presence in the daylight, Bessie knew. He was a mean man—she'd seen the proof of that with her own eyes, but did he deserve this? Did anybody? And what would happen next?

She returned home just before first light. Hershel was not asleep in their bed, and indeed, he was nowhere to be found. Did they tar and feather him, too, and leave him in a ditch somewhere? No, that couldn't be right. He'd gone to join them. The thought of him there in that crowd of ghosts made her stomach turn. The thought of what Ben might do made her knees go weak.

CHAPTER 28

Hershel was ashamed to be seen with the white casket carrying the robe and hood, so he made his way carefully in the dark to the river's edge and threw it in. He watched it float, bobbing along until it hit a submerged rock or a tree stump and sank. *There goes Bessie's ten dollars,* he thought. Now if he could only rid his conscience so easily of what he had done. He couldn't face Bessie, so he went to Bobby's boarding house and asked to sleep on the floor.

All night, he dreamed about Bessie's words and Ben's injuries. He couldn't believe he'd been a part of such cruelty—to burn blisters on a man's back and then cover them with chicken feathers. Thank God it was pine tar they used, since it was liquid at a low temperature compared with roofing tar. Still, he knew the pain it would have caused, especially when it wouldn't come off, short of turpentine. He guessed it would have to wear off, but how long would that take?

His sympathy for Ben was now equal to his sympathy for Sarah—maybe more. And then there was Bessie. She'd said she couldn't live with him anymore. Would she really go through with it? Where could she go? The house was his as the miner in the family, but her brothers and her mother and his father and, of course, his children all lived there. His thoughts grew dizzy going round and round in circles. His back ached from lying on the hard floor as well as from the weight of the guilt he now carried.

Bessie lay down for what she hoped would be a few hours of sleep, but her muddled thoughts kept her just dozing. Where was Hershel? He'd never been away from home on purpose for a whole night like this in all their years together. Where could he have gone? Had something happened to him? Was he all right? He always called her a worrywart, and she guessed it was true. She thought about the last words she'd spoken to him before he went out. It was so completely unlike him to be a part of the spectacle she'd witnessed. Had he really become one of them? If he had, could they continue their lives together?

Hearing her mother in the kitchen, Bessie rose from her sleepless bed. Everyone had the day off from work, and she'd looked forward to a family streetcar ride to Shinnston for ice cream. Now she only hoped they could talk out this problem.

"Morning, Bessie," said her mother. "What time did you get to bed? You look all wore out."

"I stayed with Sarah till almost daybreak. Ben's in bad shape with burns from that pine tar. I have no idea how anyone would get that stuff off. You know how your hands feel if you pick up a pinecone—all sticky? It doesn't wash off, and the only thing I know to get it off is turpentine or alcohol, and that would make his burns worse."

"I never heard of such a thing. Why would those men do that?"

"They say they're protecting women from their husbands, but with Ben's temper and a little whiskey, it's hard to tell what he'll do."

"Did she need protection from him?"

"If you want to know the truth, he's been beating her up nearly every weekend for no reason other than he's drunk."

"How come I didn't know that?"

"She covers it up, doesn't scream, doesn't yell, and keeps to her house as much as she can. Hershel and I heard him last weekend breaking dishes and slamming out of the house, with her cowering behind the door."

"The bastard."

"So the Klan came after him, and now everyone has to pay for it."

"What do you mean? What have you got to do with it?"

"Well, as much as I hate to say it, Hershel was in the middle of that whole thing last night, and he hasn't come home since."

"Bessie, you can't mean that Hershel took part. He's not that kind of man, and you know it."

"All I know is that he took that white suit and left this house."

Hearing a footstep on the porch, Belle stopped in the midst of pouring a second cup of coffee. Bessie had gone to wake the children for their breakfast. Hershel came in the door, hanging his head and looking as devastated as Bessie had looked. "Where's Bessie?" he asked.

"She's in with the kids," she replied. "You've got some explaining to do. You know I've loved you like a son, but something's terribly wrong here today."

"Yes, I know. I can't tell you how sorry I am for what a fool I've been. I just hope Bessie will forgive me and take me back."

"Didn't know she'd given you up."

Just then Walter, now seven years old, came running into the kitchen and grabbed his father around the waist, squealing, "Ice cream, ice cream, ice cream." Bessie, never looking Hershel in the eye, said, "Walter, sit down and eat your oatmeal and hush."

Hershel took a porch chair out to the backyard, where he hoped to have a private conversation with Bessie. If she chose not to talk to him, he didn't know what he'd do. He needed to explain that he didn't know what the Klan had planned for Ben, and that if he had known, he would never have been a part of it. He needed to explain that until last night, he didn't know about all the people they hated. At the Clarksburg meeting, they'd only mentioned alcohol and wife beating. In his anger at her for telling him what to do, he hadn't listened. When he thought about their hatred of Negroes, he felt ashamed to remember how kind Molly had been when Bessie had the flu. When he thought about their hatred of Italians, he felt ashamed to remember that his friend Domenic had died along with Orie in the Monongah disaster. When he thought about their hatred of Poles, he felt ashamed to remember their dear neighbors, the Olas from Poland. Bessie must understand, so he went in search of her now before it was too late.

Jeremiah was napping on the front porch. Belle had taken everyone else except Bessie on the streetcar for ice cream. Hershel found Bessie lying down, her face streaked with tears. He stood in the doorway looking at her, so she said, "Come in if you want to."

"Oh, Bessie, how can I tell you how sorry I am?" he said.

"So tell me."

"I've been trying to make things better, but I've just made everything worse."

"What do you mean by worse?"

"I've taken the false word of strangers for the truth that was before my eyes. I went to a meeting in Clarksburg, and all they talked about was wife beating and bootleggers. Then I went to a parade in Fairmont and heard them talk about Catholics, but I thought they weren't all like that. I didn't know about all of the hate they practice till last night. I should have listened to you, but I was too full of pride at belonging to this group to pay you any mind. When I saw what they did to Ben, I came to my senses. I tried to sleep on the floor at Bobby's, but I kept seeing your face and hearing you say you wouldn't want to live with me anymore. I kept seeing what happened to Ben, and I felt sorry for him. I thought about Molly and poor Domenic and Mama and Papa Ola, and I couldn't bear the shame of it all. I was a fool, and I'd deserve it if you never looked at me again. But I couldn't stand that, Bessie. I need you and this family as I need air to breathe. Can you forgive me?

"Where's your white suit?"

"I threw it in the river."

"Well, that's better than making a quilt out of it. I wouldn't want anyone I know to sleep under such a filthy thing. So, Hershel, are you telling me you're through with the Klan?"

"Yes, I am, and I wish I'd never heard the word. I have Bobby to thank for introducing me, but it's my own damn fault. He had enough sense to say he'd have no part of them."

"Will they let you go that easy?"

"I hope they'll say good riddance."

"And what if they don't?"

"Please just believe me when I say I'm through with them. My only worry is that they're mixed up with this mine. If my job's in danger, I'll have to find a new one."

"Let's hope it doesn't come to that. I'll say my piece now and we'll be done with it. If you had come home last night all proud of what you'd done, or even if you didn't like the violence, but accepted the hate, I truly could not have stayed with you. I'd have had to take Orie's money and try to find a way to support the children. The man who left here last night could not have been the man I married. But you are the man I married, and I'm glad you came to your senses, as you say."

"So are we okay?"

That question was left unanswered by the whirlwind that was Walter, bursting through the door, squealing, "Daddy, daddy, Grandma got us two scoops apiece!"

Bessie watched in vain for Ben to go to work for the next two weeks. She didn't dare go near the house to ask about his burns, and Sarah never came out in the yard at all. Their pump was not visible from Bessie's back porch, so there wasn't even a way to see if she came out to get water. Bessie had fretted over Sarah's fate once Ben woke up, but there seemed to be nothing to be done. She heard no crashing dishes. She heard no sobbing. She heard nothing at all, which seemed even more ominous. Finally, one day, the mailman knocked on her door. Home delivery had begun, which eliminated that part of Bessie's job at the company store. "Do you know what happened to your neighbors? The mail's piling up in their box, but they don't seem to be at home."

"No, I haven't seen them in a couple of weeks. I just thought they were there all this time."

"Guess I'll wait a few days and then start sending this mail back where it came from. Seems like a waste of postage to me, though."

Hershel was relieved that he'd had no more word from the Klan. Even if he always felt like someone was watching him, so far, no comment had been made. In the middle of the third week since Ben's punishment, another miner caught up with him as he walked home. It was the same one who'd told him about the meeting that night.

"How's it goin', brother?" said the man.

"All right, I guess," replied Hershel.

"No more trouble with that neighbor of yours?"

"Looks like they've moved away. I haven't seen any signs of either one of them."

"Robert asked me to check on you. Seems a barge going down the river dislodged an object that might have belonged to you. One of our boys was on that barge, and he brought it directly to Robert. The article of clothing inside was marked 'tall.' Now, not many of our folks are tall, and the ones who are all seem to be in possession of their belongings. Any thoughts about that?"

Hershel stopped in his tracks. "I might as well tell you straight out—I don't intend to come to any more meetings or any marches or any punishments. I quit."

"Well, son, joinin' up was easy—all it cost you was ten dollars. You might think what happened to your neighbor was a little harsh, but have you thought about all the good we do? We take good care of widows and orphans, and we're trying to stamp out bootleggers and moonshiners. I'd say you should give it some more thought. Besides, after you've taken an active part in one of our events and seen all our faces, quittin' might not be so easy."

"Is that a threat?"

"No, I don't make threats. But I do make promises, so you better watch yourself around here. Never know what loaded coal car might just break away and run you right over. Coal mining is a dangerous business. We all know that. Accidents happen all the time. Enough said." And with that, he turned and walked off in the opposite direction.

CHAPTER 29

Instead of going straight home, Hershel went to the rooming house to look for Bobby. He needed to know how his friend had gotten away from the Klan when he didn't seem able to himself. He didn't know where to turn. He found Bobby in his room with a half-empty glass and a bottle of whiskey on the windowsill.

"I saw you comin' up the road, and I knew you'd soon be at my door," said Bobby. "Have they threatened you yet?"

"Well, they said it was a promise, not a threat, but it was a threat, just the same. How did you know?"

"I heard the same thing. Then they said if I'd bring them someone who'd stick with them, they'd leave me alone. That's when you asked about them, and I thought my troubles were over."

"My God, Bobby, why didn't you tell me right off what they were?"

"You weren't in any mood to hear it, Hershel. You were all worked up about your neighbor's wife, and that's all you cared about."

"Oh, maybe you're right, but I'm sure as hell not about to trick somebody else into joining up."

"Now, look here. I didn't trick you. You asked."

Hershel slumped down onto the floor and said, "Okay, you're right. I asked for it, but now what do I do?"

"The only ones I knew were Robert and the two others in the car that night. How many of them did you recognize?"

"The biggest surprise to me was the bigwigs at the mine. My boss wasn't among them, but there were business owners and mine superintendents—people I'd never expect to see putting on those white robes. I guess that's why they want to keep it all so secret."

"Wonder why they would even care about your neighbor's wife."

"I don't think they give a damn about her. I think they just wanted to show what they could do, and they did it right out in public so everybody would be warned not to do or say anything to make them angry."

"Well, you better be careful at work. They could kill you and nobody'd be the wiser."

"Yeah, I know."

"How about a drink to take the edge off?"

"No, Bobby, I've got to keep my wits about me."

"Well, I'm just gonna make friends with this bottle of rye—prohibition or no prohibition."

When Hershel returned to work the next day, his boss, Jack, took him aside and gave him the same warning. "Rumors are flying that you better watch yourself. I don't know what they've got against you, and I don't want to know. Just be careful," he said. Hershel had been underground long enough to know where the dangers lay. He'd never been in a situation, though, where someone might set out to harm him. They'd begun wiring a new section of the mine, and he was grateful to have his electrician's job back. Still, that meant he'd spend most of his time working alone.

Hershel sat down to eat his lunch and looked forward to the coffee Bessie had put in a new container called a thermos that would keep it hot, or maybe just warm. He loved his coffee, and he'd just taken his first sip when he heard footsteps coming down the tunnel from both directions. The miner he'd met up with the day before came into view. "So, Hershel, have you thought about what I told you yesterday? Have you changed your mind?"

"No, I haven't. I want no part of the Klan. Tell me something, though. What makes you want to stick with a bunch like that?"

"Like what? I reminded you about all the good we do."

Hershel rose to meet this fellow eye to eye. "How many different kinds of people do you hate? I've heard it's a hell of a lot."

"We just want to make sure America stays in the hands of real Americans. We don't want all these foreigners, these Pollacks, these tallies, these Jews taking over, taking away our rights as decent citizens."

Just then, Tommy, the electrician's helper, approached from the other direction. "Hey, Hershel. Jack sent me to see if you need any help."

"Hi, Tommy. No, I just stopped for lunch."

Turning to the other man, Hershel said, "No change of heart here, and you can send that word along to Robert."

"Well, you had your chance," he replied as he started back down the tunnel.

Hershel finished his shift and headed home. He and Bessie had been sort of tiptoeing around each other for days, and he worried that she would never be the same cheerful and loving person she'd always been to him. Instead of talking it through, he just remained silent. The warnings went unmentioned.

"Daddy, Daddy, did you save me anything in your lunch bucket?" cried Walter, running down the road to meet him.

"No, son, not today."

"Let me carry it home anyway," he said. "I want one of these when I grow up."

"Now, Walter, we've talked about that. You need to do good in school so you'll have a good job and never have to set foot in the mines. I reckon you could carry your lunch to work in one of these no matter where you work."

"Yeah, I reckon so," said Walter as he began to swing the bucket by its handle just as Hershel remembered doing as a child. Running and hopping and jumping over puddles, Walter beat his father home.

A week passed, then another, and before long, over a month went by without any more threats. *Maybe it was just idle talk,* Hershel thought. *Maybe they just wanted to scare me so bad I'd never tell who they were.*

Still, he constantly looked over his shoulder. Still, he dreaded the sound of a footstep on the porch after dark. He and Bessie spent no more evenings in the swing, so he had time on his hands after supper. She busied herself with the children and didn't seem to miss him at all. She and Belle carried on whispered conversations that ceased abruptly when he came into the room. Ben and Sarah had disappeared without a trace, and new neighbors moved in next door.

Two months after the warnings, Hershel and Tommy reached the end of the new tunnel, and together, they tested the completed wiring. Once they knew it was done correctly, they shut off the power to wait for the inspector who would need to sign off on the work. Unless they opened up a new section, Hershel's job as electrician would end and he'd go back to loading coal. The new automatic mining machines made the work harder, because they never stopped cutting, so there was no rest between explosive shots. The only time the shoveling stopped was when they filled a car and rolled it out to wait for an empty.

With his mind on these possible changes to his work, at the end of the day, Hershel started his long walk back to the mine entrance. Tommy had hurried on ahead. He had a hot date, he said, and needed time to get spiffed up. On his way in that day, Hershel had noticed some loose rock along one rib or wall of the tunnel. Now he heard an unusual sound. The light on his hat didn't reach very far into the darkness, but a couple of other lights seemed to be bobbing around ahead. Then he heard the sound of running feet and a loud crack. As he approached, the wall broke loose, taking a section of the roof with it.

Hershel awoke flat on his back in complete darkness, the only sound dripping water. It did no good to open his eyes; there was nothing to see. He was covered in a thick layer of coal dust that he tried to wipe from his face. His rescue training had taught him to remain still until he could figure out if anything was broken. His right hand worked, but the left seemed weighted down. When he tried to move, a sharp pain coursed through his left side. He couldn't reach for his pocket watch, so he didn't know how long he'd been there. If too much time passed, the odds of living through this would grow small, so he hoped he'd only been out a few minutes.

Bessie knew something was wrong when Hershel didn't come home for supper. She'd heard no disaster siren at the mine, and no one had appeared at her door with bad news. Maybe he'd gone to Bobby's. Running up the porch steps to Bobby's rooming house, she lost her breath and had to stop for a minute. *Better slow down,* she thought. Sitting down on the top step, she saw Bobby coming up the hill, so she waved and started toward him.

"Bobby, do you know anything about Hershel? He hasn't come home from work."

"Oh, boy," he said. "I knew something would happen."

"What do you mean, 'something would happen?'"

Taking her by the arm, he said, "Come in the hall, Bessie. We can't talk out here."

She wrenched her arm away and shrieked, "Something would happen?"

"Okay, okay, now, calm down. There might just be a simple explanation for this. Let's go to the mine and see what we can find."

They saw no lights in the mine office, and no one seemed to be around. The first-shift men had all gone home, and the second shift had already started. "Where's the siren?" Bessie asked.

"Now, you can't just set off the siren without knowing anything's wrong."

"I intend to get somebody's attention, even if I do have to blow the siren."

"You wait right here, and I'll try to find somebody."

"I won't wait long, so you better hurry up," she promised.

Bobby found a flashlight in the equipment shack and started into the mine. After a few minutes of walking, he heard a coal car rumbling ahead. If men were working, he thought, nothing could be wrong. But where was Hershel? Asking those he passed, he got no answers, only questions—who's missing? where did he work? When he heard the siren go off, he thought, "Oh, God. Bessie's done it now." As it turned out, he'd missed the fire boss, who'd gone out by a different heading and who had discovered a large slate fall in the new section being wired. No one knew if anyone might be beyond that slate, but a search had to be conducted just in case. Men began coming out to see what the problem was and how they could help. Bessie stood, wide-eyed, and managed only to say, "My Hershel's missing. He's an electrician," setting in motion a flurry of activity.

Riverview had a rescue team, of which Hershel was a member, so those arriving knew what to do and how to do it. Fortunately, this rescue involved no explosion or fire, but a mountain of broken timbers mixed with slate and coal that had to be moved carefully. The coal dust and methane gas that came down with the roof and wall could explode under these circumstances, so the first step would be to water down the dust and try to dissipate the gas with the mine fans. There were water trolleys in the mine, but none anywhere near the new section.

Lying in the dark, Hershel tried to hear any sounds coming from the other side of the rubble. He'd felt pain in his left ear and discovered something sticky on that side of his face. Only a scrape, he hoped. He tried speaking out loud, but the sound was muffled. Maybe he should start tapping out the code he'd been trained to listen for when he was the rescuer. But what could he use? He had one arm and leg free and nothing in reach.

Struggling against whatever was holding him down, he began feeling for any object he could use for tapping. Nothing on his right side. Kicking out with his right leg, his foot landed on his hat, but he couldn't manage to bring it close to his hand. Reaching up overhead, he felt the edge of his lunch pail. Now if he could only grab the handle, he'd have something metal. He could tap on the bucket with the handle and make a faint noise, but a noise, nevertheless. Every effort to bring the pail closer seemed to roll it farther away. With a lunge that shot pain through his whole left side, he managed to find the handle and bring it within his reach. The small piece of cake he'd saved as a treat for Walter fell out onto his face as he swung the bucket over, and he laughed to himself. The thought of that cake would keep him alive, he vowed.

The rescue team had now assembled just outside the mouth of the mine and was waiting only for the last equipment check to be made. They could ride on a motor for the first mile inside, but they had to walk the next mile for fear of a spark setting off the dust or gas. A water trolley had been brought to the rubble pile to dampen down the dust, and the level of gas was being monitored, but they took no chances. Tommy had been located and had come at once to help find Hershel.

"When I left him, he was putting away the tools and about ready to walk back out," he said.

"Did you notice anything as you left work today, Tommy?" asked the fire boss.

"Well, there was some loose rock just about where this roof fall is piled up."

"Anything else?"

"No, I don't reckon. I did pass a couple of fellas I didn't know walking in. Must have been second-shift guys. Sure hope they weren't back there, too, when it fell."

When the team arrived, the first order of business was to maintain silence and just listen for a few minutes. Then they began carefully moving the larger pieces of rubble from hand to hand, like a fire brigade exchanging buckets of water. It was slow work but safer than bringing in a machine to move the slate and coal. Smaller pieces were shoveled up, clearing the way inches at a time. Every ten minutes, they stopped to listen again. After three hours, they'd begun hearing a faint sound from beyond the fall tapping out the code for, "I'm alive." Tapping back, "Okay," they restarted their efforts with a new sense of hope that at least one person was still holding on.

Hershel kept tapping till he finally heard a reply. His clothes felt damp, and he knew that rising water in the mine could kill him before they broke through. If only he could see. If only he could stand up. He thought how lucky he was that no track had yet been laid in this new part of the mine. Being knocked onto tracks would surely have broken his back. He lost all sense of time passing, but with rescuers on the way, he began to wonder about all of his injuries and how long he'd be out of work. He had a houseful of people to provide for. Surely, they wouldn't put them all out of the house if he couldn't work. Running his hand over his face, Hershel noticed that the sticky blood had dried on his cheek. He felt the grit of coal dust in his eyes. Feeling around with his good hand, he found Walter's cake and thought again that it would save him. He lost consciousness just as the light of a rescuer's helmet shone on his face, seven hours after the tunnel had gone dark.

"Hershel," the man shouted, "we're here!"

CHAPTER 30

Word finally came that he'd been found alive but injured. The whole family had gathered outside the mine entrance, and Russell raised a cheer. "Best wait to see what they mean by injuries before you do much of that," warned Belle. Still, if he was alive, maybe they'd all have a chance to celebrate. A light drizzle had begun, and they'd come out without umbrellas. Still, no official saw fit to invite them into the office to do their waiting.

"We mean less to them than those mules," muttered Bessie. "And we both work for them."

"Hush now, Bessie. You can't afford to get yourself all worked up," said Belle.

"Here, Mama, put my coat over your head," said Ivy.

"No, child, you'll catch a cold," said Bessie. "Now that we know something, why don't you kids go on home? Your supper's in the oven, so maybe it won't be all ruined. Please do that for me."

Russell agreed and urged the others to come along. He'd go with them, he said, and let Jeremiah know what they'd learned.

"Ivy, you make sure Walter has his supper, and I'll be along directly," said Belle.

The first thing they heard was the sound of a motor approaching the mine entrance and echoing off the walls. Hershel lay on a stretcher, his eyes closed and blood on his face mixed with swaths of coal dust. His left shoulder didn't look right, Bessie thought, but it was hard to tell about his injuries. He was black from head to toe—a sight she wasn't used to seeing. He always carefully washed his face and hands before he came home.

"Where will you take him?" she asked.

"We're not sure if anything's broken, so we'll take him to the miner's hospital in Clarksburg. I'm worried that he hasn't woke up since we found him. Don't know how long he'd been out."

"I'm coming with you," she said, "and don't you tell me I can't."

"It's against the rules, ma'am," he said.

"The rules be damned. I'm coming with you."

"Sonny," said Belle, "you better just get out of the way or there'll be hell to pay."

Under his breath, he said, "No skin off my nose."

Bessie rode sitting on the floor in the back of the ambulance with Hershel, listening to his occasional whispers. She heard her name over and over, along with Walter's. They'd covered him with blankets and had offered one to her when she began to shiver. They turned on the siren when they got near the city, and the sound of it was more frightening than the silence. People began pouring out the doors as they pulled under the portico at St. Mary's Hospital, a place Bessie knew well. Hershel was whisked to the emergency department, but when Bessie tried to follow, a tall nun in black and white took her arm and led her to the waiting room. "We'll let you know something soon," she said.

How many people am I going to lose? she thought. *And why have I been so cold to him lately? Why couldn't I have trusted him when he said he was finished with the Klan?* The thought of the Klan brought a sudden chill— did they do this? Why would they? He'd never said anything about being afraid, but then, he hadn't mentioned the Klan again after that awful night. Her life seemed to be falling apart before her eyes. What if he didn't recover? What if he could never work again? How would they live? Where would they live? She waited, sat down, stood up, paced, looked out the window, peered out into the hall, and still had no news.

After three hours, a doctor and the tall nun came bustling into the room, and she braced herself for what they might say. "Now, you're Mrs. Martin, is that correct?"

"Yes, I am. How—"

"Sit down please," he interrupted.

"Just tell me."

"All right. Here's what we know for now. Mr. Martin had a dislocated shoulder, which we've put back into place, a possible skull fracture, and a number of contusions."

"What is that word, *contusion?*"

"That's what you'd call a bruise—bleeding under the skin. We couldn't see them till we removed the coal dust. His left arm and leg are badly bruised but not broken."

"Is he awake?"

"Yes, he has regained consciousness. He's awake."

"Will he be okay?"

"Much depends on the extent of his head injury, but we think he'll live."

As they stood to leave, the doctor turned and said, "One thing was odd. He had a small piece of chocolate cake wrapped in wax paper gripped in his right hand. Don't know if he intended to eat it or if it had some sort of meaning to him, but we had trouble taking it out of his hand."

"Can I see him now?" asked Bessie.

"Yes, come with me," said the nun.

They'd propped him up in bed with his shoulder and arm shrouded in a sling. He still had smudges of black on his face and arms, but they'd put on a clean hospital gown over the dark-blue bruises. His head was bandaged, and he had a patch over his left ear. His filthy clothes were stuffed into a paper bag by his bed. He seemed to be sleeping, and she was afraid to hug him, so she just took his hand and softly said his name. "Oh, Bessie," he said, "where am I?"

"You're in St. Mary's in Clarksburg."

"Last thing I remember was holding on for dear life to Walter's cake."

"Walter's cake?"

"I'd saved him a treat in my lunch bucket, and when I finally got hold of the handle and swung it over my head, the cake fell out. I thought it was a sign."

"What do you mean, 'a sign?'"

"Oh, Bessie, I was pinned down in the dark and couldn't move. When I managed to get some metal to use to tap out the code, the cake came with it. I felt like it would save my life."

"The doctor said they had a time getting it out of your hand."

"What else did he say? They got me trussed up here like a hog."

"He said they'd fixed your dislocated shoulder, but I guess it will be awful sore for a while. That's the second time—same shoulder. Then he said you had a head injury and a lot of bruises. I can see them under that nightshirt they got you wearing. How do you feel?"

"They gave me a shot of something, so I'm kinda groggy, and I can't hear very well."

"I'll let you rest now."

"Don't go. I may drop off every once in a while, but pull up a chair and stay with me."

Bessie stayed until the nurse said she could stay no longer. The sun would be coming up soon, so she decided to try to find some breakfast and wait for visiting hours to start again. She had important news she'd been putting off telling Hershel—a baby was due in five months. Since their argument about the Klan, she hadn't been willing to share much of anything with him, especially not this sort of thing. Her mother had guessed two months earlier, but that was right in the middle of their troubles. Fortified with two cups of strong coffee, she returned to the hospital.

His bed was empty when she entered his room. In a panic, she rushed to the nurses' station. "Where's my husband? Where's the man in room 220?"

"Now, don't be alarmed. He's just gone for some tests. Have a seat in the waiting room and we'll let you know when he comes back."

Again, she waited, sat, stood, paced, and finally, they brought him back. He'd had an x-ray that could help them figure out what had happened to his head.

"It didn't hurt at all," he said. "They just sort of shined a light on my head, and then it was over."

"Did they say when we'd hear back from it?"

"Somebody's got to look at the picture they made and tell the doctor what he sees. Then they'll tell us, I guess. Are you okay, Bessie? You look tired."

"Well, I've been up all night worried to death, so that might account for looking tired," she said with a smile.

"Come sit down."

"Hershel, I've got something to tell you that I've been putting off."

"Okay, what is it? Are you still mad at me?"

"No, I'm not mad at you. I've begun to remember how much you mean to me and to our children. We all stood outside the mine in the rain waiting to hear—Mom and Ivy and Orie and Russell and Wilbert. We left Walter home with Jeremiah—don't know who was taking care of who with those two. We couldn't bear to think we might never see you again, so we just waited and hoped. Oh, Hershel, I'm sorry I've been so cold to you these last few months. Can you forgive me?"

"It's me who needs forgiveness, Bessie. I've known that ever since that terrible night with Ben and Sarah, but you didn't seem to want to talk about it after that. Can you forgive me for being such a damn fool?"

Squeezing his hand, she said, "I think we're both forgiven from this moment on. Now I have good news. We're having a baby in about five months."

As he tried to take her in his arms, a pain shot through his injured shoulder. "Oh, Bessie, I'm so happy. You know how much I love children. You've known for a while, then?"

"Yes, and Mom guessed awhile back, but I was just too stubborn to tell you. Another thing to be forgiven for, I guess."

"Well, I know now, and that's all that matters. If only I knew when I could go back to work. The electrical work is all done, and I suppose I'll have to go back to shoveling coal."

"You can't do that kind of work with your shoulder like it is."

The doctor came through the door with a black see-through piece of paper in his hand. "Well, we know now about your skull fracture. It's just a hairline break that will repair itself in time. See this right here?

It doesn't explain your hearing loss, though. Was there a loud sound associated with your accident?"

"Just before the roof fell in, I heard a loud cracking sound."

"Well, that could have damaged your eardrum and caused the bleeding."

"Will my hearing come back, doctor?"

"I don't know. I've looked in your ear, but x-rays can't be used to see inside. They just look at hard substances, such as bone. Perhaps in time, your eardrum will heal and your hearing will be restored. I think you can't count on it, however."

"When can I go home?"

"Now, don't get in a hurry. With what you've been through, you need bed rest for at least a week. After that, we'll talk about it again. We'll send a note to your employer not to expect you back for perhaps two weeks."

"Doctor, you don't understand. I have a family to keep, and I can't afford to be off work that long. Just let me go right now, and I promise to rest up at home for a few days."

"It will take longer than a few days for your shoulder to heal enough to even take off the sling. How could you possibly work like that?"

Bessie now spoke up. "Hershel, please just do what the doctor tells you. We'll manage at home with my income and Russell and Wilbert's part-time work at the company store. If you go back too soon, you'll end up right back in here again."

"She's right, you know," said the doctor. "Now I'll call the nurse to give you something to ease that painful shoulder."

After Bessie went home, Hershel tried to get out of bed by himself and discovered that his legs refused to hold him up. Luckily, the nurse was coming in to give him his sponge bath and managed to get him back to the bed. "Hard to tell the bruises from the coal dust, Mr. Martin," she said.

CHAPTER 31

In the two weeks since Hershel's injury, no word at all had come from the mine—no questions about his condition, no questions about when he would return to work, nothing. He'd stayed in the hospital for a week but still had not regained his strength. Bobby visited and took news back to the rescue team that their efforts had paid off. He and Hershel tried to piece together what had happened.

"Hersh, what do you remember? Did you see anybody that day?"

"No, I couldn't say that I saw somebody, but I did see headlamps ahead of me in the tunnel when no one should've been there. I heard some scraping noises and the sound of running feet just before the roof-fall. The doc thinks the loud crack when it all came down is what caused my hearing in my left ear to be so bad. The noise is the last thing I remember, till I woke up in the hospital."

"You think somebody caused the roof to fall?"

"I can't say one way or the other. Guess I thought those warnings had just blown over, that they didn't mean it. I can't believe you could get away from them and they won't let me alone."

"I never saw what you saw. You just know too much."

"Wonder if I should go to the police?"

"If they're members, too, you'd just make it worse."

"What should I do, then?"

"Maybe you could just go to the mine office and tell them you're not quite able to come back to work and see what they have to say."

When Bessie got home after work, she opened the mail and found a notice of eviction. "You are hereby notified that we have disallowed your continued residence in the company house located at 535 Main Street, the cause being that no miner is currently employed by this company," it read. "You must vacate said property within ten days."

Oh my God; oh my God; oh my God, she thought. *What can we do?* It was too late in the day to do anything at all but worry. She called all the grown-ups to the kitchen table and told them what had happened. Hershel's anger flared as he swore he wouldn't let them do this.

"I'll go to the office first thing in the morning," he said. "Aside from being hurt on the job, I've done nothing to justify being fired."

"How can we move in ten days? Everything we own is here," said Bessie.

"And where would we move to?" asked Belle.

Russell and Wilbert wondered if their part-time jobs at the company store were in danger, too, not to mention Bessie's job as well. Of course, if they had to move out of Riverview, they'd all have to find jobs elsewhere. Belle had been insisting that her two boys find ways to continue their education; she wouldn't have them going into the mines. Maybe they could work their way through Glenville College. They'd both finished high school and seemed to be just drifting along ever since.

"You boys hitch a ride to Glenville tomorrow and ask about school. No time like the present," Belle said. "And no use sitting around here feeling sorry for ourselves."

Hershel approached the mine office the next morning determined to make things right. He worried that whatever had caused this trouble was his fault. How could he have been so foolish to put his family in such danger? Their home was being taken away in ten days, now nine days. How could he live with himself if that happened? His shoulder ached the farther he walked, and his head throbbed. His hearing had not recovered, and he had resigned himself to the possibility that it never would.

"I need to speak to whoever's in charge," he said to the woman behind the outer office desk.

"And who may I say is calling?" she said.

"I'm Hershel Martin, and I've been off work for a couple of weeks because I was hurt in a roof fall."

"Oh, yes, Mr. Martin. How are you doing?"

"Fair," he said. "Not there yet, but okay."

"Just a minute. I'll see if anyone can see you."

He'd not been asked to sit down, and she was taking an awful long time coming back out. Finally, the door opened and she said, "I'm sorry, Mr. Martin, but there's no one here to speak to this morning. Perhaps if you come back this afternoon, we can help you then." In a silent fury, he turned and headed toward the door. No use taking it out on her—it wasn't her fault. "I'll be back," he said.

Slowly walking back home, he turned over in his mind all the things he could not control. If the company found a way to just fire him like that, they'd have nothing to fall back on. They'd have no home. All his life, he'd dreamed of having a home that no one could take away, of having a piece of land. There'd never been any chance of those things when they had to live in a company house. Now even that was being taken away.

He just couldn't go home, so he wandered down by the river. He found a rock warmed by the sun to sit on and thought about the turns his life had taken. His temper had gotten him into trouble any number of times, even though he tried hard to control it. Anger had turned him against school early, and he'd paid for it all these years. He'd turned it on himself when Jane died such a violent death and again when Lucy died long before her time. He and Charlie hadn't been able to get along until it was too late, and he resented Bill's success.

He'd settled into a happy life with Bessie and the children, but now he seethed with rage that his own failings had put them in this awful position. His anger at Ben's treatment of Sarah had caused him to trust strangers who only pretended to agree with him. Worst of all, he hadn't talked it over with Bessie, who would have seen through all of their promises. If he couldn't get this straightened out this afternoon, they'd have seven days to pack up and move—but move where?

When he reached home, he discovered Bessie sitting in the kitchen when she should have been at work. "Well, Hershel, it's official. Neither one of us has a job," she said.

"What will they do to us next?" he asked.

"I guess they've done their worst—half killed you and then fired you. What did you find out at the mine?"

"No one would talk to me. They said I should come back this afternoon."

Bessie sat with her head in her hands. Hershel sat down beside her and took both her hands in his. "Bessie, we'll get through this as long as we don't give up hope. It's all we got."

Hershel saw a man he recognized from the night of the tar and feathering when he got back to the office. The guy tried to escape being seen, but Hershel said quickly, "I need to talk to you." Others sitting in the waiting room looked up, so, reluctantly, the man turned and said, "Come on back here, then." Doors on either side of the hallway were closed, but the man led him into the last one on the left and said, "Sit down, and I'll be back in a few minutes." The room was sparsely furnished with straight chairs around the walls and an oblong table in the middle. The single window looked out on a truly bleak scene—a slag heap that seemed to sway toward the river bank beyond. After twenty minutes, the man returned accompanied by two others. One pulled up a chair and sat at the table. "Now, what is it that you want from us?"

"For starters, I want to know why I've been fired from my job and put out of my house."

"Well, on the day of your accident, you had finished the wiring of the new section, so that job simply ended. Your doctor has shown no indication that you've recovered. In your condition, you can no longer work as a coal loader, so there's nothing here for you."

"I'll be good as new with a little time. And, by the way, it was no accident. Someone set me up to be killed that day."

Half rising from his chair, the man said, "Now, hold on. You can't go around making accusations like that. Do you have any witnesses to back up these ridiculous claims?"

"No, of course I don't, but that's how it happened just the same. I should have been alone in that tunnel, but lights up ahead showed me there were others there. Then they ran away, and the roof fell in. I'd been threatened, twice, by a man who works in this mine—once on my way home and again in the new section I was wiring. I'm wondering what the sheriff or the union might have to say about all this."

Slamming his fist down on the table, the man shouted, "If you're making threats against us, they'll do you no goddamn good!"

"Look, I came here directly from the disaster at Monongah, and I've been a loyal employee for eleven years. You can ask Jack about my work. There's a group in this town that punishes people, and might even kill people if they've a mind to. I think you may know who I mean."

"That's a lie."

"It's the God's truth. Now, I'm willing to go peaceably and find myself another job, but I can't do it in eight or nine days or whatever I've got left. I can't see my wife and family out on the street with no income and nowhere to go. But if you want hell raised, I'm ready to raise a whole lot of it."

"Just what are you implying?"

"There's a newspaper in Fairmont that might be real interested in the goings on in this little town." As Hershel started to rise, the two men standing by the wall moved toward him, but the man at the table gave a subtle gesture, and they moved back.

Sweat beading on his forehead, he took a deep breath and said, "Sit down, now. No need for that, no need at all. In light of your excellent work record and the fact of your injuries in our mine, we'll give you thirty days to vacate the house and a good reference for a job somewhere else if you'll just forget all about these foolish charges you seem determined to make."

It was Hershel's turn to take a deep breath. "If you'll give me something to show we have the house for a month, and if you'll have that lady out there type me up a very good reference right now, I'll do as you ask. And by the way, I'll need money to move."

"You do drive a hard bargain. I'll give you fifty dollars right now if you'll just get the hell out of here."

"Make it a hundred and you've got a deal."

Hershel knew he'd have to be careful. They seemed worried enough about what he might say or do to give him both time and money. The sooner he was gone from Riverview, the better. Now, he just needed a job. Bessie insisted on putting the money in the bank and borrowing a horse and wagon to move, like they had done before. But where could they go? The thought of the poorhouse haunted them, and so Hershel and Bessie set out the next morning to see if any jobs were to be had.

The streetcar ran to all the mines along the river between Clarksburg and Fairmont, so they went to each one in turn but quickly found none to be hiring. They'd decided to go to Monongah only as a last resort, and now that was their last hope. They counted up the years since the disaster that had taken so many lives—thirteen now. Hershel dreaded the thought of working there again, but, as his mother had always said, beggars can't be choosers. No choosing was possible, though, as they were not hiring either.

"Bessie, how about a cup of coffee?" said Hershel.

"You have coffee and I'll have tea," she said. "They've got both at the company store."

As they entered the familiar store, "Well, look who's here," said a familiar voice. Jamie Lee came out from behind the counter and gave Bessie a hug. "What are you doing here in the middle of the day?" she asked.

"We're looking for work, and there doesn't seem to be any on offer today."

"This mine hasn't been hiring for quite awhile now. Not since the war ended, really. Are they laying off at Riverview?"

"No, but Hershel's had some serious injuries, and he's looking for an electrician's job. He's been second electrician, and they've finished that job now at Riverview."

"Well, you know they're opening up a new mine at Owings. You might try there."

"Where is that from here, Jamie?"

"If you get on the streetcar back toward Clarksburg and change at Gore and go to the end of the line, you'll have about a mile to walk. You could probably get there and back before dark. Can you walk that far, Hershel?"

"If it means a job, I can walk anywhere. Thanks."

When they got to Owings, the first thing they noticed was the lack of company houses. There were a few scattered dwellings, but they were far too grand for ordinary miners, so they must belong to the superintendents. The community bustled with construction activity, but it was much smaller than either Monongah or Riverview. They made their way to the mine office and looked for signs listing available jobs but found none. Walking into the office, they discovered the woman who had been clerk of the Relief Committee in Monongah, Mary Jo Calabrese, sitting behind the desk. "Small world, Mary Jo," said Bessie with a smile. "Well, hello. Mrs. Morris, isn't it?" she replied.

"I've been Mrs. Martin for quite a few years," said Bessie. "This is my husband, Hershel."

"Pleased to meet you. And my name is Smith now. What can I do for you?"

"I've been an electrician at Riverview, and they've finished that work there, so I'm looking for a job. I have a good reference letter if you'd like to see it," said Hershel.

"Oh, I have no authority to do that, but I can tell you there are a couple of openings. We're just getting underway here, and they want this to be a modern mine."

"Who would I have to see?"

"Mr. Jessup does the hiring, and he's in the mine right now, but he should be out at the end of the shift at 4:00. Would you like to wait?"

"Yes, we'll wait," said Bessie. "Tell me, Mary Jo, are there no company houses here?"

"No, none have been built yet since we're so new. Not many have been hired on, so it hasn't been a problem."

"Will there be no part of the contract that says miners have to live in company houses?"

"No, not under these circumstances. Maybe that will come later. Ah, there goes the whistle. Mr. Jessup should be here soon."

Riding home on the streetcar, smiles on their faces, Hershel and Bessie had trouble believing their good luck. The glowing reference letter had so impressed Mr. Jessup that he'd offered a job on the spot. After they'd agreed that Hershel should report for work in two weeks when the newest section of the mine was ready for wiring, he and Bessie hastened their steps back to the streetcar before the last one ran for the day. Now they'd have to find a house to buy—one with at least an acre of ground.

CHAPTER 32

Russell and Wilbert had set off early in the morning to ride the streetcar to Clarksburg and then try their luck at hitching rides the sixty miles to Glenville. Belle had raided her savings to give them money to stay overnight if need be. Russell, the oldest, at nineteen, took no real interest in school, but Wilbert had graduated early with good grades and was excited about this possibility. The trip took longer than they expected, so they didn't arrive in Glenville till nearly four in the afternoon. The college itself was a sight such as they'd never seen before—a tall stone building with a tower stretching into the sky, taller than any coal tipple for sure. Rushing to the administration offices before they closed for the day, graduation certificates in hand, they were invited to wait. All day, they'd waited for rides in the autumn heat, but now, at least, they could sit down.

"Well, young fellas, are you here to enroll?" asked a portly gentleman coming toward them with his hand outstretched.

"Sir, we're here to see what it would take to come to school here," said Wilbert. "We are low on money, but willing to work our way, if that's possible."

"Well now, come in my office and we'll talk about that. Do you have your school records?"

"Yes, sir, we've come prepared."

"Commendable, commendable. Now, let me take a look."

The afternoon sun moved slowly across the sky as Bessie and Hershel planned their next steps. Bessie, at age thirty-four, had seemed to tire more easily with this baby than she had with her others. Hershel was still recovering from his injuries and couldn't do any lifting. Moving would be hard, but the bigger kids were still out of school and could do most of the packing. Belle could supervise while Bessie and Hershel looked for what they hoped would become their new home.

"I've never lived anyplace but a company house, have you?" Hershel asked. "Where do we even start to look for our own place?"

"No, I've never known anything but this kind of life. The thought of our own home seems like nothing but a dream."

"Let's go to Monongah tomorrow and ask Bill what to do."

The boys returned home late the next afternoon with news, and the family gathered to hear it. Wilbert had been offered a position keeping the furnace running for the big tower building that held both offices and classrooms—what they called the Lighthouse on the Hill. In return, he would have his classes and his meals and lodging paid for two years, long enough to get his teaching certificate. Of course, he would have to maintain his good grades and work hard at his job. Russell had harbored no wish to become a teacher, so he'd returned empty-handed.

"What do you want to do, Russell?" asked Hershel. They'd both always been good boys, but he wondered how Russell could keep from going in the mines with no other job prospects.

"Well, what I'd really like to do is be a policeman—maybe a state trooper."

"Are you old enough?"

"No, you have to be twenty-five, and you have to be able to ride and take care of a horse."

"What's a horse got to do with it?" asked Belle.

"Somebody told me there aren't enough paved roads to have cars, so troopers ride horses and then take care of them—feeding and grooming, whatever that means."

"That means brushing their coats and keeping them clean. We lived near a farm when I was a girl, and they had horses. They let my brothers ride, but I wasn't allowed just because I was a girl. I showed them a thing or two, though." Belle smiled.

"What did you do, Mom?"

"I sneaked in the barn one night and took one of the ponies out for a ride—no saddle, just me and the horse."

"Then what happened?"

"Well, we had a fine ol' time, and when we got back, there stood the lady of the house with her hands on her hips, just daring me to ride on up."

"Was she mad?" asked Bessie.

"She was more shocked than mad. She said that any girl who could ride just hanging onto the horse's mane should be able to ride like the boys. From then on, I was allowed to ride, too. My own mama wasn't too happy about it, but she never said no. Guess she knew I'd just do it anyway."

"Always been a wild girl at heart, eh, Belle?" Jeremiah grinned.

"Hush up, you old coot," she replied.

Hershel turned the conversation back to more serious matters, saying, "Russell, looks like you need to find you a farm to work on till you're old enough to join up."

House hunting was not working out. Bill had said that Bessie should keep an eye on the newspapers and make inquiries at all the local banks. They'd already used up ten of their thirty days with no prospects in sight. No properties were available in Owings, so they couldn't just move to where the new job was. The sorting and packing was coming along, but soon, school would start. Ivy had two more years, and Orie had four. For Bessie, school had to be an important part of their thinking. Hershel had quit school in the third grade and she had gone through the eighth, but she was determined these two would finish high school.

The headline of the *Shinnston News* stated, "State Police Build New Barracks in Shinnston." Further down the article noted that the former police residences in a community called Haywood Junction were to be sold. What would these residences be like, Bessie wondered. Would they have bars on the windows or look like jails? Would they be suited only for bunk beds along the walls? Would there be kitchens? Checking the streetcar schedule, she found a stop near this Haywood Junction that she'd never noticed before. It was nearer to Shinnston than she thought, so if they lived there, the children could still go to school. "Hershel!" she shouted. "We have a ride to take."

They rode to the stop at Haywood Junction. Helping Bessie down onto the cinders along the tracks, Hershel asked those waiting to get on the car which way to go to the houses for sale. "Walk that way about a half mile," said a man, pointing down the dirt road. "You'll see signs. They been kept up pretty good, but don't think I'd want to live in one," he said. "Never been too fond of lawmen," he said with a grin.

Looking ahead, Hershel saw a line of houses on both sides of the road, four to each side. They looked similar to the large, square company houses in Riverview, but they lacked porches in the front and back. I could fix that, he thought. A tree-covered hill rose behind the houses on the right, but the land seemed to drop away behind those on the left. There were plenty of trees there, but he was looking at treetops, so the gully must be very deep. Coming closer, he realized it was not a gully, but a valley that ended just where the road wound around the bend. He heard a loud roaring from down in the valley that sounded to him like a huge mine fan, so there must be a mine underneath these properties. He hoped that wouldn't be a problem, but it was nothing new for anyone living in a coal camp.

Bessie could see that the first house on the right had already been sold. The "For Sale" sign had the word *Sold* stretched across from corner to corner. She pointed this out to Hershel and told him what it meant. The "For Sale" sign on the second house indicated it was still available, so they walked up the steps from the road to try to look in the windows. The house sat on a fairly steep hill, so they had to go around to the back to see inside. The sight that met them as they rounded the corner was one they would never forget. Beyond the house lay an untouched, flat stretch of hillside covered in broom sage, and above that lay woods that went all the way to the top of the hill. "Look what a perfect garden spot that would make," said Hershel. "And there's even enough room for an orchard," said Bessie. Whatever the house looked like, they could make do, if they could just find a way to have this land.

Quickly, they looked in the windows in the rear of the house and discovered that one room was, indeed, a kitchen with what looked to be piped-in water. They could see into only one other room, which was empty, but the house appeared to consist of eight rooms, four up and four down. They could see the entrance to an enclosed stairway up to the second floor. Bessie took down the information on the sign, and they walked more quickly this time back to the streetcar stop. They'd have to go to Monongah and Shinnston tomorrow to see how much money they had in each bank, and then they could inquire about the house. Exhausted from excitement and all that walking, Bessie rested her head on his shoulder and closed her eyes till they had to change streetcar lines. She slept, but he dreamed of the way those woods might look in October—red and gold and yellow leaves against the light brown of the sage. His mother's sketches of leaves and flowers were only in black and white, but he remembered how she'd loved the colors of fall.

The next morning, Bessie wasn't feeling well enough to go anywhere, so Hershel had to go alone to check on the bank accounts. Unable to read any piece of paper they might hand him, he never felt comfortable in banks or offices of any kind. Since she hadn't put his name on the Monongah account, they wouldn't even tell him the balance. Still, last time she'd asked, it was about $1,200, and it would have grown a little more since then.

Prepared to be turned away again, he tried to distract himself by looking out the streetcar window on the way to Shinnston. The maple leaves were changing colors already—looked like it would be an early autumn. If they had another bad winter, he hoped they'd be in a good, tight house. He'd been trying to seal up the cracks in the company house at Riverview all these years, but they just kept coming back. Winter wind seeped in every room, and the windows coated over with ice on the inside. As close as they lived to the mine, the ground trembled with every shot that went off, rattling dishes and waking up babies.

As he entered the Bank of Shinnston, he saw a friend of Bessie's working as a teller, so he headed for her window. Recognizing him, she made short work of finding their balance of $550, counting the "moving money" from the Riverview mine. He might not be able to read, but he could cipher. Writing down the numbers, he figured they had about $1,700 to spend. Now he'd go to the state police headquarters and ask about the house.

The new barracks were located just south of Shinnston in a big, open field next to the Masonic Cemetery. He figured he could save streetcar money by walking, which took longer than he expected. The bruises on his left side had turned from black to red to yellow, but his leg began to ache as he approached the headquarters. A young man came out the door and said, "Sorry, sir, but we're closing up the office for the day."

Hershel asked, "Is there anyone still here I could talk to about buying one of the houses at Haywood Junction?"

Scratching his head, the man said, "I think they're only here in the morning, so you'll have to come back."

Worried that someone would beat him to the house, Hershel said, "Can I make an appointment or something? I'm real anxious about that property."

"Tell you what; I'll put a note on the bulletin board. Give me your name and tell me what you want, and I'll say you'll be back in the morning."

That completed, Hershel said, "Thanks. I'll be back."

Bessie felt better after resting all day, and she beamed over the news. They both knew time was running out. Half of their thirty days were gone. "Yes, I'll come with you tomorrow, and we'll buy that house, you'll see."

Hershel slept very little that night, between dreams of the roof falling in and dreams of having land of his own. He remembered hearing his mother and father's whispered fears of losing their home during a strike. He remembered his own fears of his dear Bessie having to live in a tent, or worse. He remembered the Olas, who spent their last days in the poorhouse because they were evicted from their company house in Monongah. *This chance might not ever come again,* he thought as he drifted in and out of sleep. Finally, morning light began to fill the window, and he rose to face this most important day.

They rode to the streetcar stop nearest the state police headquarters and walked the rest of the way. "Are you all right, Bessie?" he asked.

"Yes, Hershel, I can't be anything but all right today."

They entered into a long hall lined with open doors. Hershel pointed to a bulletin board and asked Bessie if she could see a note with his name on it. "There it is," she said. A woman came out of one of the offices. "May I help you?" she said.

"Yes, we've come to see about buying one of the houses at Haywood Junction," Bessie said.

"My word, they're going like hotcakes," she said.

"Oh, we can't be too late. We want the second one on the right side, the uphill side," Bessie said.

"Well, now, let me see. I have a note here from a Hershel Martin, who wants the same one."

"That's us; this is Hershel," Bessie cried.

"Oh, I guess that's better, then. Have a seat, and I'll find the paperwork on that house."

After a few anxious minutes, they saw her coming down the hall, followed by a man in a blue uniform. "Betsy tells me you want to buy a house from us."

"Yes, sir, we do," Hershel said. "How much does it cost?"

"Well, it's actually quite expensive because it has running water. Several people have asked about it but couldn't afford it."

"We've been saving for a long time, so just give us the price," said Bessie.

"I'm afraid the two acres of land are $70 each, and the house itself is $1,500."

Adding the numbers in his head, Hershel said, "That comes to $1,640. Is that right?"

"Why, yes, it is."

"Can you hold it for us for a day or so? By that time, we'll be able to see it on the inside and get our money from the bank," said Bessie.

"We must have the entire amount up front, so if you need to secure a loan from the bank, we can give you a few days longer if need be."

"Oh, no, we won't need a loan. We've saved the money," said Bessie.

"And you know, of course, the property must be in your husband's name."

"Fine," said Bessie.

"Excellent. Betsy will find the key for you. Let's get this paperwork out of the way, but if you change your mind, you must let us know immediately. You'll need to bring us a bank draft made to the order of the State of West Virginia in the amount of $1,640."

The paper signing took a while, which gave Bessie time to have second thoughts since they hadn't even been inside the house. Of course, they wouldn't really have it till they delivered the money, and getting it out of two different banks would probably take some time. The thought of the money in Monongah made her wonder what Orie would think. He and Hershel had been close friends since they were trapper boys together, and he'd always talked with her of having a house of their own. He would approve, she thought.

"Hershel, are you sure we're doing the right thing?" she said as they rode home.

"I think we're doing the only right thing we've done, or I've done, in a very long time. Just think of all the reasons. We have to move; that's not a choice we can make. My new job starts on Monday, and there are no company houses in Owings. The children will go back to school in a couple of weeks, so they'll need to be settled before then."

"Yes, you're right."

"In terms of your brothers, Wilbert is set on being a teacher and even has a job at the college. Russell needs to learn to ride a horse so he can be a policeman, but his job now will be finding a farm to work on till he's old enough."

"I'm so glad they won't have to go into the mine. Mom's always been determined about that, but sometimes it can't be helped."

"We have so much to be happy about, Bessie. Our Emma Jane is as much of a rascal as her big brother Walter, and we'll be having a new little one soon.

"Mom says this one will be another boy. Don't know how she knows these things, but we'll love it, whatever it is."

"Well, maybe all her knowledge comes from her days as a cowgirl." He grinned.

"Could be. She and Jeremiah keep a running argument going about who knows the most about everything. I hope they'll like the house."

"It seemed sound on the outside, and even if it needs a lot of work on the inside, we can make it right. It may look like a barracks for a while, but when I put on a front porch, it will look like a home. This is our chance, and we're taking it."

RESEARCH SOURCES

Beckley West Virginia Exhibition Coal Mine

Center for Disease Control (CDC) Institute for Occupational Safely and Health. Coal Mining Disasters.

Chalmers, David Mark. *Hooded Americanism: The History of the Ku Klux Klan*, 3rd ed, Duke Univ. Press, 1987.

Clipping files at West Virginia State Archives Library for *Fairmont Times*, *Fairmont West Virginian*, and *Pittsburgh Dispatch* newspapers.

Duffy, Jim. "The Blue Death." *Johns Hopkins Public Health*, Fall, 2004.

Frazier, Claude A. and F.K. Brown. "Labor's Blue Eyed Angel. *West Virginia Historical Quarterly*. West Virginia Division of Culture and History.

Herring, Mary H. "The Why of the Klan." *The New Republic*. Feb. 23, 1923.

Hoover, Judith D. "'Miners Starve, Idle or Working': Working Class Rhetoric of the Early Twentieth Century." In *Who Says? Working-Class Rhetoric, Class Consciousness, and Community*. William DeGenaro, Ed. Pittsburgh: Univ. of Pittsburgh Press, 2007.

"KKK and WCTU: Partners in Prohibition. http://www2.potsdam.edu downloaded 8/8/14.

Lang, Susan E. *Extremist Groups in America*. New York: Franklin Watts, 1990.

McAteer, Davitt. *Monongah: The Tragic Story of the 1907 Monongah Mine Disaster*. Morgantown: West Virginia University Press, 2007.

National Communication Association's Voices of Democracy: The Oratory Project; Mary Harris 'Mother' Jones, "Speech at a public meeting on the steps of the Capitol, Charleston, West Virginia (15 August 1912)

Mine Safety and Health Administration. *Pictorial Walk Through the 20th Century*

Skog, Jason. *The Monongah Mining Disaster.* Minneapolis: Compass Point, 2008.

Wayne State University Archives of Labor and Urban Affairs.

West Virginia Division of Culture and History Archives

West Virginia University Libraries, Oral History Archives.

READER'S GUIDE

1. As Chapter 1 began, what did you think might happen? How were you surprised?
2. Can you imagine such devastation? How did reading Chapter 1 affect your interest in reading the book?
3. What did you learn about child labor that you didn't already know?
4. What did you learn about life in a coal camp? Company houses? Hard times?
5. Were Hershel and Lucy inevitably drawn together? Have you known anyone with tuberculosis?
6. Have you ever had a neighbor like Grandma Ola? What did she mean to Bessie?
7. How does the introduction of Belle into the story change things?
8. What does it mean when the mine roof "talks?"
9. How was the move to Riverview both good and bad for the family?
10. What effect does payment of wages in "scrip" have on the family?
11. How did the introduction of Mother Jones affect the story?
12. Did you wish Hershel had not become a rescuer? Why did he do it?
13. What did you learn about World War I and the flu pandemic?
14. How did the introduction of Sarah and Ben affect the story?
15. What did you learn about the Ku Klux Klan that you didn't already know?
16. What role did little Walter's cake play in Hershel's survival?
17. Were you surprised that people could be fired and evicted when they were injured on the job?
18. Overall, how did Hershel's lack of education affect his life?